I SLAMMED FACE FIRST INTO THE SIDE OF THE VAN.

The paunchy cop, Donner, held me by a fistful of locks, his .45 pressed into the side of my skull. Nash, his partner, patted me down, relieving me of my piece, my wallet, and badge.

"Don't even think of moving, you son-of-a-bitch," Donner wheezed into my ear, enveloping me with the smell of his whiskey and tobacco-fouled breath. "You must have known we'd catch up to you sooner or later, blood. You're gonna answer some questions. Just make sure I believe every word if you care anything at all about your health."

Nash spoke with a flat, dry voice. "Shouldn't have gone on television implying what you did."

"Someone inside the department is working with you." Donner fumigated me again with his bad breath. "You're gonna tell me who it is. Or I'm gonna accuse, judge . . ." He pressed the barrel further into the softness of my right temple, tightening his grip on my hair. "And execute!"

A DANCE IN THE STREET

CHARLES SHEA LeMONE

AVON BOOKS NEW YORK

*Dedicated to the loving memory
of my mother and father, Edna and Charles.*

*Special thanks to
George W. Brown, Julia A. Ross and Jim Morris.*

A DANCE IN THE STREET is an original publication of Avon Books. This work has never before appeared in book form. This work is a novel. Any similarity to actual persons or events is purely coincidental.

AVON BOOKS
A division of
The Hearst Corporation
1350 Avenue of the Americas
New York, New York 10019

First Avon Books Printing: March 1993

AVON TRADEMARK REG. U.S. PAT. OFF. AND IN OTHER COUNTRIES, MARCA REGISTRADA, HECHO EN U.S.A.

Printed in the U.S.A.

RA 10 9 8 7 6 5 4 3 2 1

Chapter One

Los Angeles is at her most beautiful during the rainy season, but that was hard to appreciate on a night when a fierce storm sent buckets of rain down the windshield, almost neutralizing the wipers on L-92, my Independent cab.

It was 4:15 A.M. I was cruising east following Sunset Boulevard—on a new morning in the middle of January, when everyone could justify their irritability, quick tempers, short rides, and bad tips. A result of the post-holiday blues.

I wasn't concerned that before heading home I might go another hour or two without catching a fare. I thought better when I drove, and that night seemed like a good night for doing both—driving and being introspective. In two more days I'd be celebrating—or more like acknowledging—my thirty-fifth birthday.

At that time of morning, the dispatcher's static-filled voice only occasionally broke the silence. I anticipated little help from him. I had my regulars, but only two or three might call at that hour.

I was considering the possibilities when a woman ran into the glare of my headlights. Braking, L-92 skidded on the slick boulevard.

She was waving her arms above her head, running

across the flow of traffic near Las Palmas Avenue. Fortunately, I got control of the skid, and she didn't get run down. Other brakes squealed, but by the time a black-and-white prowl car pulled to a halt at a stoplight, traffic was back to normal and she was in the backseat, clutching a petite purse and a soggy manila folder. She clung to them like warmth against the chill of the night.

The bleak weather and the late hour made her seem extremely young and fragile. Her hair was blazing red and braided, tied with a violet scarf. She wore a light-weight cotton jacket and tight faded jeans drenched to the bottoms of her running shoes.

I reached behind and reclosed her door, locking it shut.

"I need a ride to the Valley," she said, straining to hide the tension in her voice, her eyes darting nervously.

"You in a big hurry?"

"Who wouldn't be on such a night! You want the fare or not?" she demanded, dragging tiny, rakelike fingers through her wet braids.

Putting L-92 into drive, I slid away from the curb while asking, "Where in the Valley?"

She rattled off the address, checking my face against the I.D. photo with my name, Solomon Priester, on it. Then she withdrew into herself.

Making for Cahuenga Pass, taking the side route where Wilcox ends, I knew that any further questions would have to wait.

Seven years of driving for dollars had taught me a lot about knowing when to close my mouth. Being black and having grown up in an East Coast tenement, I realized the preciousness of silence. Wearing long, thick Rastafarian locks that have been unclipped since the first day I went into business gives me a sliver of added depth for understanding the unspoken. Glancing in the rearview mirror, I could almost sense her feel the same no-need-to-fear-each-other alliance.

Taking a left, I ran parallel to the Hollywood Freeway. With no other traffic to contend with, I studied her.

Shadows did not alter the keenness of her features—the deep-set eyes under a V shape of curly, unbraided bangs; the long, thin nose that contrasted with the fullness of her lips; and a well-rounded chin that gave her face perfect balance.

She caught my eye and stared back, unblinking.

Just then a light-colored BMW roared alongside, the tires spraying street sludge. It blazed by facing the lights of the oncoming traffic, then roared back into the lane in front of me, inches from crash time. Angry horns fractured the night, and before their sounds faded, the BMW was gone. Its rear lights were a blur, swallowed in a whirlpool of blackness.

"Where's that ass coming from?" I asked myself, relaxing my grip on the steering wheel.

"What?" Her voice on edge. "Were you talking to me?"

"Yeah, I asked where you were from."

"All over."

"All over," I challenged in a friendly manner. "What are you, about fourteen years old?"

"You gotta be kidding." Her laughter rang hollow. "You get paid for the laughs, too?"

"Sometimes," I said. "On top of driving this cab, I've got a badge and a license to dig into other people's business. You know, like rent a ride, rent a badge—either way, it pays the rent."

"Sure . . ."

I laughed to myself, knowing that she didn't believe me. But it was true, I carried a private investigator's license and a gun. Unfortunately, seldom did my moonlighting call for more than observation stakeouts. Dull, sleepy hours that required more coffee than imagination. My first-owned cab, K-13, had been my link to undercover work for Pops Orosco, a local snoop. Similar outings and classes led me to become a full-fledged private detective looking forward to the day when I could work full-time as an investigator. But whether the girl in the backseat knew this or not, I was determined to find out as much as I could. So I picked up the conversation.

"Why do you look so glum tonight?" I said, braking slightly to adjust to the synchronization of the lights. Beating a yellow signal, I made the jump onto the northbound freeway.

She sighed a big whoosh of air. "The work I do."

I decided to say nothing. Instead, I let out a true sigh myself. A sigh that expressed neither sympathy nor judgment.

"I work for one of the party lines, 976 stuff. But this was supposed to be a clean company that a roommate told me about. Just regular stuff. No X-rated, hard, or heavy crap."

"So what happened?"

"I don't know, some of the calls get out of hand. I guess some of the guys get too drunk and don't know what they're saying. But hearing creeps talk about violence doesn't do anything to turn me on." She paused. "It just makes me sick!"

"Maybe it was just a bad night."

"It's been going on for a week!"

After exiting the freeway and hanging a right on Van Nuys Boulevard, I went for the obvious. "You sure looked scared when I picked you up. Almost like somebody was chasing you."

"Maybe there was!" Her voice had a hard, stabbing quality to it. "But who cares?"

The heavy rain persisted as we neared the address she'd given me. I slowed to look over my shoulder. Our eyes met in the dark interior. Hers appeared as black as mine.

"You can act like it doesn't matter," I said, turning my eyes back to the road, "but you were really scared shitless when I picked you up. Something or someone bent you out of shape."

I watched her struggle to find more words, then she gave up and squirmed uncomfortably into the deeper shadows of the backseat.

"This is the block?" I demanded impatiently.

"Up one more," she said softly.

Suddenly, with a sigh, I found myself speaking a line from a William Blake poem, " 'What is the price of experience . . .' "

"The yellow house on the right. The one in back."

"Here?"

"Yes, that's it." Her voice was girlish now, innocent.

I braked and put the cab in park, reading her the fare and reaching for one of my Independent Taxi cards with my number, L-92, on it. But before I could give it to her with one of my business cards, the correct amount of bills fluttered down beside me on the front seat. Then she shocked me.

" 'Do some men buy it for a song, or wisdom for a dance in the street?' " She had followed through with the next line by Blake.

Quickly, she was out the back door, slamming it shut. Then she was a stark figure dashing across a bare, narrow lawn, heading toward a small house set on the rear of a lot.

While filling out my tally sheet, I waited to see a house light appear. Five minutes passed as the rain slackened into a drizzle. I waited another five minutes, then shrugged, thinking perhaps she had gone straight to bed. Maybe she preferred the dark. Either way, it was approaching 5 A.M., and I decided to stop booking and head for home.

Pulling away down the tree-lined secondary street, I noticed a light-colored car shaded from the streetlights under the arms of a large oak. Smoke from the exhaust was the only indication that someone was inside. I cruised by at a crawl. It was a cream-colored BMW. Tinted, rain-splattered windows hid the interior from view. I tried to get a make on the license plate. The lettering was indiscernible, but it was a dealer's tag.

Two long blocks later, I swung right and sped down an alleyway. Doubling back on Magnolia, I was hoping to recapture any detail associated with the light-colored BMW that had blasted past me on Cahuenga. Seeing two similar cars in such a short span of time, and the girl's behavior, all added up to the probability that more than coincidence was at play.

I drove by the spot where the BMW had been parked; it was gone.

At the intersection, two hundred feet away, I parked in a manner that allowed me to watch the street in both directions, while keeping an eye on the entrance to the girl's house.

I turned the sizzling static of the shortwave off and increased the FM by a notch to the sounds of 103.9. Something about the hour, the weather, and the tone of the deejay's throaty voice caused me to desire the makings for rolling a big spliff. Almost two years had passed since I'd smoked my last joint. Yet, unrelenting, the urges remained.

Memories of other days.

I picked up the *Los Angeles Times* and went to the half-completed crossword puzzle and pondered on ten across. The clouds had shifted, and only fine droplets washed down the windshield. Then the deejay—as though intentionally driving icepicks of unwanted memory through my heart—lowered the stylus on Sade's classic arrangement of "Give It Up."

I recognized the instrumental intro as one of

Jocelyn's favorites. I pushed the digital tuner until 94.7's signal came through. The song playing was too sentimental to fill the void I felt. So I popped in a homemade cassette. Recent and rare reggae sounds came forth. I settled to the beat, listening to the timeless message of the words. But there was no erasing the emotional tugs that had already gone to work, forcing me to remember and regret.

Close to three years ago, Jocelyn and I had met at a reggae concert in Topanga Canyon. After sitting together, we were surprised to discover that we knew many of the same Canyon residents. We soon found ourselves in a group of about a dozen festive-minded people. Wine and herb were plentiful. I indulged in both, but Jocelyn refrained, sticking exclusively to her cooler of tea.

There were other differences between us. We talked about them, but without lectures or conditions. But our arguments grew intense three months later, when I had an accident while driving her RX7.

She was riding with me and had asked as we left the party among the last of the stragglers, "Are you sure you can drive?"

"I drive better when I'm a little intoxicated," I had flippantly answered.

I escaped with no injuries, but Jocelyn was less fortunate. While none of her injuries was severe, I'll never forget the black eye she wore for so long. Being a model and an actress she had to put her career on hold. I continued to drink and drive—socially and while at work—keeping L-92 on the road. But I did it more conservatively, I told myself.

Then, the fatal crunch came. A twenty-four-year-old railroad worker, high on crack and loaded with liquor, with numerous driving-under-the-influence violations, hopped a curb and took out seven people.

Jocelyn was one of them.

By not drinking or smoking, as I pledged at her funeral, I forced myself to create an immense gap between myself and the railroad worker or anyone like him. The best anyone could hope to do, I concluded, was to maintain whatever integrity they hadn't already lost.

After twenty-odd minutes, I completed the crossword puzzle.

I toyed with the idea of giving up this foolish stakeout of a noncrime scene. But for some odd reason, I felt I'd regret doing that.

Then I decided to follow my instincts. I grabbed the handle of my foot-long Magna Light from beneath the driver's seat and stepped from the cab.

The rain had stopped falling, but the storm drains and house gutters were alive with runoff. A few birds chirped, their notes emphasizing the stillness of early morning.

The street was one of those that ran for five blocks and never again appeared on a map. One side of the street was occupied by new apartment complexes and condominiums. On the girl's side, there were private dwellings. Most of the homes were dark. A few nightlights shone from within.

I turned onto the stone walkway leading to the little yellow house. Approaching slowly, I tried to think of an explanation should she suddenly appear, safe. After climbing the rotted, wooden steps, I hesitated on the porch. From there, I could see that the door behind the aluminum screen had been left wide open.

I switched the flashlight to my left hand and reached under my vest for my Cobra .38 snub-nose revolver. I put my thumb on the hammer. Even though I was wearing my driving gloves, the coldness of the steel sent a chill through me. Easing past the squeaky screen door, I stepped into the darkened house. Except for the echo of the screen door closing and the sound of my own breathing, the house was quiet.

Momentarily, I stood in one spot, training my ears for the slightest sound within. Satisfied to a degree, I eased the door partially closed behind me.

"Hello," I called out softly.

No response. I clicked my flashlight on and swept the room with its beam. The living room was small. Even at first glance, there were signs of a struggle. A wooden coffee table with a broken leg stood upended. Nearby, a vase with fake flowers and a large ceramic ashtray and its contents lay scattered on the floor beside a lamp with a busted bulb.

To the left of the kitchenette was a short hallway. I followed it cautiously while grisly expectations stained my imagination. Fighting to steady my nerves, I advanced slowly toward the three doorways that branched off the hall.

Quickly, I checked out an empty bathroom, cold and still.

The second doorway revealed a bedroom. I swept the room with light. An unmade bed took up most of the space. On top of a dresser stood a framed photograph of a full-figured brunette posing in a swimsuit. Her stomach was sucked in to deemphasize the twenty or more extra pounds she carried. She wore a suggestive smile on a face that seemed younger than her body. Among the baubles decorating the dresser top were keys on a plastic key ring with the name Karen engraved into it.

One more room, I told myself, inching toward the end of the hall. My senses heightened with uncertainty. Hoping that it, too, would be unoccupied, I held my breath. Pushing open the slightly ajar door, I gripped my revolver tighter.

At last I sighed, and began to breathe normally.

A single mattress lay in the center of the room. There were no other furnishings. A large pink foot locker, an overnight suitcase, and a duffel bag, spilling their contents of clothing, made an untidy yet unsuspicious picture.

I began searching the possessions that I was sure belonged to the scared little girl I had picked up on Sunset.

There wasn't much to search. There were no baubles, bangles, or beads to wade through. Just austere necessities. Not even an extra purse in sight.

I removed an empty glass from the top of the foot locker and opened it. More clothes, most of them brand-new with price tags still attached. Below, I uncovered a dozen books. Half of them the works of William Blake. One book's pages fell open to the picture of an angel in flight.

For some reason, this saddened me.

I replaced the contents, thinking there was nothing more to find. However, beneath the mattress I made an interesting discovery. Inside a plastic sandwich bag was an eighth of an ounce of sensimilla, rolling papers, a brass roach clip, and several roaches of assorted sizes. More important, there was a pocket-size address book. There were only a few notations in alphabetical order. With my driving gloves on, flipping each page so I could copy the list was a challenge. I used my tongue, glad that I wasn't leaving any fingerprints.

There was something childish about the handwriting I was copying. Large letters were scrawled on the small pages. Listings were on a first-name-only basis. Under H, I found "Home" where the names would normally appear. There were an address and a telephone number but no city or zip code. The street name sounded ritzy but didn't ring a bell.

I put the wrinkled plastic baggie and its contents back as the sun peeked through a high, rectangular window. A phone I had missed began to ring, and I knew it was time to leave.

Retracing my steps, I wondered about the manila folder that seemed to have disappeared with the girl. Then like a desperate, empty-handed burglar, I made my exit from the back door. I tried the lock after shutting it behind me. It opened with a soft click. I left it the way I found it—closed but not locked.

As I walked away, the phone was still ringing.

Back in L-92, I found my beeper had recorded a message. It was from Ramona, a favorite customer. I got on the cab's two-way radio and called the dispatcher's office to find out if Ramona had called there when she was unable to reach me directly.

"You guessed right," Randy, the night dispatcher, said. "She put in a call for you about ten minutes ago. But you're right on time though, bro, 'cause I was just about to flag L-39 to do the run."

"Don't!" I said. "I'm on it."

He gave me the address, which I recognized as a private strip joint on La Cienega. I wasn't worried about being late, because Ramona habitually called early enough for me to watch her last performance before driving her home. After arriving at the club, I used her name at the door. Then I made my way along a dimly lit corridor whose walls were strung with posters of strippers doing their thing. I followed a pair of stairs to the basement.

"She'll be on in a couple of minutes," one of the scantily clad dancers acting as a hostess said. "Follow me. She has an empty table up front."

"That's okay," I said. "I'll just wait here in the back."

The black-and-white marble bar was unoccupied. The mirrors behind provided an excellent view of the stage, where a tall, thin, surprisingly buxom black woman was doing her act for a dozen zombie-eyed customers. The bartender, a young Tom Selleck clone, came to find out what I drank.

"Picking up Ramona," I told him.

"No problem," he said with a smile and a wink. "At eight dollars a pop, I can dig it."

He set a glass of water in front of me and went back to cleaning and restocking his station. The black dancer ended her act to lukewarm applause.

"Next," she said into a hand-held microphone while gathering her undies, "for your enjoyment, we proudly present Ramona and Raul!"

The lights chilled to an aqua softness, then blazed red, and olive-skinned Ramona slinked onto the stage. The funky music she'd chosen began to play. Raul, a five-foot-long boa constrictor, was draped around her neck. The audience responded with a collective sigh, then with jubilant whistles, catcalls, and avaricious applause.

Ramona stood a shade under six feet. The sequined, skintight brief she wore had a reptilian design, making it difficult to tell where Raul left off and she began. Tossing her long hair back, she smiled at the crowd and began her gyrating dance while her full-moon breasts threatened to burst through the sheer material. Her narrow waist emphasized her round, fleshy hips.

I'd seen her arousing act many times before, but each performance projected an element of newness. Animalistic newness.

She was somewhere between thirty-five and forty years old. When she was onstage, no one thought of her age. She spotted my reflection in the mirror, smiled, swung her hair in a circle above her head, and turned her tight, grinding bottom toward me.

Watching her charm the audience as Raul flicked his tongue at the footlights, I recalled our relationship.

More than a year ago, she had arrived in town. The

first call she made for a cab produced me. Right away, she began telling me her life story.

Her father, an Italian trumpet player, had worked for a circus, where he had met Regina, an extremely tall and robust Armenian acrobat. When Regina became pregnant, they left the circus, and Ramona was born. She regretted having never known the circus life.

On my fourth trip to her house, she invited me to join her upstairs. A half a day later, I emerged—tired and loved out.

It became routine for us. She'd call for a ride, which meant I'd watch the last show, drive her home with the meter off, and literally be her captive until she was ready to surrender me.

One night, when we reached the door, I said, "Let's skip tonight," having had a rough day.

She cursed me—long and strong.

"From now on," I told her, "call someone else when you need a ride."

"Fine," she spat back. "From now on, drive your cab somewhere else!"

A few days later, she called to apologize. "If someone treated me like that," she said, "I'd be mad, too. But I don't want you to dislike me. Can we still be friends?"

She finished her act as the audience begged for more.

Ten minutes later, she glided up to me, carrying Raul in his elongated wooden-screen cage.

During the ride, sitting beside me and the silent meter, she lit a cigarette with a dying butt. Blowing smoke out of the window into the early light of morning, she sighed. "What a night!"

"Hecklers?"

"No way! I know what to do with them, quick!" She knocked ashes from her Newport into the wind. "It was Raul."

"Raul?"

"During the second act, he wouldn't let go." She re-crossed her stockinged legs, turning to stare from her window at the rolling freeway traffic. "I thought he was trying to kill me."

"What?"

"He's never done that before."

"Yeah. That does sound strange."

"No shit!" She tossed the partially smoked cigarette. "I was scared as hell. And onstage, too! When we came to the part where he's supposed to uncoil so I can hold him up—you know the part?"

"I know the part."

"He just wouldn't let go." She trembled so intensely that my skin crawled.

"Maybe you should look into getting a new partner."

She was quiet, thoughtful for a few moments, then responded, "No. But me and him are going to have to have a long talk. That's another reason I called you to-night. I figured if he tried that same shit again, you'd help me." She turned her big brown eyes toward me. "You would have helped, I know."

I took her hand.

We stopped in front of her apartment on Bunker Hill. The clouds were thick, the sky hazy lighted purple.

"Don't tell me," she said.

"What's that?"

Her lips crinkled into a half smile, "You have to go home. Feed your fish?"

"Good guess," I said. "It's been a long day for me, too. And I can hear them calling me now, 'Come home and feed me, Poppa!' "

She laughed, tugged at a handful of my locks, and gave me a big wet kiss on the cheek, "You're nuts like me."

When I slid Raul's cage out of the backseat, it felt

heavier than usual. She gave me a peck on the lips as I handed her the cage.

"You behave yourself now, Raul," I said, scratching a fingernail across his screen opening.

A few brilliant rays of sun were breaking through dense, low-hung clouds. I took the Silver Lake exit off the Hollywood Freeway and swerved by the reservoir which we neighbors refer to simply as "the lake." At any time of day, it offers a refreshing view, like a fantasy apparition holding the rest of the city at bay, sealed off from the hectic, sometimes savage, lines of its borders.

I swung right on Glendale Boulevard, hung a left a few blocks later, and ascended into the hills. At the end of a cul-de-sac, I pulled L-92 in front of my garage. I didn't bother to put it inside because it already needed a wash.

Seventy-two carved stone steps led up to several homes and, behind them, the bungalow I rent. Two landings and twenty-six wooden steps later, I came to my front door.

My gigantic aquarium seemed to beckon like a beacon, its lights brighter than the sun shining through the curtained windows. I fed and admired my exotic collection, thinking about the crack that Ramona had made. She had been right. My mind had been elsewhere, but it had not been on my fish. I had been lost in thoughts of the girl who had finished the Blake line, disappearing in the rain.

Often, I would walk around the lake or climb some of the nearby hills. It helped to limber up the stiffness in my muscles and joints that idled while driving. But that morning the mere thought of any further physical or mental exertion sent a shudder through my tired body.

I fell directly into bed. And unlike most nights, sleep came instantly.

Struggling through my subconscious, the thunderous sound of pounding rushed me into a premature, groggy awakening. A harsh, booming voice reached my ears, shredding all connections to the world of sleep.

The pounding on the door continued, louder—near splintering.

"Make it easy on yourself, and open up! We know you're in there, blood!"

Chapter Two

Shaky-legged, I stumbled from my water bed. My digital bedside clock read 9:39. The neighborhood dogs were baying louder with each passing second.

Wrapping a robe around my birthday suit, I stumbled toward the racket that had shaken me from a deep sleep. Even in my fog, intuition told me what to expect. The pounding at the front door ceased abruptly. Then, just as surprisingly, a puffy pink face appeared, pressed grotesquely against my sliding-glass side door. The panes rattled from his weight.

Catching my eye, he snorted. "Police! So don't even think about any dumb shit!"

"Okay! Okay! You can see I'm coming!" I raised my arms.

Another plainclothes cop, tall and gaunt, stood directly behind the take-charge guy with the gruff voice. By pushing his slicker further back, he exposed the butt of a revolver, worn at his hip.

I acknowledged the act. "Come on in," I said, sliding the unlocked door open.

"Step back," said the paunchy one. "And put your hands on your head."

I took three steps back, following his instructions to the letter. "What's this about?"

"It's about you!" The stocky man with the pink face flashed a badge. "Lieutenant Pete Donner. Homicide."

"Homicide . . ." I mumbled to myself, aware of their keen, work-weary eyes combing me and the room, noting every nuance of my reactions, searching for the slightest sign of paranoia or guilt.

"We've got some questions for you," the slender man said, after identifying himself as Joe Nash.

"What kind of questions?"

"We'll get to that." Donner poked his face close to mine, giving me a whiff of his stale breath. "First, we want you to take a squat so you're easier to watch."

Nash nodded in agreement. I sat on the brick-red leather couch, part of a set that had cost, with interest, more than two-and-a-half weeks' earnings.

"If this is going to be a long talk, I'll get you guys some coffee."

"You shuddap!" Donner shot back. "If we want something, we'll help ourselves."

"Just trying to be polite," I said.

"This isn't a social visit." Nash spoke dryly, rocking on the balls of his feet.

"Let's cut the shit." Donner sat, leaning toward me on a matching leather loveseat. Eyeball to eyeball, he asked, "Between approximately four and five o'clock this morning, where were you?"

"Driving my cab." I shrugged. "That's how I make a living."

"Is that the best you can do?" Donner smiled with his lips but his eyes remained hooded, void of any humor. "I don't call that cooperation, and that's what I'm expecting from you."

"Why shouldn't I cooperate?" I asked. "There's a ride sheet in my cab. If you haven't already looked at it, it'll tell you where I've been for the last two weeks. I've also got copies around here somewhere that cover the last six years. What do I have to hide?"

"If you believe that"—he leaned closer—"then why the bush-beating half-answers?"

"Is that what I'm doing?" I asked.

In the impending silence, I studied both men. Donner, with his thinning, dishwater-yellow hair, was probably in his late forties. He looked ten years older. He wore a perpetual snarl—used so long his lips seemed molded that way. It was a fervent, unrelenting expression that had me guessing him to be a man who hated and distrusted anyone younger than himself.

On the other hand, the skeletal likeness of Nash sent out a completely different reading. He shifted on the balls of his feet, constantly uneasy. A complacent, grim smile indicated the possibility that he might possess a sense of humanity—unlike Donner.

"You can play cat-and-mouse." Donner broke the silence. "And we take a little ride down to Parker Center for some more in-depth questioning. Or you can do yourself a favor, save yourself the hassle." He rubbed a caressing palm over a tightly balled fist. "Either way, I don't give a fuck!"

"I think you do," I countered, "or you wouldn't be so evasive with your questions. I still don't have any idea what the hell you want from me! I mean, you woke me up! I didn't wake you up. So, break it down. Why me, huh?"

Donner did his best to restrain his anger. A gnarled hand reached out in the direction of my throat. It paused, as though in slow motion, then backed away, finding a matching hand to clutch. As Nash took the diplomatic lead, Donner slowly cracked his knuckles.

"A murder victim was discovered early this morning. According to information we have, the deceased was last seen in your cab."

"And who was the deceased?"

"You make a guess," Donner spat. "Between four

and five o'clock this morning. How many fares did you have?"

"The young girl?" I found my voice with great effort. "Her?"

"Yes," Nash answered solemnly. Then, prompting himself with notes jotted in a small spiral pad, he continued. "Kim Stouffer was the name she used. Seventeen. Red hair. Was staying somewhere in the Valley, in Burbank or . . ."

He flipped a page. In a faint voice, I found myself offering the correct city name. "Van Nuys is where I took her."

"Right you are," Donner said. "And how's the rest of your memory?"

I shook my lowered head. Visions of the previous night rushed back to me with a haunting clarity. I could hear her last words to me, ending the line of poetry. Then there were personal considerations—I'd searched her house. But I had no intention of sharing that information with the pair stripping me naked with their eyes. Why did the newsbearers have to be them? Would they understand my motivation for entering the house, suspecting something terrible? Chalking up a victory for the powers of instinct, I also nursed deep pangs of regret, wishing instead that my suspicions had been wrong.

With their piercing eyes on me, deciphering and pondering every minute gesture, I responded in reasonable time.

"I gave her a ride. My last of the night," I lied. "Picked her up on the strip, near Las Palmas."

"Then what?" Donner asked, his tone wrought with insinuation. "It was a real wet night, I bet?"

"Then I did what I always do with my customers, I took her where she wanted to go," I answered, having raised my voice for the first time. I added on impulse, "Maybe you should take me downtown. I might feel more at home there than you're making me feel here. 'Cause I don't like the idea of someone killing that girl any more than either of you."

"Especially since you were the last known person to see her alive." Donner gritted his tobacco-stained little teeth, squinting dark beady eyes. "Which—by the way—makes you, Mr. Priester, a prime suspect. Tell us, were you pimping her on the side?"

I felt like smacking the shit out of him, but reason won, and I finally spoke. "That would be your first guess!"

Across Donner's shoulder, I could see the hands on my kitchen clock. They read 9:44, which meant that the inquisition had taken only a scant five minutes. It seemed infinitely longer. I felt an irrational urge to run.

"Her being my last customer may make me a suspect," I said. "But that doesn't make me a criminal. And, from what you've told me—plus what I know— you've got no substantial reason to arrest me. But, then again, if you think differently, take me down and book me. For what? Driving a cab?"

Without warning, Donner struck. A powerful back-hand came from his lap. It caught me square on the side of my face. I rolled as best I could with the blow, but before I could brace myself to retaliate, he had a hand-ful of my thick locks, pulling my head back across the arm of the couch. He applied a choke hold, using more than enough pressure to assure me that my life was in his hands.

"I could kill you, son-of-a-bitch. That what you want, blood?"

I looked up at him with all the indifference and dis-dain I could muster, not giving him the pleasure of see-ing me ask, much less beg, for anything from him.

"Pete, come on, man!" Nash was pulling at him. "It ain't worth it." He repeated, "It ain't worth it. Buddy, come on, buddy. Look at me! It's your partner, Joe, talking to you!"

Nash continued to plead, and eventually the pressure from Donner's arm and the death grip on my hair relaxed. A moment before I lost consciousness, he let go.

I slumped into the couch, gagging and spitting.

Donner slammed open the sliding door, disappearing beyond my watery vision, heading toward the exit. I went down to the floor on one knee. When I tried to rise, a powerful, viselike grip ripped at my stomach muscles. Dry heaving, I collapsed back on the couch. I tried to sit up and felt Nash helping me. I pushed him away and sat, head between my legs, my lips dripping an acidic bile.

Nash looked the helpless, inadequate dupe, saying, "I don't know whether to say I'm sorry—or what?"

"Then don't say anything!" My voice was oddly strange. The pain of speaking made me cough again. "Just get the fuck out!"

He stood, unmoved.

"We know you have an investigator's license," he said indifferently. "But I hope you're smart enough to stay out of harm's way and meddle somewhere else. Preferably as far away from this case as you can."

Cautiously, eyes steadily on me, he backed toward the open door. "So long now," he chimed, sliding the door shut. "See you around."

Loud as my aching throat would allow, I growled, "Not if I see you first!"

Exactly twenty-two minutes later, I was showered and dressed, and peeking out my front window. I'd lived on the hill for five years. Strangers and anything unusual stood out. The gray old warrior of an undercover Plymouth was easily visible, parked on a perpendicular street that faced my cul-de-sac. Its presence might have gone unnoticed, except that the rear end jutted out beside a pastel-pink house.

I had watched Donner and Nash drive away after their visit. They'd hung a hard left on Glendale, peeling rubber, causing all the dogs in the neighborhood to start barking and howling again. I figured that there was an even-steven chance they'd stake me out. Maybe even come back sooner than expected.

I could only hope for better luck than that, and also wish that they had no backups covering them.

I tied my hair down with a black silk scarf, then crowned myself with a big, wide, gray apple jeff, cocked over the left eye. I smiled, pleased with my reflection. I attributed it to my Philadelphia upbringing; dressing up or down was a sport.

I grabbed a duffel bag–size pack that I'd earlier crammed full with extra clothes and camera gear. After surveying the back of my house, I decided the hills behind it looked safe. Besides, I figured Donner and Nash would be looking exclusively for the cab to tip them off to any missions that I might be contemplating.

Climbing out of the kitchen window and inching downward, I used the rainspout that ran the length of the wall to scurry the thirty or so feet to the rain-soddened ground.

The footing was wet and slippery, but soon enough I made my way around the base of a rugged, undeveloped ridge that abutted my bungalow. Using the roots of a camphor tree like climbing ropes, I pulled myself to the top of the rise. Resting there, I checked to see if I had been followed. All seemed quiet.

Facing the other direction, below a dramatically darkening sky, the L.A. River, the Golden State Freeway, and the tracks for the Southern Pacific Railroad sliced north and south. I pulled a two-tone blue fisherman's slicker out of my bag and slipped into it, pulling the hood up. With the mirror-reflecting sunglasses I wore, I was convinced that I looked like someone other than me. I tested the theory, starting my climb down to Riverside Drive.

I kept Silver Shadow, my customized Dodge van, stored in a rental garage a short bus hop away in Atwater. I kept it there because my garage entrance was too low for the seven-and-a-half-foot clearance needed for the boomerang antenna. Less than fifteen minutes after secreting away, I pulled the tarp off my silver-striped black van and reconnected the battery cables I had left disconnected to prevent electrical drain. It was showroom-new. I had bought it five years ago, chalking up less than twenty-four thousand miles.

I spent so much time running my solo shifts with the cab that getting away from it all proved to be wishful thinking. But any lingering regrets about buying the van disappeared as the engine kicked over, purring like a playful panther. I discarded my disguise—the slicker, the jeff, and the black scarf—letting my locks fall free, and rolled into the wet streets.

I used a pay phone while having the van's tank filled. I got through to my answering machine. There were three messages, all of which had come while I was sleeping or after I'd snuck away. The first one was a hang-up; so was the third. But the second call made my ears tingle.

Courtney, the morning cab dispatcher, sounding urgent, came across the line. He mentioned the time of day, a time when I had still been snoozing.

"Sol, babe, looks like you've got some problems. Twice this morning we got calls from so-called police officers. After checking them out, one was real business; the other a phony trying to get your address. I don't know what the hell's going on, but I hope you get this message in time to make some sense out of it. Odd stuff, first thing in the morning. But take it easy if you can, babe, and stay in touch." Click.

I dialed another number—Kevin Carter, a detective with the Rampart division. He was a friend I occasionally played basketball with at Silver Lake Park. There was no answer at his house. I got the number for the nearby precinct from an operator.

"I'll see if he's in," the detective who answered said. "Who should I say's calling?"

"Tell him it's Banker," I said, using the nickname that Kevin referred to me by because my favorite shot was a banker high off the backboard.

A few seconds later, he was on the line.

"Sol," he said, getting straight to the point, "I hear you've managed to get yourself into some trouble."

"Some," I said, "but any trouble is more than I need."

"So how can I help?"

"I've got a few facts that I didn't feel comfortable sharing with the officers that came to the house. But if we can get together, it might prove helpful to both of us."

"Where and when?"

We agreed to meet in ten minutes near the Riverside Drive entrance of Griffith Park. The rare sound of thunder boomed in the distance. Heavy pellets of rain fell from the winter sky as I rushed back to the van.

Rolling in the pouring rain, I factored in the tidbits I'd learned. It would seem that not only was the police department interested in my whereabouts, someone else was also prying into my life. I threw all of the limited facts I'd gathered into a stew, boiling in my overly percolating mind.

I came to the conclusion that the report linking me with the drop-off had come from the BMW that was casing the scene. If a watchful neighbor had made such a report, it seemed plausible that the same person would have been aware of my return. However, there were no indications that anyone knew I had returned and entered the house, making myself privy to the address book and its contents.

It made sense. I'd spotted them, they'd spotted me.

They could easily trace me to the L-92, but I was left lingering in a dangerous no-man's-land while they were scot-free.

I parked off of Riverside, near the children's pony rides. Soon after, Kevin pulled up. He parked his Pontiac Le Mans and trotted through the rain toward me.

He was fashionably dressed as usual, a tall mulatto, about my height, a shade over six feet, slightly bowlegged. He had been born nearly forty years ago, growing up not far from the park where we played ball.

He slid into the front seat beside me. I turned off the reggae tape I was half-listening to. We shook hands firmly.

"So what've we got?" he asked, resting his pale green eyes on me.

"First, tell me about the girl. How did she die?"

His eyes narrowed and his normally handsome face contorted in a grimace. Knowing that he had been involved in the investigation of the infamous Hillside Strangler slayings, I braced myself for the worst.

"From what I hear, it wasn't pretty, I'll tell you that." He hissed a sigh. "A guy walking his dog came across the body early this morning off Mulholland, between Laurel and Coldwater Canyons. It appears that she was tortured. She had cigarette burns on her thighs, breasts, and eyelids."

I muttered a curse.

"The medical examiner is speculating that the torture preceded her death by an hour or more. Cause of death, strangulation. The crime lab is fairly certain that the strangling was done by a pair of large hands." He paused. "Of course, everything I'm giving you is secondhand."

"How about footprints, tire tracks, anything near the scene?"

"So far, nothing. They figure she was tortured somewhere else, then flung down the hillside. Luckily, a purse found a mile away turned out to be hers."

He removed a pack of gum from his jacket pocket. I took one, and he slid two sticks into his mouth.

"What about you," he asked. "What've you got?"

I began, starting at the top: A frightened young girl got into my cab, clutching a manila folder. She mentioned intimidating calls as a reason for her uneasiness. Seeing the BMW that I'd nearly crashed into parked on her street, I'd been suspicious enough to enter the house.

At that point, Kevin whistled, "You really know how to stick your neck out, don't you?" He shook his head and spat out the window. "I almost wish you hadn't told me that."

"Well, I did!"

We locked eyes. He didn't think I was guilty any more than I did.

"Go on," he prompted.

I told him about the signs of struggle in the house, and my fears that the girl with long, red, braided hair had been abducted. "No signs of her, or the manila folder she seemed so attached to."

I skipped telling him about the list I'd copied from the address book. Much as I trusted Kevin, I kept that piece of information like a down card. Patiently, he listened while I brought him up to date. I tried to simplify my retelling of the confrontation I'd had with Lieutenant Donner and Nash. But I labored too long on the side effects.

"I've heard a lot about Donner. Plays hardball,"

Kevin said distastefully. "Once upon a time, he might have been a good cop. Now, I'm not so sure."

"Neither am I," I said. "But if you could check out the BMW, I think we might be a lot closer to knowing what went down."

He questioned me about the car and its license plate, jotting down what I told him.

"A dealer's tag. White, pale blue lettering," was the best I could offer.

"I'll run it through the computer and ask around," he said. "And maybe I'll find time to talk to Donner about how he dealt with you."

I smiled but said, "I appreciate the thought, but I think we'd better keep knowing each other under wraps for the time being."

"You're probably right." Kevin raised an eyebrow sagely. Then he asked, "How can I contact you, later?"

I gave him my beeper number.

"Well." He sighed, putting his notebook in a pocket. "This isn't a whole lot to go on, but you never can tell. I'll have to use a lot of discretion, though. But with a case like this, everybody'll be buzzing with a hundred and one theories. Especially if the press bites onto it."

Before we parted company, I told him about my suspicions that the girl's job as a party line hostess might somehow be connected with her death. I again mentioned the threatening calls she had spoken of.

"Seems as though, in some way, she touched you," Kevin observed, stroking his clean-shaven chin.

Immediately, the Blake phrase popped into mind.

It had been a line I had heard that very day while listening to a New Age talk show. That the young girl had ended the quote was uncanny enough. That she was dead, murdered, made it all the more meaningful. But those were emotions I couldn't express to Kevin. Too unprofessional.

"She was just a young girl," I finally explained, "out of her element."

He accepted my answer. "I'll put everything you've told me on the front burner and see what I can do." Then he cautioned, "Be supercareful, bro'. Could be you've jumped in over your head."

Chapter Three

I ordered a cheese omelette, hash browns, toast, and tea to feed a stomach that hadn't seen any fuel in more time than I cared to estimate. With two plates and a lukewarm, brim-filled cup, I sat down at a rickety Formica-topped table, across from Umberto Orosco, an old, weary-looking man who preferred the name Pops.

It wasn't the culinary reputation that had brought me to the Alcoholics Anonymous meeting house in Glendale. I had come hoping to find Pops, who made the place his second home. I was now an infrequent visitor. Pops was my mentor, a retired private detective who rotated his time between the racetrack, the back of the exotic fish store that his wife had operated for over thirty years, or here, where I found him, at the Hospitality House.

It was half an hour before the next meeting, and he was characteristically sucking on a long, filter-tipped cheroot while nursing a cold cup of instant coffee. His dark, bloodshot eyes wore their usual seen-it-all gaze.

"So what brings you this way?" his raspy voice asked. "Certainly not the food."

"Just came by hoping you'd be here," I said, taking a preliminary bite out of the eggs, which tasted like cardboard.

"Serious business?" He studied my eyes intently. "I'd bet."

"You'd win, too, Pops."

He knocked dead ashes toward the floor, asking, "So what's bothering you?"

"I don't really know how to begin," I said with a mouthful of toast.

"To begin, begin," he said philosophically, pushing the racing forms lying in front of him aside, resting a scrawny arm on the table, letting me know that he was in no hurry.

I babbled on, doing my best to reconstruct the series of happenings that had made me a suspect in the commission of a hideous crime. I soon ran out of words.

Pops chewed on his upper lip and the ends of his scraggly mustache for a disproportionately long time. Screwing his face up, he gambled on a hypothesis.

"Instead of worrying about yourself," he declared, "you're feeling guilty about her dying—like with Jocelyn."

"Perhaps. But . . ."

"Much as you loved her, you didn't kill Jocelyn. And you know that!" Pops was emphatic. "And you're no more responsible for this new girl's death than I am. But I know that's true. You . . . you don't seem to want to accept that, though. You just refuse to let go. That's the real problem."

Pops remained silent, gnawing on the plastic filter of his cheroot, waiting for me to respond.

"Well." I addressed him in a flurry of emotion. "You're right on one count. I haven't been able to bury the past, to go on—like you're always telling me to. However," I continued, "this new girl is another story altogether."

Pops shook his balding head like I'd missed the point. He surveyed his empty cup with glazed eyes—focusing on it as though to aid his memory.

"I've always been fond of the bottle," he started, barely audible, "ever since I can first remember. My mom and dad were the same. But anyhow, when I was just a pup, I met this real nice girl named Suzie. Sweet Suzie is what I called her." His crinkled lips smiled through his mustache in reflection. "She was some girl. Told me I was the first. And I still believe her."

He fondled his empty cup.

"I came into some money and had a steady job at the time. So I figured she'd jump at the thought of marriage. Well, I proposed to her, but, surprisingly, she laughed and turned me down. Said, 'You enjoy the high life too much. You're a good man to party with, Berto, but I could never consider marrying you.' "

He paused, satisfying himself that I was still there, listening.

"It took a long time for me to realize how much she must have loved me to be so outspoken, so honest. But"—he smiled mischievously—"do you think I gave up?"

"Most likely no."

"Absolutely no. I wasted three good years of my life trying to woo her into changing her mind. Now my motto is: 'Amen and a whole bunch of women!' "

He held his empty cup up like it was filled with champagne. "But you know what I'm driving at," he said. "You can't live like all the good is gone out of life and not expect it to be true. This little girl, whoever she was, is gone. And Jocelyn . . ."

"Don't start!" I could feel my stomach tighten. "Please!"

"Okay! Okay!"

He studied me for a long time. "Did you contact your buddy on the force—Carter?"

"Yeah, we met earlier. He's checking into a possible lead on the BMW."

"Good. You may need someone like that on your side."

"True," I said, as though reading his thoughts, which weren't painting pretty pictures. "But I really don't know where to start on this case. I—"

"Case!" Pops's bitter laughter interrupted me. Then he slammed an aged fist on the table. "That's what I was afraid of. Suddenly, this is your case?"

"Whether I like it or not, it's been dropped in my lap."

"Don't act rashly, Sol. Just take care of yourself. Let the cops handle it. That's what they get paid to do. Besides, they sure won't appreciate any help from you. Just stay out of the way."

"Sounds like what Donner's partner advised me to do," I said, shifting my eyes from the intensity of his gaze, "but you know I can't do that."

"You're a real funny guy," he said, narrowing his beady eyes in seriousness. He checked his Rolex. "There's a meeting starting soon. So listen up, because I'm only going to run through this once."

"I'm all ears."

"Two things you haven't learned. One: You're too damned impulsive. Always looking for the big case. You can't see the trees for the forest. It's like that Cochran woman ordeal when you ran in—"

"Look! Do we have to relive that?"

"No," he said. "But you are going to hear the last thing I have to say. Number two: Before you have a case, you need a client."

Ignoring Pops's recommendation, I skipped the group meeting and got back to Silver Shadow just as the parking meter ticked its last beat.

I snaked up Outpost Drive, encountering a single car coming down. I swung a left on Mulholland, enjoying the lay of the land. Exclusive Mulholland Drive runs the rim from the Cahuenga pass some twenty-two miles to the Pacific Ocean, bordering downtown Los Angeles, eclipsing the glamor-seeking lights of Hollywood, cutting a monumental ridge between the basin and the San Fernando Valley. Numerous celebrities built mansions along the rim. Yet many a criminal had historically chosen to deposit their garbage, bury their evidence, or leave their victims along the banks of the same Santa Monica mountains.

Someone had written—somewhere—that Los Angeles was a constant sprawl of suburbs in search of a city. Perhaps it was this very essence of the city that had kept me so attracted to it.

When I was born, my mother and father were still living in the heart of a North Philadelphia hot spot of crime and degeneracy. Tenements rotted on the barren, twilight border of demolition, but my father's TV repair shop kept us anchored, roofed, clothed, and fed.

I saw the drunken family feuds that spilled blood into the streets, the gang-warring teenagers who followed suit, spilling more blood. There were the schoolyard bullies that never seemed in want of replacements when they'd been outgrown, outpoliticized, or straight-out defeated. I could still recall the third-grade class picture of me with seven fresh stitches over my right eye. Regardless of my mother's constant pleas to move from the neighborhood, my father had stubbornly stayed. His shop was more important. But after getting robbed twice, my father had had a change of heart. Suddenly, he felt as unsafe as my mother and me.

I was fifteen when we moved, and though the house we moved into was a row house—like most Philadelphia houses—we did have a front lawn. It wasn't a big lawn, but it was suburbia to me.

Working with my father in the new shop during the evenings and on weekends had became something that

I was not only required to do but had actually begun to look forward to. I cherished the praise I got when I learned something quickly, discovered something new, or completed a job sooner than expected.

My father was a quiet man with distinguished looks. His inner thoughts were hard to guess. However, I remember him drumming one thought into my head, as though, beyond the technical, he could only offer one philosophy worth teaching.

"Being a black man, you got to be twice as good as the white man if you want him to give you work. But even if he does give you a job, you're still working for him. Why do that when you can really be free in the truest meaning of the word, and work for yourself?"

I never fully understood his uncharacteristic ramblings, until I was twenty-nine years old starting a shift—not driving for someone else, but in my first-owned cab.

As I was coming out of a S-shaped curve, emergency flares and orange reflecting cones caught my attention, bringing me back to the present. Creeping around a ridge that faced the hazy, rain-saturated valley, I spotted the cordoned area.

"This is the spot," I told myself, imagining the girl's tortured body being flung over the hillside.

As far off the road as possible, tilted on a slope, a county-issued sedan was parked. Two uniformed officers were present. Both looked bored and unaffected by the rain. I knew the view well. It was near a point that had a turnout because of the many sightseers and lovers who stopped there to suck up the view. I kept rolling. No need to stop, I told myself, not if I could trust Kevin Carter to fill me in.

Twenty minutes later, I did stop at Sloane's Tavern, a West Hollywood drinking den. It provided a not too rowdy, yet lively, background din.

I dialed the "Home" number that I'd copied from the dead girl's address book. Four rings, and an English-accented woman answered.

"Hello," I said energetically, "this is Marvis Burns with the Department of Water and Power. It seems that your meter is out of kilter, registering five hundred gallons a day more than last year's average."

"Tchh, tchh."

"No need to worry though, we think we've found the problem."

"Well, thank heavens."

"It's just a faulty water valve."

"A water valve?"

"Yep," I said. "A problem like that can cause a lot of headaches till you narrow it down."

"Well, honestly speaking, I'm just an employee here and—"

"That's all right." I brightened. "We'll send a man out there tomorrow. Will someone be home?"

"Certainly, someone is always here."

"Good," I said. "Let me check the records I have in front of me." I gave her the address, reading it from my notes. She concurred. I repeated the phone number.

"Yes, that's correct."

"In the city of . . ." I cleared my throat, rustling the pages of a telephone book near the receiver.

"Palos Verdes Estates." Her condescending voice filled me in.

"And the utilities are paid by . . ." I said, waiting.

"Mr. Rupert Collingsworth," the housekeeper righteously announced, "who is not in at the moment."

"That's no problem, but do you have a work number that I can reach him at?" I asked. "We need his confirmation."

"Hold on a moment." She set her receiver down with a loud clatter.

I tapped on the side of the phone, pounding out an

anxious beat until she returned. I wrote the phone number down, repeating it, and thanked her before disconnecting.

I dialed the number. A receptionist answered.

"Collingsworth and Associates Law Offices."

I asked for the mailing address and jotted down a Long Beach address.

As I was cruising down Melrose, my beeper sounded. It was the third time the pager had interrupted my thoughts, but unlike before, this time the message came from someone I wanted to hear from—Detective Kevin Carter. He was at the number shown on my message display and answered on the first ring.

"Detective Carter."

"So what's new?" I asked.

"Lots, but nothing I'd call good."

He had checked out a host of BMW dealers before hitting on anything. Then he came across the Wescott Auto Leasing dealership on Ventura Boulevard in Reseda. Their logo was white with light blue lettering. More importantly, they had reported the theft of a cream-colored BMW sedan.

"What time was the theft reported?"

"Ten this morning. Although when reporting it, the manager mentioned the possibility that the car had been stolen sometime during the night. It was found downtown this afternoon. They dusted it thoroughly for fingerprints, but that proved to be waste of time. It had been wiped clean."

"Have you tried matching the tire treads with any tracks found anywhere near Mulholland?"

"I'm sure that's in the process," Kevin assured me. "But there's something else you might find curious."

"What's that?"

"When the officers that were sent out arrived to talk with the dead girl's roommate, there were no signs of a struggle recorded. Nor any indication from her that there might have been signs of trouble before they got there."

"Hmmm . . ."

"Could it be you were in the wrong house?" He laughed.

"Not a chance!"

"And forget the name, Kim Stouffer. That name has proven to be as phony as the I.D. she was carrying. But someone who knew her is powerful enough to see that her true name is withheld—with what I'd call a serious vengeance."

"Anything more?"

"That's about it, but . . . I've got to run. Be in touch."

The congested midday traffic, affected by anything unusual, was slowed by the rain. Yet an hour later I turned off Pacific Coast Highway, climbing the curving, secluded roadside hills of Palos Verdes Peninsula, heading toward the estates perched high above the sea. With the help of my Thomas Guide map book, I soon found myself parked in front of the address that the dead girl's hand had listed.

Several peacocks strutted outside the stately wrought-iron gates of a private road that led to the huge estate. The peacocks were the offspring of imported predecessors who had ranged for decades in the wild after escaping from captivity as pets. Their presence was appreciated by some, but scorned by the majority, who saw them solely as aggressive neighborhood pests.

I watched their proud pecking and colorfully rousing displays. They acted as though they owned the grounds, scrutinizing me and the van with a skeptical, malevolent awareness. Hearing their shrill, piercing screams, I better understood the complaints of those who were awakened by such unnerving cries.

The rain seemed obliterated by the height of the hills.

Through the mist, the mansion appeared to be a glorified representation of an era long gone. There wasn't much of the house to be seen above the professionally sculptured landscape, but the impending quiet and the deserted streets painted a picture of opulence at its apex—pesky birds and all. I wondered why a girl born to such exclusivity would choose the gutter-soiled streets to be her eventual tomb.

I recalled the North Philadelphia house that my family and I had known. Although my father had owned that entire corner tenement house, he rented out the second and third floors. The shop took up more than a third of the first-floor space. Behind it sat our tight little apartment. My bedroom was no larger than a cramped storage room. But the feeling of security had overridden the confining closeness. There was comfort in feeling that a home life, a warm haven, existed, blocking out the gangs, the drug-infested nightmares of the streets.

I hadn't fled from home. Why had she?

Envisioning the frightened young girl wearing the fugitivelike face I'd seen in my rearview mirror that morning, I shuddered.

A bold young peacock pecked at my door. The surprise jolted me. I found myself staring into tricolored silver-dollar-size eyes. I laughed and searched the van for feed. A forgotten bag of trail mix served the purpose. Careful of my fingers, I slipped the contents outside. My guest devoured the offering rapidly. A mouth on a long-stretched, almost hairless, neck begged for more.

As I drove to Long Beach, I heard an all-news radio station report covering the murder. They referred to the victim as a Jane Doe, alias Kim Stouffer. Again, I felt emotionally connected to the deceased girl, especially listening to the impersonal voice delivering the report.

Standing near the Pacific shore like an example of the recent enthusiastic commitment to civic development, an immaculate architectural statement of a high-rise building rose. In the lobby, I found the listing I was searching for and caught the first available elevator to the top floor.

The pale blue carpet seemed virgin-new. At the end of the well-lit hall, I met two impressively wide doors. I swung them open and stepped into a plush, empty waiting room. I tapped the bell at the vacant reception counter, marveling at the view that the windows afforded.

From a hall behind the receptionist's desk, two street toughs in Rodeo Drive color-coordinated attire emerged. One was a tall Hispanic, the other was a dark black man with slick processed hair. Belying their refined clothing, both their faces looked like they had seen action inside a ring. They spotted me, and a momentary wave of shock—and/or recognition—swept across both men's eyes. They made their exit while sizing me up. With the same defiant indignation, I eyed them back until the doors closed behind them.

A feminine voice beckoned hello, and I swung around to find a gorgeous blond receptionist, now at her post. She looked to be in her early thirties and was dressed as though she were stepping out to a formal affair.

"May I help you?" Her voice strained at being polite but instead came across as haughty.

"Yes," I said. "I'm Solomon Priester, and I'm here to see Mr. Rupert Collingsworth."

"Do you have an appointment?" she asked, knowing full well that I didn't. "Mr. Collingsworth and Associates can only be seen by appointment. If you'd like to schedule one—"

"Why don't you dash down the hall," I interrupted her, "and tell your boss that I'm here to see him about his daughter." I gave her a toothy smile. "Let him decide. Okay?"

If looks could kill I would have been listed in serious condition. She laid a hand on the intercom and contemplated buzzing him, but instead she did as I had asked and hurried down the hall. She returned promptly, instructing me to sign in at her desk and follow the hall to the last office on the right.

While signing in, I read the two previous signatures: Tarzan of the Apes and Andre the Giant were scribbled in competitively sloppy styles. I smiled, wondering whether it had been the Hispanic or black thug who had chosen the moniker Tarzan.

Following procedures I'd learned working with Pops, I had stopped at a local library and looked up what information was available on Collingsworth. There were numerous articles, all glorifying him. He was a respected citizen who had served three terms on the Long Beach City Council before retiring from politics. He had gained a reputation as an All-American offensive tackle for a UCLA championship football team. He had turned down offers to play professional ball to study business law at Stanford. After graduating at the top of his class, he had used a meager inheritance to venture profitable real estate investments. Success seemed to have been waiting for him at every turn. His reputation appeared unblemished.

I read a clipping announcing the birth of his daughter, Jennifer Adrian Collingsworth. She would have turned seventeen that spring had she been allowed to live.

The only melancholy notes were accounts that his childhood sweetheart, and wife of nineteen years, had suffered a stroke. After years of convalescence she had died seven years ago, from a massive hemorrhage.

I stepped into his spacious office, closing the door behind me. The expression on his face revealed nothing about his thoughts. He struck me immediately as a distinguished, gray-haired news-commentator type, trusted by a national audience.

"In what way may I help you?" He spoke in a disinterested manner.

"I presume you're already aware that your daughter was the victim of a murder committed sometime this morning," I said as tenderly as possible.

"Yes." He sighed deeply, lowering his glassy blue eyes. "I was contacted this morning."

"Mind if I have a seat?" I approached his large mahogany desk.

"But ..." He cleared his throat, ignoring my question. "What does that have to do with you?"

I sat, pulled my badge from a pocket, and flashed it toward him. "I'm a private investigator. Solomon Priester."

"I don't understand," he said, perfunctorily acknowledging my badge. "Who are you working for?"

"That's confidential," I lied.

For a fraction of a second, he appeared baffled. Then he straightened his already well-placed tie and regrouped his domineering presence. "I'm still not clear as to what this has to do with you." He heavily stressed the last word.

"I can understand," I assured him. "An explanation's due."

"Yes ..."

"Early this morning, I picked Jennifer up in a cab I own. She was a frightened little girl who appeared to be running from something. I dropped her off in Van Nuys but couldn't get rid of the hunch that I might have been able to help her. Now it's too late."

"Wait a second." He shook his angular head with its etched-in-granite features. "There was a report about some cabdriver picking her up. But from what I've been given to understand, that same cabdriver, you as it turns out, was at the top of the list of possible suspects." His voice grew in volume and intensity. "Now you're sitting here in my office asking me questions?" he said incredulously.

"The police questioned me already. I couldn't swear that I'm off the hook in their eyes, but regardless of whether they realize it or not, I know I'm completely innocent." I spoke frankly. "Or why would I be here?"

His entire manner seemed to come unglued. His eyelids blinked in rapid succession. Tanned, thin nostrils flared like wings. "As far as I'm concerned, until proven otherwise, you are still a suspect." He spat out each syllable. "Now get out of here!"

"I only have two questions for you," I said calmly. "One: Why do you think Jennifer traded her upper-class security for the streets?"

With surprisingly quick speed, the fifty-two-year-old man rose to his full six-foot-five-inch height. Leaning thick hands on his desk, he glared across it, down at me. "If I weren't a lawyer—who should know better—I'd pick you up and toss you out on your ass!"

"You'd find that easier said than done."

"Out! Dammit! Out!" He left his side of the desk, coming my way.

"As I said, two questions. I've only asked one," I said, languidly rising, looking up into his hate-filled eyes. "Secondly, what kind of business did you have with Andre the Giant and Tarzan—the muscle freaks that were leaving here when I came in?"

"I've had quite enough of you!" He grabbed me by the arm, but I pulled away from his steellike grip, escorting myself toward the door.

"Later," I told him, "I may regret putting you through this. But I'll tell you straight out, no one is going to stop me from finding out who killed your daughter. Not you or anyone else!"

"I'll trust the police to sort this whole mess out,

without your meddling interference. And I won't be surprised to see you arrested and jailed."

I turned at the open door, facing him squarely. "I don't think you really believe that," I said. "But it is unusual to meet a lawyer who's so confident in the police."

We stared at each other, grimacing. Then I left Collingsworth with his heavy arms hanging slack at his sides. As I passed the receptionist, she wore the expression of someone whiffing the first signs of a backed-up sewer.

"Be prepared to see me again," I promised.

After racing back to Silver Shadow, I paid the slow-moving parking attendant. A quarter of a block away, I positioned the van so that I could reconnoiter all the traffic leaving Collingsworth's building.

It wasn't long before Collingsworth peeled out of the underground parking facility in a bright red Ferrari. Agitation was written in bold print on his face as he sped past me. Following, I did a quick U-turn and made a light just as it was turning from yellow to red. I needed all my driving skills to keep pace. Staying far enough behind, yet close enough to not get lost in traffic, I continually denied him the chance to evade me.

We progressed into Torrance. Almost out of sight, the Ferrari finally pulled into the parking lot of a Security Pacific Bank. Rather than follow him into the lot, I stopped at the curb in a red zone. From my knapsack I gathered my Nikon and fitted it with a powerful zoom lens.

In a huff, Collingsworth left his parked car and hurried toward the entrance of the bank. Outside, Tarzan and Andre met him. Acknowledging their presence with a nod, Collingsworth entered the bank.

Ten minutes later he emerged, walking straight up to the conspicuous duo. Gesturing wildly, he addressed them. I shot a half dozen shots, catching him as he forcibly pushed a thick envelope into a waiting hand. Finally, he walked away from them, heading toward his Ferrari.

A congratulatory look passed between the two thugs. As they peeked into the envelope, I took more shots. Forsaking Collingsworth, I followed them with the camera to their car, a black BMW.

I kicked the van's engine over and punched into gear, cutting into traffic behind the black sedan. I focused and took several shots of their license plate as they pulled onto Torrance Boulevard. A few blocks later, my luck petered out as I lost sight of them speeding onto a freeway onramp. No amount of guesswork or speed could make up the difference. I got on my citizen-band radio, hoping that someone might sight the vehicle, but none of the channels I tried provided any help. They had escaped, lost in the wake of rush-hour madness.

Twice, unsuccessfully, I tried to reach Detective Carter.

The San Diego Freeway trip into the Valley was a long, tedious one. It gave me plenty of time to think. The van's captain's chair is about as comfortable as any seat can get, so I endured.

The sun had long since set as I crept along, bumper to bumper through the Sepulveda pass, rolling down into the Valley. Lights from the interweaving highways, boulevards, and streets sparkled lucidly. Thanks to the rains, the air was uncommonly fresh and unspoiled.

It was 6:10 when I pulled up across the street from the little yellow house stuck in the back of a lot. There were lights shining from within, though the curtains and shades were pulled shut. I stretched my muscles in the back of the van to overcome the fatigue trying to convince me to go home to bed.

I stared at the face of the house, thoughts rushing by faster than I could harness them. There were so many questions, multiplying with every second. The talk with

Collingsworth had stirred up more confusion. I hadn't anticipated him greeting me like a prodigal son, but neither had I expected to find him fraternizing with the likes of the two thugs with whom he was later to rendezvous. Then there was the fat envelope.

Cash? If so, how much, and for what?"

From the manner that the two hoods had signed in at his office, it was apparent that they had no respect for Collingsworth, his reputation, or his position, though his wealth might impress them.

It had to be money, I surmised. They were shaking him down, extorting or blackmailing him. He had certainly seemed like he was paying for something that he'd rather not. But if extortion or blackmail was, indeed, part of the scheme, what was he hiding?

Collingsworth's attitude at the office had come across as defensive, and threatened. Where was the remorse for his daughter? Where was the sadness and grief associated with losing a loved one? Especially by such abominable means. Instead of spending the afternoon in mourning, he was running scared and angrily to his bank to make a withdrawal.

Very suspicious but not a crime.

Again I thought of Detective Carter. I looked hopefully at my beeper as though that might cause it to sound.

My attention returned to the house on the back lot.

Again, another puzzle. The living room had been violently disturbed. Yet when the police had shown up, it was neat, no signs of struggle. Perhaps the roommate, Karen, could explain.

I took a deep breath, got out of the van, walked up to the front door of the yellow house, and knocked politely.

Chapter Four

"Who is it?" Her voice trembled.

"Is Kim here?" I asked the face of the door.

After a slight hesitation, the paint-flecked door broke open, spilling light. Soon, she was studying me through the metallic haze of the screen door under the red glare of a porch light, stepping closer for a better look. She was much thinner than the photograph she kept on her dresser top. She was now a picture of emaciation with a robe wrapped around it. However, her smile was the same—inviting.

"Hi. Kim's not here."

"Oh, where is she?"

The smile disappeared. "You a friend of hers?"

"Yeah, of course."

"Want to come in?" she said, solemnly unlocking and opening the door between us.

"Sure. Something wrong?" I asked, stepping into the house. The fresh, musty smell of herb was thick in the air. "You seem upset."

Her hazel eyes saddened and tears were welling long before she could find the words to speak. Then she finally blurted, "Kim's dead!"

"No!" I clapped my hands in front of me and sat down on the cheap plaid couch. "No!"

"She was killed." She stood there in the middle of the room, hugging and clutching her ribs. "Sometime last night. The police came this morning. They found her. On Mulholland. Messed up bad!"

"Who could have done something like that?"

"Nobody I can think of."

"When was the last time you saw her?"

"Last night. We work for the same party line." She sat in a bulky armchair. "She always rides home with me. But she just disappeared about 4:30 this morning. We weren't suppose to get off until 6. I remember the time she left because I was there on the line by myself, rerouting the calls to the girls that work at home."

She wiped her nose on her knuckles and sniffed, hunching up her frail shoulders in the burgundy velour robe. A neighbor's stereo blasting some Grateful Dead could be heard drifting through an open window.

She reached for a frosted cup near her hand, asking, "Can I get you some wine?"

"No, thank you, I don't drink."

"Some pop, tea? Something like that?

"You're Australian aren't you?"

"My! That's a good guess. Most people can't figure out where I'm from. I've lived everywhere, really. England, Stockholm, Spain. A few years here, a few there. My family moved from one country to another like there was no tomorrow."

"How old are you?"

"I'll be twenty-six next fall."

"On second thought, I will have some tea."

"Great! I like Rastamen, you know. I think they're neat."

She went into the kitchenette, grabbed a small pot, ran some tap water into it, stuck it on the stove with the flames high, and walked back toward me with a shoebox top containing the makings of some potent-looking blond-haired herb. She placed it on top of the broken coffee table. Minus its legs, it sat flat on the floor. She grabbed rolling paper from the large ceramic ashtray that I'd last seen upturned. Now it was filled with spent cigarettes, matches, and a one-inch-long roach being held by Jennifer's brass roach clip.

"This is some real good shit!" she declared, squatting and sitting cross-legged on a floor pillow.

More Grateful Dead sounds filled the silence.

"How long have you known Kim?"

" 'Bout a year," she said, crunching up a big bud by grinding it between a thumb and a forefinger. "How'd you meet her?"

"Gave her a ride once."

"She was a nice girl. On the street when I met her. But you know how it is when you see somebody down on their luck and you say to yourself, maybe there's some way you can help them out." She licked the glue on the paper and rolled it tight. "You help, if you can. Not that you expect anything in return."

"Sure."

I picked up a book of matches and struck a light. She pushed the fat joint toward me instead.

"That's okay," I said, holding the flame for her.

She took a strong hit and held it in as long as her lungs could. "You know, Kim wasn't her real name," she said after exhaling a cloud of smoke. "That was just her working name. But I could tell by the way you asked for her that you were really a friend. Funny, though, she never mentioned partying with anyone like you."

"What was her real name?"

She extended the joint my way.

"No thanks. I've got a long drive."

"It's really good shit, you know?"

"That's what I'm afraid of." I made my eyes large with fright.

She laughed and coughed, "You know, you're all

right! Even if you won't have a drink or a puff on this really good ... good ..." Her eyes suddenly widened as she remembered the boiling pot on the stove.

Soon, I held the cup of tea, switching it from one hand to the other when it got too hot.

"So you want to spend the whole night talking about Kim or what?" She gave me that patented smile meant for cameras or arousal, loosening the barrette that held her hair in a ponytail. "I mean, how much did she charge a big, fine-looking fellow like you anyway?"

"I'm not a trick. Just a guy she met."

"Oh, pardon me." She sounded disappointed, yet threw her hair back, shaking it loose. "What kind of work do you do?"

"I'm a private investigator."

"No shit!" she said in a gush of wonder. "That sounds exciting!"

"Right now, I'm looking into the death of a girl named Jennifer Adrian Collingsworth."

"Jennifer!" Her eyes narrowed. "You knew her name, didn't you?"

"True, I ..."

She slammed the joint into the ashtray and leaned as far forward as she could, as though ready to spring. "Why'd you do that? You could have told me you knew who she was a long time ago."

"Yeah, maybe I could have," I said, setting the hot cup down. "But would you have been willing to talk then? To trust me?"

She thought for a moment. "Why should I trust anyone, 'specially you?"

"Because nobody else seems to care whether Jennifer lived or died."

"Is her father paying you?"

"No! I believe he'd rather have me doing something else."

"That's the smartest thing you've told me," she said.

"Because if I didn't know anything else about Jennifer, I know she hated him."

"Why?"

She dropped her intent gaze and shook her head, "She wasn't much on talk about her past, especially in connection with him."

Again, her eyes began to well with tears. She came to me and wrapped her arms around my neck and began to sob uncontrollably.

"I'm scared." She trembled.

"I can't blame you. But I've got a feeling any danger that you might have been in has passed."

I held her and waited until she had cried herself out and had begun to relax.

"I have to go blow my nose." She excused herself.

When she returned, she never again asked me who I was working for, but she told me a lot. With no semblance of time or order, she talked. Jennifer had lived with her initially for two weeks. She had left a major phone bill which was never paid. She had moved in with a manager of the party line, Bryan Mann. Whenever they would argue and fight, Jennifer would come back to Karen.

"Does this Bryan character still work for the company?"

"No," Karen answered. "They fired him about two weeks ago for missing too much time. That's when she moved back here. He's still unemployed as far as I know."

The phone operations consisted of various specialties—covering every niche and fringe of sexual fantasy imaginable. Recorded and live programming was available twenty-four hours a day. In two years' time, Karen had worked all but the gay lines. She gave me advertisements, listing nine numbers.

"What's really a trip," she said, laughing, "is, most of the women who work out of their homes are fat old ladies, probably breast feeding their kids while trying to sound like they're nineteen-years old."

"That's interesting," I said, then asked, "When's the last you heard from Bryan?"

"Not since this morning. When I got home. I was running in because the wind was blowing like hell was on fire. And ..." She hesitated.

"And what?"

"I was wondering if the back door was unlocked. Because Jennifer had taken my key to get a copy made."

"And ..."

"The phone was ringing. I tripped trying to get to it. But it kept ringing, and I thought it might be Jennifer in trouble."

"Trouble ..."

"Because of the way she just vanished. And the crazy calls she was getting."

"What kind of calls?"

"Sick." She turned her nose up. "Sadistic ones!"

"You ever receive similar calls?"

"No," she said. "Only when she was there. We taped some of the calls, though. Whoever it was seemed to be trying to get her goat. But I think that was because the rest of us didn't let his crap bother us."

"So who was it on the phone when you picked it up this morning?"

"Like I said, it was Bryan. Looking for Jennifer."

"What's he like, this Bryan?"

"He's tall, thin, kind of handsome. Wears glasses most of the time and has a mustache and beard. He's the executive-looking type. Somewhere between twenty-four and twenty-eight years old, I guess."

"Sounds like you like the guy."

"Haaa!" She grunted a hollow laugh. "At one time maybe. Just seeing him. But Bryan's an asshole that nobody liked working for. He'd shortchange you in a second."

I felt I had reaped all the fruit the tree would freely bear. It was time for an answer to the one question I wanted answered.

"So why did you hide the fact that they—whoever killed her—probably dragged her out of here?"

Her head recoiled with a startled snap. I reached into the ashtray and picked up the roach clip.

"This is hers. Isn't it?"

"What!" she snarled, then shot back, "It was! But I liked it, and she gave it to me. Okay?"

"Fine!" I said, rising. "I've had enough. And looks like you have, too!"

I tossed a card for my private investigation business across the coffee table. It slid off and came to rest near one of her bony knees.

"Were you the first contact she had for putting her ass on a mattress for pay?"

"No, but that just goes to show how much you know," she said without masking her irritation. "I met her through a john that asked me to give her a hand. Yeah, she was particular, and felt guilty doing what she did. But she was a working girl nevertheless, long before I met her."

"How can I get in touch with the boyfriend?" I asked, knowing that no listing for a Bryan had appeared in the address book I'd uncovered.

"I don't know," she said, picking up my business card. "He never called back. The last number he had was disconnected before she moved back here."

She walked me to the door.

"You still haven't explained why you straightened the living room up."

"I was scared and sleepy," she said. "I knew something was wrong. The front door was open and the place was a mess, but I couldn't go to sleep worrying what the police might think if they came and found the place the way it was. I thought it might end up with me getting deported. I'm not a legalized citizen, you know?"

"I can appreciate that, but one thing I need to know, can you get your hands on a tape of the freak caller that rattled her so much?"

"It should still be in one of the desks at work. We tried to scare him off by saying that we were taping him. Not that it did any good."

"Please, call me when you have it. Or if you hear from Bryan."

"I'll call," she said, clicking the door shut.

I relished the cold wind. Refreshingly, it slapped my face.

Much as I wanted to believe otherwise, Jennifer was hardly the innocent young girl I had tried to imagine. I had suspected otherwise but had refused to face the truth. She had been tarnished, consumed, and ultimately spat out. But it did trouble me to know that she had been aware that she was gambling with her life, or why would the words from the Blake poem have been anything worth memorizing?

I could still hear her repeating the words.

" 'Do some men buy it for a song, or wisdom for a dance in the street?' "

Having not seen her when she spoke the line only added to the impact—like words from a ghostly spirit.

I parked Silver Shadow on Glendale Boulevard and began hiking the hill. L-92 was parked exactly where I had left it. I thought of the money lost by not leasing her for twelve- or twenty-four-hour shifts to the drivers that I trusted. But lately I'd become the sole operator, driving the fat hours of each shift, forsaking any semblance of a social life.

As I came to the foot of my bungalow, I heard the gushing sound of water. It was seeping by the gallon from beneath the floorboards and running down a support post that elevated the house.

Drawing my gun, I took the steps quickly. I swung the door open, crouching and aiming. All was silent and still, except for the sound of the running water, and my feet splashing in it.

I flicked on the lights. The room had been thoroughly tossed and trashed.

My aquarium was still intact, but a large, empty bottle of Clorox bleach floated on top of the murky water. All of my precious fish lay belly-up, dead. I could taste the death in the water. My mind exploded like an automatic weapon with a thousand round clip, firing nonstop.

Burned into the living room wall were the words, "Get Back, Jo Jo."

I knew immediately that the water lapping at my shoes was more than any water bed could hold. Through the ransacked house I ran to each sink, unplugging the drains, turning the faucets off.

I used a mop to push runoff out the front and side doors, while assessing the damage as total. The leather couch and loveseat had been slashed and gutted, stuffing strewn everywhere. The twenty-five-inch TV tube had been shattered. My new stereo unit and all of its accessories were battered and ripped apart. Albums and tapes were torched. The few paintings I owned had been cut to ribbons. Every lamp, every endtable, every knickknack had been smashed. Cherished books floated or sank, water-logged. The same painstaking detail had been applied to the kitchen. In the bedroom, a smashed computer monitor lay like a wide mouth groaning. There was the water bed, still leaking, and my entire wardrobe torched, lying nearby in a heap.

I sat on the frame of the wasted bed, put my head between my legs, and covered my eyes with trembling hands. I didn't want to look at the destruction. I wanted to step out of the house, come back, and find that it had all been a bad dream. My fish, still alive.

The sound of the phone ringing edged its way through the fury building in my mind. I sloshed through the debris, finding the phone. Picking up the receiver, I held it to my ear. Harsh laughter grated like fingernails on a blackboard.

"Thought we'd leave your phone live so we could welcome y'all home." The voice had a rhythmic southern black drawl to it, hissing sinisterly.

"Who is this?"

"Someone what got an eye on you!"

The line went dead. I cursed into it anyway.

I found a shoebox and placed my lifeless fish inside it. They had lost their iridescent glow. Saying a prayer in the name of each, I buried them in a flat spot in the back of the house. I had no control over the tears that ran down my face. I cried for the little boy within, wishing he'd had an older brother. I cried for the outrage that I always felt when some defenseless person came under the bully's attack.

I wanted to choke the ground. Rip out its Adam's apple.

The sun was shining brightly in a sparkling bright Kodachrome blue sky. I carried the last of my vandalized belongings down to the trash bin. I'd restuffed and covered the leather couch with a couple of blankets. It was now the only piece of furniture in the room except for the empty aquarium. I was painting over the message burned into my wall when I heard footsteps climbing the stairs.

With gun in hand, I met the startled expression on Detective Kevin Carter's face.

"Do you greet everybody like this?" He eyed my piece.

"Lately," I said. "Come in. I think you'll see why."

The bare room with wet, warped floors made quite a statement. I went back to covering the Beatles phrase etched in the wall. "I've been cleaning up since I got in last night."

"Dammit!" He looked around at the emptiness, his eyes coming to rest on the aquarium. "Shit! They completely wiped you out."

"They did. The question is—who?"

"Got any ideas?" Carter asked, after a lengthy silence.

"One or two." I covered the last of the stains and tossed my brush into a tray of paint. "I guess you heard that I went to see the father, Collingsworth?"

He snorted. "That was one of the reasons I stopped by. He made fuckin' sure we heard about it."

"Well, fuck him anyway." I grabbed a rag to wipe my paint-stained hands.

"He tried to get a warrant issued for your arrest. But the best he could get was a restraining order. You should be receiving it before too long." His eyes squinted intensely. "How did you zero in on him, anyway?"

I told him about the address book and my decision to withhold the information from him.

"Anything else you been holding back?" he asked with venom in his voice.

I shook my head negatively. "But somebody obviously thinks I know more than I should."

While he jotted in his notebook, I told him about my meeting with Collingsworth, then the bank rendezvous with Andre and Tarzan and the fat envelope that changed hands. I closed by mentioning the call I'd received from a southern-accented black man. A voice I was willing to bet belonged to the thug I'd first seen at Collingsworth's office.

"If it hadn't been for the call, I'd be suspecting Lieutenant Donner and crew." I gave him the roll of film from my Nikon. "Develop this and you'll have their tag number, too."

"Another BMW, huh?" he said, pocketing the roll of film. "I still haven't had a chance to check the one that was found downtown. I'm trying to think of some excuse that doesn't tip our hand before I have it requisitioned from the impound. But most likely, we'll find traces of the girl's hair and clothing that come up positive. If it wasn't for that possibility, I'd be pissed as hell about the information you withheld."

"Maybe I was wrong. But you seemed so upset when I told you about searching the house, I figured I'd better keep that to myself. Besides, what if you had told me to back off and not check on the home lead. I might have missed out on Collingsworth and whatever connection he has with these two punks." I gripped the exposed roll of film, now in his breast pocket.

"You're probably right. But if they pull you downtown for questioning, you're on your own. I know nothing from nothing."

I told him about my visit with Karen, the roommate, asking, "What's the word on this Bryan fellow, the boyfriend?"

"The department's got an APB out to pick him up for questioning. We've had his apartment staked out, too. So far though, no luck."

We were both pacing a wide circle around the couch.

"I know one thing," I said. "There's something funky going on with Collingsworth. It may not have anything to do with his daughter's death, and then again it might."

"I'll check with that Security Pacific in Torrance. Any recent big withdrawals'll stand out. And unless the license or car was stolen, I'll find out who owns the black sedan. Whoever it is has some questions to answer, too."

"There's another thing that keeps bugging me. The

manila folder that she was clutching when she got in the cab, where is it now? And what was in it?"

Kevin shrugged. "Who could guess?"

"Maybe whoever owns the party line might have some answers."

"That's a thought," he mused. "Although they've been questioned. I've already raised a lot of eyebrows, considering this is not even my case." He half-smiled. "It looks like I'll be leading the league in plugging up the holes." He lost his smile and sighed heavily. "Soon someone is going to want—make that demand—the identity of my anonymous tipster."

"Well, either we give up or face that situation when it comes."

"I'm glad you're so confident," he said, with no enthusiasm.

"I've got to be," I said, looking around at the emptiness that I used to call home. "Even if I'm no longer a chief suspect, or being paid to find out who is, I'm definitely involved!"

In due time, we wrapped up our briefing, and Kevin left.

Since my answering machine was broken, I took my phone off the hook and lay down for some much-needed sleep.

My stomach woke me a few hours later. I ordered a pizza. It arrived as my phone rang for the first time since being placed back on the hook. It was Courtney, the cab dispatcher.

"Hold on," I told him.

I paid the delivery man. Munching on the vegetarian pizza, I went back to the phone.

"I haven't been able to get through to you," he said in his usually exuberant tone, "And I needed to know you're all right."

Without going into great detail, I brought him up to date.

"I haven't heard you on the airways," he said in his fast, clipped manner. "So I figured you must still be up to your neck with this cop shit. I'm calling just to let you know we're behind you. Randy and all the guys. Anything we can do, let us know and it's done."

"Thanks, Courtney," I said, chewing another mouthful. "Right now, though, I don't know when I'll be back. I've got a lot to sort out."

"I understand. But how about L-92? Lots of good drivers are looking to lease. Give me the word. While you deal with all this bullshit, at least a few bucks'll be rolling in."

"Yeah, makes sense. Who you got in mind?"

"I know Shorty's looking for some part-time or steady work. Wallace smashed his ride up yesterday. You know how reliable Shorty is. He practically drove full-time for Wallace."

Barry Short, known as Shorty, had been driving ten years longer than me. Every time I encountered him, I was always amazed at his courteousness. He never seemed to be in a hurry, but he was always visible, night and day. Several times, I'd been parked behind him at the airport and watched him nonchalantly pick up a good fare like it was nothing less than he expected. "Some drivers never run out of luck," I found myself thinking more than once when we crossed paths.

"Tell him to give me a ring," I said. "He's driven for me before, so he knows where I'm at."

"Will do," Courtney said spritely. "Hope to hear you on the hot wire soon."

I was Saranwrapping the remaining pieces of pizza to put into the refrigerator that no longer worked because of a sliced electrical connection, when the phone rang again.

It was Shorty.

"I'd like to hit the streets tonight, if I could."

I agreed to let him drive.

"Give me a couple of hours," he said. "And if it's okay, I'll pick it up about 3 o'clock and keep it for a good twelver. Then we'll take it from there."

"I'll leave the key downstairs in the mailbox," I said. An inner voice urged, No. "Better yet, knock on the door, up top."

"No problem." He laughed. "Them steps ain't that long. Long, but not that long."

For the few hours it took for Shorty to get there, I either paced the floor or tried to find comfort on my blanket-covered couch. To say I felt stressed and frustrated would be a supreme understatement. A multitude of emotions whirred unceasingly through my brain cells. Snippets of scenes, brief hunches, and snatches of conversations played and replayed themselves over and over again.

I didn't know where anything stood. All I knew was that I wanted to feel hope. Hope for an eventual outcome. Any outcome.

Then the empty aquarium would demand my attention. Then I would see images. The body. A tortured body. A tortured young woman's body. Now dead. No more to live. And as I looked around the room, every bare space seemed to heighten the fact that someone had died.

My missing belongings paled to insignificance.

I was alive. Yet I knew, if given a chance, I'd have thrown myself headfirst into any hazard, if I thought it would have saved her. Now that it had come to light that the car parked near her house had probably been the one that had spirited her away, I knew I could have changed the outcome. But, as Pops might have said, all that's hindsight.

I saw Shorty coming up the steps. He was a wiry man but not really short, standing at about five feet nine. It was his surname that mostly inspired his nickname. I met him at the door with the cab key and a gas-oline charge card.

"She's about a half-tank down," I told him. "Fill her up and bring me the receipt."

"Sure thing! And hey, man, thanks for giving me a play. Having as many kids as I do, right after Christ-mas, you know I need the bucks," he said, jingling the key. "Want me to drop it with the lease money in the mailbox or bring it up top?"

"You better bring it up," I said. "And good luck."

I was lying back on the couch when I heard the ex-plosion. It shook the house, rattling the windows until it seemed they would shatter. Though the thundering sound seemed to come from everywhere at once, imme-diately I knew the source.

Flames and blackened smoke spewed into the air.

Chapter Five

I raced from the house to find sweltering flames and tar-black smoke licking the air. As I rushed headlong down the uneven steps to the bottom of the walkway, a torrid heat enveloped me. Then the gas tank exploded into an inferno. Only the shape suggested L-92, with Shorty inside. Someone grabbed me as I struggled, dazed, to pull Shorty's crisp, blackened body out of the flames.

More neighbors gathered. I wondered where they had been when my place was sacked.

"Let me go," I screamed.

"Think about what you're doing!" Rob, a portly man, said as he relaxed his bear hug.

More people flocked to the scene. I closed my eyes, and the sound of the sizzling flames magnified. Amid the smell of gasoline, rubber, vinyl, and paint, the unmistakable scent of flesh assailed my nostrils.

All around me, whispering voices asked, Why did something like this happen?

The fire department finally arrived and doused what remained of the fire-ridden debris. I gave a statement to the police officers in a black-and-white.

From my front window, not much later, I saw the press arrive. They conferred briefly with the men from

the bomb squad and talked to a spokesman from the
fire department. Then they raced up the walkway. A
half-dozen reporters, and camera operators jostled for
space on the deck leading to my front door.

I was feeling such rage and turmoil, I considered re-
fusing to talk with them. As though they sensed this,
the racket at the door heightened. An inner voice rationalized that a meeting with the press might serve as
protection, however minor.

Opening the door, I recognized a few of the faces
from the tube. It was spunky little Collette Carter from
KABC who fired the first question. "Mr. Priester, could
you shed any light on why someone would choose to
plant a bomb in your cab? Outside your home?"

Cameras whirred.

"I could! First, why don't you step inside?"

I extended the invitation to the entire contingent. Ob-
ligingly, they elbowed their way through the doorway.
Waiting until all of them were inside, positioned, and
satisfied with their light readings, I spoke directly to
Collette.

"This was once a regular home. Until yesterday, I
had a TV, stereo, the works." I stripped the blankets
from the shredded couch. "This once had a matching
loveseat which can now be found downstairs with the
trash." I pointed at Collette Carter's feet. "Right there,
I had a pretty blue Asian rug. Now also waiting for the
trash man."

"What's this got to do with your cab being blown
up?" Lee Miller from KCBS asked.

"Because the man that died out there is not the first
but the second person to be murdered who was associated with my cab. And—"

"Yes, we heard you were questioned by the police
about a girl's murder." Lee Miller pursued his line of
thought even though the other reporters tried to upstage
him. "So how do you explain all of this?"

"What was the girl's name?" Collette asked, thrusting her mike toward me, on tiptoes because of her modest height and the crowd pressing in on both sides.

"It figures this way," I said into Lee Miller's mike. "Someone murdered a girl, and because I happen to be the cabby that picked her frightened butt off the street, it seems that somebody's uneasy that I might know more than they want me to." I jumped directly into the question that came from Collette. "She called herself Kim." I surveyed the other faces. "Any more questions?"

"Who do you think might be behind all of this?" a Latino reporter asked, a note of sincerity and concern in his voice.

"Right now, I'm suspecting everybody!"

He looked confused.

"What I mean is this: The police woke me up yesterday morning. Real rough, too. And since then it's been hell on wheels. A good man, just because he leased a cab from me, is now dead. Dead! And I know he died in my place. That bomb wasn't meant for him! See?"

"Are you going to file a complaint against the officers who questioned you?" Collette asked.

"They know who they are."

"Yes, but . . ."

Purposefully, I moved a step away from her, "What I know is, my home and my livelihood have been savagely attacked—by somebody out there!" I pointed to the cameras.

Again, I took a question from the Latino reporter. "What was the driver's name—the man who lost his life in the blaze?"

"Not now. His family has to be contacted first."

"Someone suggested"—Lee Miller smiled, amused—"that you moonlight as a private detective. Could you dispel those rumors, Mr. Priester?"

"That's my business."

"What?"

"I think I've answered enough questions. You piece it together. That's your job, isn't it? Piecing things together."

There was a moment of silence. They stood lamely as though waiting for the end of a gag, then they all fired questions at once.

"Out!" I shouted, pushing them back toward the door. "Go!"

"If you change your mind," Lee Miller said, "and want to talk—"

"That'd be news!" I slammed the door behind them and pulled the curtains shut. Before they were completely drawn, I saw Collette, sticking her tongue out at me.

I raced onto the porch, not knowing what I would do if I caught her. But there she was, waiting for me to make the next move. I froze.

"We need to talk," she said, sassy-like, with a hand on her hip.

"Not now!" Again I slammed the door. Right then, I didn't want anyone to see me.

The ringing of my phone jarred me. I answered and heard the click of a receiver. Yet holding the phone in my hand was a reminder. There was a call I had to make. Though I wanted to put it off, I knew I couldn't.

As I had hoped, I was the first to contact Shorty's wife. She went into hysterics. There was the sound of children crying in the background. I didn't know where to begin to comfort her. I tried and failed miserably.

I double- and triple-checked Silver Shadow, not wanting to join Shorty before I found out who killed him. Unlocking and opening the passenger-side door, unlatching and lifting the hood were long, suspended moments. Climbing under the van with a flashlight and inspecting every nook and cranny should have assured me that it was safe to switch the ignition on. But a tingling of apprehension, warm sweat, and fear mounted.

Snorting like a bull, I turned the ignition key. The engine kicking over had never sounded so sweet.

I was warming the big engine when I noticed Donner and Nash's junker. It pulled up the boulevard at a creep, hazard lights flashing. The nightly traffic raced around them. In the fast lane, they came to a halt at the corner of my street. As though parked, the junker sat there, oblivious to the honking horns of the impatient traffic. A street lamp and an overhead light in the car shone on the unmistakable faces of the odd couple. They were quite visible, engaged in an animated discussion.

I shrank further into the dark obscurity of the van.

From the driver's seat, Donner pointed up the hill, toward my house, shouting something. Nash shook his head, disagreeing. For a few minutes, they continued their argument. I was about to pull into traffic, hopefully unnoticed by them, when their unmarked car suddenly swung into a tire-screeching U-turn. Soon their stick-on flashers were at work, their siren blasting. Oddly enough, the sound reminded me of the cry of peacocks and of Shorty's wife.

Hollywood Boulevard's traffic lights are calibrated so that at any speed—slow, moderate, or fast—traffic is mandated to stop and go. Stop and go was, however, contrary to my orbiting thoughts.

I steered, but it was like the van was on automatic pilot. Cutting north on Argyle, I retraced my way back east on Franklin. No one seemed to be following when I filled up a vacant parking space in back of Smoody's Blue Note.

Even with my windows up, I could hear the music rocking through the open vents of the club. I knew from the raw edge of the sound that it was live. And I didn't have to guess who was on drums.

Smoody was somewhere in his late forties or early fifties. According to him, he was born drumming on the south side of Chicago, where his parents managed a nightclub. They had live bands on weekends, and when he was too young to remember, he started sitting in on drums. Since then he'd played pop, rock, moderate and progressive jazz, the blues, country, rumba, samba, and reggae—always learning and teaching.

He was a favorite for studio work because he picked up the licks so quickly. Therefore, he could lay claim to being on hundreds of recordings. His strong bass foot could motivate a crowd, but his specialty was the way he whipped the high-hat cymbals, making them chime and chatter.

All his contemporaries knew that when you worked with Smoody, you not only had to be ready to work, you had to love it, too.

The East Hollywood club was the fruit of a long-time dream.

"A club where the cats can play for themselves," he explained as his inspiration one day when we were sweating to put it all together with hammers and saws. I had helped him install the sound system, worked with him on building the stage, been there on opening night.

For the first few years, it had been rough going, but now he no longer wondered whether the club would survive. It jumped seven days a week. There was open-mike night, a night for blues and one for jazz, but on the weekends when the crowds packed the place, they came to hear the Third World sounds of reggae.

When I walked in, I realized how long it had been since I'd crossed the club's threshold.

A quintet was working on a dub of the late Peter Tosh's composition, "I'm the Toughest." Ernie Hopson, known more for his tenor-saxophone virtuosity, seemed to be biologically connected to the soprano he blew.

Smoody gave me a big grin, as if he'd been expecting me. But he always did that. I had to strain but managed to return his smile. Immediately, he went back to counting off the changes for the young bass player, who seemed to be the only one having trouble with the piece. I was surprised to see that in the year or more since I had last seen him, Smoody had begun to grow natty locks.

A hefty barmaid came over to the table to take my order.

"Nothing, please. Just came to see Smoody."

From the top, the group went through the piece, while I tried unsuccessfully to reach detective Carter on the pay phone. The jam ended, and Smoody met me outside the phone booth, giving me a big hug and lifting me off my feet.

"So how's life treating my favorite Rastaman?" he asked.

"Not too good," I said, interrupted by Smoody's tall and attractive wife, Patty, who rushed into the club from their private quarters, wearing an apron and an anxious expression.

"Baby, you got to come up and look at the news." Her green eyes froze, startled upon seeing me, like I was someone who could be in two places at once. "You're about to come on the news."

"Like I was saying," I continued, addressing Smoody. "I've got big problems."

"Let's take a look," Smoody said somberly.

Hurriedly, we followed Patty up to the second floor. We waited impatiently through two national news features and a commercial slot before the story on me was introduced.

"Early yesterday morning," the graying newscaster reported, "the body of a teenage girl was found tortured

and murdered on Mulholland Drive. Today, that story
took a new twist. The last known person to see her
alive, a cabdriver named Solomon Priester, made the
news when his cab was fire-bombed outside his residence in the Silver Lake district. For more on this development, we go to our own Collette Carter on the
scene."

I felt my stomach cringe as I saw her standing in
front of the burned-out dregs of L-92.

"The normally quiet neighborhood of Silver Lake
erupted this afternoon with a violent explosion. Behind
me are the remains of what was once an Independent
cab. Left inside with the ashes is the body of Bartholomew Short, who was leasing the taxi from the owner
Solomon Priester, a man who happens to be the prime
suspect in a grisly murder." She stated the text with ex-
aggerated preciseness. "The suspect was interviewed
earlier. Along with the eyewitness cameras, I was
there."

A poorly focused shot of me appeared on the screen,
looking distraught and agitated to the point that I hardly
recognized myself. "The police woke me up yesterday
morning. Real rough, too. And since then it's been hell
on wheels."

"Are you going to file a complaint against the officers who questioned you?" she asked.

"I think I've answered enough questions. You piece
it together. That's your job, isn't it? Piecing things together."

Disjointed shots showed me pushing them out of the
door, shouting "Out! Go!"

They cut back to Collette, wearing a smug expression. "Rudely, we were asked to leave, unable to learn
any more about this senseless bombing."

"Bitch!" Smoody hissed.

Back in the studio, the newscaster picked up the
story. "We spoke to Commissioner Lindsey Kirkwood,

and asked him if he thought this was just an isolated incident or if there was reason to believe that the slaying of the young girl might be part of a—"

Using the remote, Smoody switched stations, hunting for another bulletin.

While he searched, Patty dug her fingers into his shoulders nervously in the pretense of soothing him. In the darkened room, illuminated only by the light of the tube, her tension was palpable. From what she'd seen broadcast, it wasn't difficult to understand her unease. It was as though at any second she expected me to either confess or go berserk.

Again, my face appeared on the screen. Outside, a siren blasted down the boulevard, drowning out the reply of my voice. Smoody adjusted the volume. The new account was more complete then the other one. But the damage was already done. Smoody searched the channels when the report ended. Soon he gave up and turned off the set.

A sudden silence that none of us seemed anxious to fill pervaded the room.

"Doesn't look good," I said. "Does it?"

Smoody smiled, standing. "I'm just a drummer." He raised his arms toward the heavens. "I drove a cab in Chicago once." He went to the portable bar near the TV and grabbed a bottle of cognac. "Want a shot?" he asked.

I declined.

He continued, "I drove one night! Only one night, and some mug pulled a gun on me. The first night! Shit! I gave him all the cash I had. Would have gave him more—if I'd had it. But I told myself right then, this bullshit ain't for me." He downed his shot and poured another. "So you pick up some whore or whatever she was and now you got the gun pointed at your head."

"True," I agreed. "It's like a gun, all right. But I don't know who's pointing it."

"How did you get here, the van?"

"Yeah."

"Parked in back?"

"Yes."

"Let's move it somewhere safer." He rubbed his hands together and left the room, saying, "Let me grab a jacket and find my keys, and we'll move it, put it in the garage."

Patty almost sprang up to follow him, but instead remained seated. After a moment, she turned to study me.

"We've been married for a little over a year." She trained her eyes on me. "One week after we met. But that's been long enough for me to see that my husband knows a lot of crazy people. I just hope you're not one of them."

"I'm only crazy enough to want to go on living." I smiled.

She smiled, too. "For some reason, I trust you."

"I'm glad someone does."

As Smoody and I walked out the door, she made sure that we heard her yell, "I'll have some food on the table by the time you two get back."

I would never go into a restaurant to order ham hocks and beans, and if offered them on a normal occasion, I would have passed. But on that night, I couldn't refuse.

"Smoody taught me how to make them," Patty announced.

The time slipped by rapidly. Smoody allowed me to run ideas by him. I also asked for his help.

"You know people, they know people," I said. "What I need is a line on who peddles false I.D. It could prove to be important."

I pulled the crumpled advertisements that Karen had

given me from an inside pocket. I had various party line numbers underlined. "Also, it would help if you can tell me anything about anyone who might own, run, or work for any of these lines."

"Hmmm," he mused, as though everything was suddenly becoming clear. "The dead girl was a voice-boxer, huh?"

"Yes, that she was."

Later, Smoody showed me a small room behind the bar and kitchen that he suggested I use until I felt safe enough to return home. It was a combination office and sack-out room. It had a desk, a phone, and a couch that folded out into a bed.

"I appreciate the thought," I said, "but I'd better go, wait to see if any calls come through."

"Don't you have call forwarding?"

"You're right." I laughed absently. "Practically all I have left is call forwarding."

Smoody sent his friend John-John to my place to put my phone in the proper mode. I insisted on giving him forty dollars.

While we waited, Smoody again showed me why he is also known as one the best physical therapists in the world. Crick. Crack. Joints that were trying to forge together as one got a breath of oxygen.

"It's been building a long time, hasn't it?" he asked as he pushed my right hip back into its socket, out of place from driving—accelerating, braking. "Better now, huh?"

It was 10:35 when the phone system was operative. I didn't have to wait long before the first call jingled through. The room was well-insulated, and even though Smoody and the boys were cooking it up with a full head of steam, their sounds were faint enough not to be disruptive.

"Hello," I answered.

"Yeah," the raspy voice announced, "It's me, Pops."

"Oh, no!" I said. "Calling to remind me of how grand I fucked up, right?"

"No. I'll save that for when we can sit down and talk," he said in a calm voice. "Sorry to hear about your driver and the cab. Tough situation, no doubt."

"Right!"

"You call me in the morning, now. Promise!"

The phone chimed the moment it hit the cradle.

"Solomon." The woman's voice sounded familiar, yet I couldn't place it instantly.

"Yeah, this is Sol. Who is this?"

"Collette Carter from KABC. We met earlier today."

My brain reeled. "That's an understatement." I mocked her. " 'We met earlier today.' "

"Listen, I can understand you being a little ticked off—"

"A little ticked off!"

"Well, you got it, a lot. I can understand you being upset, all right!" Her voice took on the superior quality that I recognized best. "All right?"

"What are you doing calling me, anyway?"

"I was actually prepared to apologize."

"Oh, really?"

"Yes. I just got a chance to see the first broadcast. I was too busy to watch it earlier. But they butchered you. That much I could see. It just happened to be a slow night for news or we might not have even followed through by—"

"And poor you, you didn't have anything to do with how they pictured me, huh?"

"Look, I don't do the editing. I'm a reporter. It's my job, and I do it well."

"Whatever happened to objectivity? Or isn't that part of journalism anymore?"

"I didn't call to argue with you."

"What else could we possibly do?" I hung up.

The phone was hardly in its cradle when the musical chimes again rang. I snatched the receiver up.

"Speak!"

There was a long pause, then I heard Detective Carter question, "Sol? Is that you?"

Chapter Six

It was 11:50 P.M. when I pulled in front of The Mixer, a redneck beer-and-wine bar in the Valley.

Karen, Jennifer's roommate, was one of the callers who had reached me during the short time I was at Smoody's. I had promised to meet her before midnight. I had also agreed to meet Kevin Carter at 1 A.M. at "the court"—which I knew was a reference to the basketball court.

I pushed through the swinging doors and walked toward the bar. The Mixer had a pool table in the middle of the floor where a game of partners was being contested. A jukebox was loudly pumping a popular country standard. One wall had a long bar lined with stationary stools punctuated with a spittoon between each stool. The clientele was a rustic breed, trying to act out their conception of real cowboys. It wasn't a place that I would have chosen for a confidential meeting, but Karen had called the shots.

One glance around the large, rectangular room told me that Karen wasn't there. I climbed on a barstool near the back end of the room where I could see everything.

Clumsily, carrying a giant bucket of ice, Karen parted the velveteen curtains leading from an alcove behind the bar. She wore three-inch spike heels, black tights, and a Danskin, causing me to think of an underweight Playboy bunny stripped of her fluffy tail. She had filled the beer cooler before she noticed me observing her across the narrow bar. At first she didn't register recognition. Then she flashed her memorable smile.

"So you found the place," she said, closing the lid of the cooler, moving to take one of my hands into both of hers.

"It wasn't hard to find." I caressed her icy cold hands, then let them drop. "What are you doing here?"

"Working." She pantomimed a stage bow. "Why, what's it look like I'm doing?"

From the front end of the bar, someone slammed an empty down. "One for me and another for my partner!"

"I see," I said.

Slinking away, she flashed a sneer at me. She was busy for a couple of minutes, filling orders and wiping up spilled drinks from the counter.

"I quit the partyline," she informed me, placing a glass of ice water down in front of me. "This doesn't pay nearly as much, but I'm just subbing a couple of hours for a friend. And I just know somehow I'll make ends meet. I always do."

"You didn't call me all the way over here to tell me that."

"Haaa!" She half-grunted. "You don't give me much credit, do you?"

"I don't have the time to figure you." I checked my watch. "I've got other appointments to keep."

"Hold on!"

She poured some tap beer, handed out a cold bottle or two, made change for the pool table, and was soon back at our empty corner of the bar.

"Bryan called." She was in my ear. "and I have the tape of that sicko you asked me to get."

"When did you hear from Bryan?"

"Just before I came in here." She looked around the room, finding everyone occupied with the music, loud conversation, the game of pool, or their own thoughts. "He was staying in some cheap motel. Then he decided it was time to go out for some groceries. He picked up what he wanted at a market when he realized—like the jerk he is—he'd forgotten to take his wallet with him." Her eyes told me how hilarious she found this to be. "Driving back, he saw the cops all over the place." She paused, eyeing the room.

"And . . ."

"He had to split with no money on him," she whispered.

"So he called you for help?"

"Yeah," she said with a wicked laugh. "He wanted to hide out at my place. Can you imagine that? I couldn't. Only a couple of days after what happened to Kim."

"Why's he so afraid to turn himself in?"

"Bryan," she squealed, "turn himself in? No way! According to what his twisted brain's telling him, when a pretty girl gets murdered, the cops always look to the boyfriend for a motive. And an alibi." She shrugged, then gave me a knowing glance. "Plus the thought of jail scares him more than cops. Seems he's already got a police record."

"For what?"

"He wouldn't tell me."

"So what did you say when he called?"

"I told him the best I could do was leave some money under the doormat for him."

"You left it?" I leaned closer.

"Of course," she said. "I always keep my word. But that wasn't enough for him. That self-centered bastard said he was short on gas and wanted me to bring it to him. I told him if he couldn't find a way to get over here, even if it's on a bus, tough shit!"

"What time did you come in here?"

"It was about nine o'clock when my friend called to ask me if I would mind covering for her. And—"

"Thanks, Karen, you've really been very helpful, but I'd better get going."

I was near the swinging doors, past several hateful glares, when I heard her heels clicking up behind me.

"You almost forgot this." She handed me the cassette.

The little yellow house was dark when I pulled up in front and cut the engine.

Directly in front of me, the lights from a car, with its searchlight, hit me square in the eyes.

Instinctively, I raised an arm to block the glare.

Suddenly, Lieutenant Pete Donner was at the side of the van. He tapped a .45 on the glass, aiming it between my eyes.

"Open up, fuck-face," he demanded. "The fun's over!"

I unlocked the door. As I stepped out, Donner yanked me by my arm, spinning me around so that I slammed facefirst into the side of the van.

"Hands high! Against the car! Spread those legs," he commanded. "Search him."

While Donner held me by a fistful of locks, his .45 pressed into the side of my skull, Nash patted me down, relieving me of my piece, my wallet, and my badge.

"Don't even think about moving, you son-of-a-bitch," Donner wheezed into my ear, enveloping me with the smell of his whiskey- and tobacco-fouled breath. "You must have known we'd catch up to you sooner or later, blood!"

"I—"

"Shut up!" He pressed the barrel further into the softness of my right temple, tightening his grip on my hair.

"You speak when I tell you to. 'Cause it seems like you've been Mr. Evasive, up till now. But you're gonna answer some questions. Just make sure I believe every word if you care anything at all about your health."

Nash spoke with a flat, dry voice. "Shouldn't have gone on television implying what you did."

"You shouldn't have been born. You little—"

Nearly breaking my shoulder, Donner cut me off. "Someone inside the department is working with you." He fumigated me again with his bad breath. "You're gonna tell us who it is! Or I'm gonna accuse, judge, and execu—"

"I don't know what you're talking about—"

The butt of the .45 slammed against the back of my head. My knees weakened. Donner held my slumping body by my hair like I was a naughty dog on a choke chain.

"We can go on like this all night," he warned. "But you are gonna tell me who the cocksucker is."

Again he pressed the point of the barrel into the side of my head. The hand that held my hair moved quickly between my legs. He grabbed both testicles and began to squeeze, laughing as he locked me in a head grip.

I unwillingly squealed in pain. "I don't know what—"

"Let him go!" From behind us, a voice penetrated the darkness. "And come slow with the gun, Pete!"

"What the—" Donner released his grip and turned toward the voice, his gun still pressed against my skull. "You!" He gasped. "You lost your mind?"

Weakly, I turned to lean my back against the van, facing the action. Detective Carter stood a few feet away. He leveled a twelve-gauge, sawed-off shotgun, scanning it between Donner and Nash.

"Pick your things up, Sol," he said. "We're getting out of here."

I grabbed my wallet from Nash and my Cobra stuck inside his belt.

"Well! Well!" Donner guffawed, glaring and pointing

an empty-handed finger at Kevin. "So now we know. You're in big trouble, mister."

"Let me worry about that, Donner," Kevin said calmly. "Take their guns and keys," he said to me.

"If you think I'm giving up my gun, Carter," Donner said, "You don't know me." He still held the gun, pointed harmlessly away.

"This isn't some Mexican standoff," Kevin said, stepping closer, undoubtedly within deadly range. "I figure it's either you or me. And without hesitation, I'll gladly riddle your wretched ass full of buckshot. I'm already working on an alibi."

After snatching Donner's cannon from his hand, I gave him a vicious knee to the balls. With pleasure, I watched him sink, cursing, to the ground. Then I stepped on his knuckles.

"No more, Sol," Kevin shouted.

Kevin threw their guns and keys into a mass of unruly hedges. I checked under the doormat, but whatever money Karen had left for Bryan had obviously been found.

"Meet me, same spot as we planned," Kevin said just before I pulled away.

I stepped from the warmth of the van in front of Silver Lake Park. Without a ceiling of clouds, the temperature had dropped near freezing. Kevin was already on the darkened court, dribbling and shooting an underinflated rubber basketball. When I walked past the gate, he tossed the ball to me.

"Sorry to hear about the bomb," he said.

"Yeah." I put up an air ball. "So was the driver's wife."

He retrieved my bad shot, "You contact your insurance company yet?"

"For what?" I said, removing my jacket and laying it

beside his. "It's a long story, but fact is, there's no Independent cabdriver in town with comprehensive."

"Damn, that's right. Now I remember reading something. What was it? A network of bogus claims sending a bunch of cab and body-shop people off to jail." Still unable to accept the truth, he spin-skipped the ball to me, asking, "No coverage at all?"

"Believe it!" I tapped his pass back to him, "Not a cent's worth."

"Tough!" He cradled the ball as he spoke. "I'm sorry to hear that."

"You always travel with a ball?"

"It was here," he said, hitting a swisher from the top of the key. "Some kid must have left it."

We shot as we talked.

I told him about my recent conversation with Karen concerning the money he'd left for Bryan.

"A tip came from a motel owner on Riverside," Kevin said. "Someone fitting Bryan's description checked in yesterday. But by the time Donner and Nash got there, he'd ducked out. Must have been in a hurry, because he left all of his I.D. and a couple of hundred bucks behind." He sank another long-range jumper.

I explained how Bryan had accomplished the slip according to Karen.

"Those photographs you took proved useful, though," he said, missing the basket for the first time in six shots. "A portrait of two rotten eggs, I'd say."

He gave me a rundown on Andre and Tarzan while I zeroed in on the basket. Armando Sanchez, the Chicano, was an ex-police officer from El Paso, Texas. He had been fired from the department after three years and several disciplinary inquiries into his behavior in the field. Preston Reynolds, the black now running with Sanchez, had chalked up a long police record as a teenager in Atlanta. At age twenty-two, while in prison for manslaughter, he had taken up boxing. After being paroled, he had two professional bouts before disappearing from the circuit after testing positive for drugs.

They had both become local residents within the last year.

"Some team," I said, sinking another shot, having adjusted my touch on the ball to the dark, the wind, and the aching in my head. "Just the kind of upstanding citizens you'd expect to be driving 'round in Beemers."

"Indeed!" Kevin nodded. "I traced the last one that you saw outside the bank. It's a company car belonging to some corporation with the dubious title of Trendset Management Systems."

"Let me guess," I ventured. "It was leased from Wescott Auto Leasing?"

"Good guess!" he said. "And I'd bet, though no fingerprints were left, traces of their hair and clothing can be found in the car that got impounded."

"Have you checked?"

"Nope." Kevin rebounded my missed shot.

"Why's that?"

"I haven't had the chance." He dribbled and laid the ball off the backboard for another basket. "I called the lab back twice while wrapping up a case that's had me spinning around in circles for months. Both times, though, I got put on hold. I think I'm being frozen out."

"Any updates on who owns the party lines? Maybe there's a connection with this Trendset group."

"There probably is." He threw the ball hard off the backboard. It bounced and rolled far from the court. "Just try proving it."

We both retrieved our jackets and plopped on the courtside bench. Kevin continued. "I'm sure that the fuckers who are really profiting have their names so buried in red tape that it would take a slew of lawyers and the IRS years to put a tag on any of them." He sighed wearily. "And none of the bastards that really count."

"Time," I said. "A precious commodity."

"Precisely," he agreed. "Especially, after what I did earlier, I may be quickly joining you in the ranks of the unemployed." He stood, stretched, and yawned.

"Makes you wonder what the world's coming to," I said.

"Sure does! Maybe in the whole scheme, we're the ones who are the chumps." he laughed. "Ever consider that?"

"No," I said. "And I'm not about to start."

"Good for you, Sol."

"By the way," I said, "thanks for saving me from Donner."

"What else could I do." He smiled. "Watch him pull your balls off?"

We both laughed. It felt good, though my head ached even more when I laughed.

"How did you happen on the scene, anyway?" I asked as we walked from the park.

"After the lab boys refused to cooperate, I decided maybe trailing those two might help. I tailed them half the night. They're so cocksure, it was no trouble. Too easy, in fact. The only time Donner probably uses the rearview mirror is to pick his teeth."

He laughed deep from the gut before adding, "They were just sitting there in front of the house for almost an hour."

"Really! Then what took you so long to play savior?"

"I was hoping you'd be able to handle them yourself."

"Yeah! Well." I stroked between my legs. "I'm glad you came to your senses."

"I guess I have more faith in you than you do in yourself."

The stiff, frigid breeze off the reservoir grew colder.

A cluster of heavy clouds moved in from the north at freeway speed.

"It's snowing somewhere," Kevin said, eyeing the accumulating clouds. "Not too far away, either."

Back in Silver Shadow, I remembered the cassette that Karen had given me. On the way back to Smoody's, I punched it in. Nerve-searing static came through the van's sound system for the first few seconds. Then an equally irritating voice filled the speakers.

"Kim, baby girl, it's me again! And I got something hard, long, black, and throbbing for you!"

Though the voice spoke in the meter of a rap artist, it sounded like the voice of a white man doing his best to sound black while speaking with a lisp.

"Not you again," Jennifer said. "Why don't you stop calling? Just hang up!"

"I'll hang up if you let me hang some grade-A meat off in your ass, 'cause I'm square bizzness, baby. If you unne'stand when a real man's talkin' to you."

"Hey, dude," another caller blurted in, "why don't you leave the girl alone?"

"What's it to you, chump ass? It's none of your bizzness how I talk to her. She's swine, and there's only one way to talk to pigs."

"If you were a real man, you'd meet me somewhere, dude, and we could—"

"Meet you, faggot," the instigator said. "What are you, about five foot two? I'll meet you anywhere. Only you got to promise to wear that pretty little red dress and those high-heel shoes I love so much! Then we talkin' square bizzness, then!"

"Just ignore him," Karen's voice came on the line. "You better get off, jerk! We're tracing this call."

"Trace this." He belched into the line, using a sophisticated booster to magnify and echo his voice. "Kim, you ugly bitch, you. I gonna roast your ass! Hear me, Kim. I gonna roast your tiny little ass till it's black and tender the way I like it. Black and tender, roasted pig's ass." He laughed satanically. "Pig's ass. Pig's ass."

"Shut up, dude. What's wrong with you?"

"Back off, punk," the amplified voice boomed. "Kim's who I'm talking to. And Kim, baby girl, I know more about you than you wish I did." His laughter rose a pitch. "I know where you live, too. It's a little pig sty. So get used to me, baby cakes, because you haven't heard the last of me. Square bizzness! One of these nights we gonna come face to face and your pig ass behind is gonna be mine. All pig ass mine!"

Either he hung up or his two minutes had run out. The other callers tried to console Kim. Soon he was on the line again. Another ten minutes of the tape held similar taunts and threats. I was glad when the tape ended. Hearing it left me more confused than informed.

It was half an hour until closing time when I got back to Smoody's Blue Note. A pretty blues songstress, backed by a trio, was performing to a half-packed house. I was surprised to see Smoody manning the bar.

"Good sound, huh?" he asked as I bellied up to the counter.

"Yeah," I agreed. "She can definitely blow."

Lost in the lyrics, I heard Smoody speaking, "The drummer's one of my students."

I gave the instrumentalists a better ear. The drummer, a young man no more than twenty years of age, outshone both the bass player and the man on keyboards.

"He's better than good!" I finally said. "Really knows how to mash it up."

"I may have to tell him I'm too busy for any more lessons." He winked, then said, "Let the house buy you a drink."

"You know better."

"Dammit! I'd forget my head if it wasn't attached to my neck."

He poured a Seven-Up on ice and set it in front of me.

"I watched the 11 o'clock news," he said, frowning and gritting his teeth, exhaling with a hiss. "They did you better. But the fact that you're a P.I. is known to the world now, bro."

"Maybe it'll be good for business." I smiled and pretended to sip the soft drink. "Since I don't have a cab anymore."

He laughed. "Solomon without a cab." He shook his head several times and then, like an afterthought, said, "I got someone I'd like you to meet."

"Who's that?"

"See the superfine one, off in the corner, with the beige top and headwrap?" He indicated the direction with his eyes. "She's Ethiopian. An artist. Always comes in—and leaves by herself." He smiled shrewdly, rubbing a thumb back and forth across his first and second fingers. "And check it out, homeboy, she comes from royal blood, and royal wealth, too!"

"I don't think now is the right time," I said, though I was definitely intrigued by the sight of her. "But thanks. I'm going to see if any messages came in."

I rewound the tape on the answering machine that Smoody's wife had set up for me. There were several messages. There was one from my mother, calling from Philadelphia. Every year she called at 6:57 A.M.. Eastern Standard Time—the exact time that I had been born thirty-five years ago on a cold January night.

"Happy birthday, Solomon. I set my alarm to call you. I guess you're out having lots of fun as usual. Call me soon. I love you. Mom."

I had completely forgotten that today was my birthday.

Lost in a wave of nostalgia, I listened as a few other messages played. Several calls from neighbors and from riders like Ramona had expressed grief concerning the bombing and the death of Shorty. Collette Carter had called again.

She had suggested that we get together informally for lunch or dinner. Surprising as that invitation had been, the last message on the recorder came as a complete shock.

"Solomon." The voice rekindled hot prickles of anger. "This is Rupert Collingsworth. I know you must be surprised to hear from me. Maybe I was too hasty in the way I reacted yesterday. However, I need to talk with you. If you're an early riser, you can find me on the beach at Malaga Cove between six and seven in the morning." There was a brief pause. "I'll look forward to seeing you,—if you can make it."

I tossed and turned. Fragments of dreams were the only indication that sleep had occasionally overcome my anxiety. When the alarm on my wristwatch went off, it was still dark outside.

The sky was only a scant bit lighter when I drove up to a parking space at Malaga Cove on the shores of Palos Verdes Peninsula. Winding concrete steps led down to a narrow, rocky beachfront as the morning fog licked at the feet of the massive perpendicular cliffs facing the water. Through the mist, I spotted a figure standing knee-deep in the surf.

It was Collingsworth, casting a line. Unsatisfied with his angling, he drew his line in, and again casted. He was repeating the same motions when he noticed me on the shore.

He waved, showing his pearly-whites as though I were a friend. His line tightened, and he fought a big catch until it was drawn into his hand-held net. Smiling, like the cameras for "Great Sportsmen" were focused on him, he waded back to shore among the rocks.

"Glad you could make it," he said, walking to his bucket, which contained two other sizable catches.

"A nice rock cod," I said.

"You know your fish, huh?" he said, clipping the hook from the mouth of his catch and dropping it into the bucket with the others. "You're a fisherman?"

"I've done some."

Seated on the damp sand, he began stripping off his hip boots. "Twice a week I come down here. Three mornings a week I jog. But nothing is more satisfying and relaxing than the time I spend here." He stood and began working his way out of his upper gear. "When I jog, I'm always looking at my watch, calculating the time and the ground I've covered. Trying to beat myself. Out here, they bite or they don't. I have no control. It's a matter of fate, and that's just fine with me."

"What else did you want to chat about?"

He gritted his teeth and bit back whatever his first impulse was to say. He wiped sand from his large hands. "The other day, you had two questions for me. Today, I'm ready to answer both."

"Why the change of heart?" I pulled my collar closer as the wind grew stiff. A seagull made a low sweep over Collingsworth's bucket, eyeing a possible breakfast.

"Last night, while watching the news,"—he stuffed his folded fishing clothes into a canvas sack—"I saw the coverage on you. Something told me that, more than likely, you're an innocent man caught in the middle. Then, I thought, maybe you could be trusted."

"Rather than held in contempt?"

"Exactly!" he said, attempting to smile. "Under the circumstances, I feel you can understand me being suspicious."

"I'm listening."

"Good," he said. "Let's start walking back. I've got to change and be at the office before long."

We started the hike. The same seagull that had made a pass over the bucket circled us so low that I felt his shadow.

Collingsworth was talking.

"The two punks you saw in my office came to blackmail me. And they succeeded. They bilked me for a hundred thousand."

I kept quiet, waiting for him to continue.

"Jennifer's mother was a sickly woman. Operation after operation for a faulty heart didn't cure her. She was left totally paralyzed after a stroke. She used to beg for me to end her suffering with an overdose of morphine."

Halfway up the steps, he stopped and confronted me. Because I was standing a step above him, we were eye to eye.

"One night when she was particularly vocal, I spotted Jennifer standing in the doorway. She was just a tot. I shooed her off and never thought any more about the incident until months later—when her mother passed away. Then something in that little girl's eyes told me that she suspected me of complying with her mother's wishes."

He sighed deeply, shoulders hunched. Then we continued climbing the steps, the roar of the ocean behind us, the seagull heading out to sea.

"I felt guilty every time I looked at her," he went on. "Because more than once I did consider heeding my wife's pleas, but I couldn't bring myself to follow through." He grimaced, making his face look many years older than it normally appeared.

We reached the top in silence. I asked, "So Jennifer must have said something to Andre and Tarzan?"

"Yes."

"But you must have already known that Jennifer had been killed."

He whirled to face me, blue eyes flashing anger. "For a hundred thousand dollars I'd pay to let the dead rest in peace." He studied me for a long time, his thick eyebrows furrowed. "Can't you understand that?"

"I guess I can," I found myself saying, looking out over the foaming ocean. "But what does this have to do with me?"

"I . . ." He shuddered. "I just don't want any of this to go any further." He set his gear and bucket down. "They'll plague me forever. You're a detective. I just want their names," he snarled. "I want the bastards' names. You can give me that. You're on the case aren't you? Maybe you already know who they are."

"Why don't you ask the authorities?"

"You think I want unfounded allegations like these open to speculation?" he looked at me dumbfounded.

"Let's say I know their names. I give them to you. Then what?"

He placed his gear in the trunk of a Lincoln Mark IV.

"I'm an attorney. You supply the names, I'll take care of it from there. But you'll be thousands of dollars richer." He slammed the trunk shut. "That should be more than enough to interest you."

"Maybe," I said, walking away from him.

"You know how to reach me," he shouted.

I turned, walking back to him.

"Did you ever stop to think that these same two bastards might have been responsible for your daughter's death?"

"How could the thought not cross my mind?" He left his key in the door, dangling, then swaggered up to me.

"I had a nine millimeter automatic sitting in a drawer beside me when I agreed to talk to those bastards." He balled his fist so tight his knuckles turned white. "Thirty minutes after I heard about Jennifer's body being found, they were on the phone. I would have used that gun, wiped them out, and asked questions later!" He was breathing hard. "But when I told them that the police had already informed me that Jennifer had been murdered that morning, it completely threw them for a loop."

He shook his silver-gray tousled head, wiping at his eyes with a handkerchief. "So I asked them, now that she was dead, what difference would it make what they said? Then the spic reminded me that they still had written statements of Jennifer's accusations, and, as he put it, 'The value was probably hotter than ever.' "

Collingsworth shrugged, "At the time, a hundred thousand seemed a cheap price to pay. On the same day . . ." His thoughts seemed to wander.

I nodded my head, evaluating all I'd heard.

"You'll hear from me, Rupert. Even if you don't like what you hear."

"Why rush off?" He stepped in front of me. "I can make a check out to you now," he offered, folding his hands nervously.

"First, I need to know if I'm with you or against you. Paying me now might constitute conflict of interest."

"My mistake," he hissed, backing away from me. "You sniff like a well-trained dog. Only problem is, you don't know how to jump when opportunity knocks."

"Something about you just doesn't ring right, Collingsworth. I'd gladly take your money if you were paying me to find out who killed your daughter, but all you really seem interested in is who's blackmailing you."

Walking away, I heard him unnecessarily gun the big engine of his car. He sped past me as I reached the van.

I was cruising along Pacific Coast Highway, passing through Manhattan Beach, when I noticed a Highway

Patrol car lurking behind. A mile later, I saw the flashers blinking and heard the siren scream.

"Pull to the shoulder of the road," the loudspeaker commanded.

Chapter Seven

Slowly, the Highway Patrol officer approached my van parked on the shoulder of the highway. In my rear-view mirror, I could see his mouth nervously twitching. Cautiously, all the while toying with his sidearm, he reached my open window. He did a quick make on me and peered suspiciously as far as he could inside the van.

"Would you mind stepping out from the vehicle?"

"What's this all about?"

"Just step out from the vehicle." His mouth squinched up as he spoke, his patience eroding. "Please!"

"Sure." I sighed deeply and got out of the van.

"Are you the registered owner?"

"Yes, it's mine."

"Then your name's Solomon Priester?"

"Yes, but—"

"Turn around, please, sir. Spread your legs and put your hands up high and lean against the van."

After I'd faithfully followed his instructions, he kicked my legs wider apart, then frisked me, relieving me of my piece. While clasping the handcuffs around my wrists, he read me my rights.

"Mind telling me what the charges are?"

"Resisting arrest and assaulting an officer," he said matter-of-factly, then hissed. "Lucky it wasn't me. You'd be dead."

Before we started rolling, he announced to his station, via his radio, that he was bringing me in. The ride to the Highway Patrol Headquarters, fifteen minutes away, was a long and tense one.

I was stuck in a small holding tank where two drunks snored. Taking up a position in a corner, hunched down on the cold concrete floor, I waited two hours before a ripened old officer came to the cell door. He read out my name and then unlocked the barred door and escorted me to the front desk.

Lieutenant Pete Donner was the first person I saw as I walked in from the holding cells. He wore a satisfied smirk on his face. While Nash signed me over to their custody, Donner slipped his cuffs on me, squeezing them unmercifully tight.

"So we meet again," he said with a wry smile. "Only this time no half-assed buddy—rogue cop to interrupt."

Lighting a Camel cigarette, he blew smoke in my face. Nash completed the paperwork.

"Your prisoner now," the watch commander said, closing a large duty book. "All yours."

Roughly, I was thrown into the backseat of their unmarked car. We crossed the city of Santa Monica and into Los Angeles without a word spoken to me. They ignored me in favor of discussing the Kings hockey team. They were still speculating on the outcome of an upcoming game when we entered the parking facilities at Parker Center.

"Still here, huh?" Donner guffawed, opening the door from me.

"No," I said, "I'm just an illusion."

He gave me a quick rabbit punch to the kidneys, then jerked me up on my toes by the collar.

"Don't rush it," he said. "We got plenty of time to get acquainted. Seventy-two hours, at the least."

Soon, I was placed in another holding tank. This one, however, was packed to the gills. It provided little or no room to sit or stand.

An uncomfortable hour passed.

Again my name was called, and I was led up a few flights of stairs and into a small room with unpainted cinderblock walls. It was empty of anything other than a scarred desk, a few chairs, and an overhanging lamp.

"Have a seat, Priester," the escorting officer ordered. He cuffed me to a metal chair, and without another word, left me alone. Unfortunately, not for long.

Donner swaggered in. He grinned as he squashed a butt out on the dirty floor and straddled a chair facing me.

"Carter, that bastard buddy of yours, has been fired." His shit-eating grin widened, then he made a mockingly sad face. "Who's gonna help you now?"

"Maybe God's got nothing better to do."

"God this." He slapped me across the face with such force that my chair tilted, crashed, and slid for several feet on the floor.

"I'll be back." He laughed, leaving me lying facedown on the floor. Managing to roll on my back, I could see him return. He carried a police baton and a telephone book.

"Nash gets squeamish about some of the work we're required to do around here," he said, sounding almost apologetic. "So I'll be working alone."

He wrapped tape and a handkerchief around the handle of his baton. Then he placed the telephone book across one of my thighs and began to whale on it with all of his might. Each blow landed squarely with a pronounced echoing thud. Squirming and thrashing against my restraints, I tried maneuvering to escape the well-placed blows. But there was nowhere to hide. He began working on my other leg. I held back the screams and curses that were building in the back of my throat.

"Go ahead and yell," he said. "No one gives a fuck, anyway. So go on, scream!"

The baton came down heavily, again and again.

"Who're you working for?"

"That's privileged information." I heard my own voice sounding distant and strange.

"You think you're a tough little bastard, don't you?"

He placed the telephone book at the base of my skull and slammed hard.

"You won't be black-and-blue but you'll be a half-dead cripple if you don't answer right." He leaned over me, his face covered with sweat.

I rolled the chair again so that I lay faceup. Thick beads of his dirty sweat dripped down, stinging my eyes as he raised the stick again.

"You gonna start talking now? Or maybe I should take a coffee break and start all over again, rested and meaner than hell!"

Without thinking, I lifted a foot and kicked him solidly in the middle of his ugly mug. The force sent him reeling back, stumbling and sliding across the room.

He jumped up quickly. Raging and cursing, he charged me, baton in hand. I shielded myself from the first blow. But from everywhere, seemingly at once, the stick rained down on me. He lost all discretion, hitting me any and everywhere—aiming mostly for my head.

Sometime during the onslaught, I blacked out.

An infuriated, beet-red Donner, bearing long, sharpened, fanglike yellow teeth, came at me again, cursing and frothing at the mouth. I struggled, and awoke. The whole world was shrouded in pitch-black darkness.

Eventually, I realized that I was lying in a puddle of cold sweat, dried and mucky blood—all of it my own. Then I ran my numbed hands across my lacerated, swollen face. Each movement sent nerve-shattering pain searing through my entire body. As I was feeling around me, on all fours, my eyes began to adjust somewhat to the darkness.

The solitary confinement cell was no larger than a utility closet, equipped with only a steel rack for a bed and a rank-smelling commode.

After I relieved myself on the commode, I tried to stand up straight, but my trauma-stricken muscles refused. I fought the urge to roll up into a fetal ball.

I had no idea how long I'd remained unconscious. Whether it was night or day, I could only guess. The ice-cold steel bunk offered no comfort. Neither did any of the other options available. At times, I paced the cold, tight rectangular room like a blind, lame beggar. I squirmed on the bunk or on the floor as minutes passed like hours.

While my body ached, my mind churned, and I was helpless to stop it. Except for the relentless beating that I'd suffered, nothing seemed to make sense. I reviewed the sunrise meeting that I had had with Collingsworth. It troubled me that he had all but absolved my prime suspects, Andre and Tarzan, of anything more incriminating than blackmail.

A slight sneeze caused my whole body to shudder in its wake. It was as if my body and my mind were separate, alien entities. While my mind sought answers— new pieces to an intricate puzzle—my body wanted to call it quits, to surrender unconditionally. The battle raged on as I prayed for sleep—any semblance of reprieve.

Sharply accented footsteps approached my cell. A rap came at the steel door, soon followed by a barking voice. "Step away from the cell door and face the back wall."

I heard the metallic clinking of a flashlight. Its cylin-

drical light peeked through a small barred spyhole—
helping make certain that I had obeyed.

Handcuffed again, I was led into a dimly lit corridor.

"Walk ahead of me and follow my directions," the
guard said, prodding my sore ribs with his nightstick.
As I shuffled dispiritedly along, each of my agonized
steps covered mere inches.

I was transferred to the County Jail. In the ensuing
process, the setting sun had a near blinding effect on
me.

At County, I again found myself deposited in a large
holding tank filled with blacks and Hispanics. A few of
my cellmates recognized me from the TV coverage of
my bombed-out cab. Though I was hardly in a sociable
mood, some of their words of consolation were heart-
felt.

I stood for two agonized hours, or more, in a line to
reach a phone. After learning that jail phone systems
don't accept credit card payments, I made my calls collect. The operator reached Kevin Carter's answering
machine.

"Sorry," she said.

I tried Pops Orosco's line, but it rang and rang unanswered. I felt fortunate to finally reach Smoody at the
Blue Note. After I gave him a quick update, he immediately understood my predicament.

"Had a feeling that something wasn't right, but you
just hang in there," he promised. "I'll get you out—
quick as I can."

"Contact Pops." I gave him the number. "He should
be able to suggest a good bail bondsman or lawyer.
Whatever it costs, I'll pay back every cent the minute
I'm out of here."

"Money's no problem," he assured me. "I'll personally sign to get your ass out of there. I've got collateral
up the ying yang, now. So don't worry, brother, I'm
there and God's with you, too!"

Eventually, I was booked, fingerprinted.

The officer who fingerprinted me added insult like salt to a fresh wound when he reminded me, announcing to anyone in earshot, "We've got a birthday boy here. Bet this is one you won't forget!"

Later I was photographed; ushered into a near-freezing shower; sprayed with a delousing chemical; given underwear, a uniform, a toothbrush, and a blanket; examined by a team of doctors, and locked shut into a communal space with an estimated thousand other prisoners in an immense space, called a ward.

The musty-smelling, book-thin mattress that I finally laid claim to felt not much softer than the naked steel bunk I'd so recently despised in solitary. Although my body shook like it would never cease shaking, I did my best to lie still on a bottom bunk in a corner of the noisy ward.

During the night, a dream assailed me in living color. Again, I stood beside L-92, smelling the stench of Shorty's burning body.

He turned to face me and say in the calmest of voices, "Don't forget me, Sol." I charged the flames—which weren't hot to me. I tore a door open and reached for Shorty to drag him out. But before I could reach him, he began to melt.

In the morning, about 6:30, the call for breakfast came.

"Come on." I felt someone nudge me gently on the shoulder. "Better get yourself something to eat."

Looking up, I focused on the face of a big cream-and-coffee-colored man sporting a shaven head and a friendly enough smile.

"I don't want anything."

"You gotta eat, least go to mess hall, 'cause that's when they take count, see if any of us chickens is flown the coop."

It took a while for me to will myself to rise and join the other men and their funerallike march. Several times, I was told to speed it up by the guards as I shuffled lamely along, as fast as I could. Through the long, cold, bleakly lit halls and down elevators, I passed hundreds, maybe thousands of prisoners returning from the mess hall. All of them—no matter how cocky and rebellious they portrayed themselves—seemed to be connected by the invisible thread of doom. They were like returned goods, quietly resigned to imprisonment as part of life's cycle of normal events.

Soupy, loveless food was dumped on my plate. Rather than eat it, I gave it to the inmates nearest me to share.

"You look bad, brother," one of the young men at the table said. "You ought to be in the infirmary."

"Long as he can stand," another inmate who looked like a gangbanger added, "they ain't got no room for him. 'Specially if it was the cops who put the whipping on him."

Later, unable to reach Smoody, I got in touch with Pops Orosco. Smoody had called him already, so there was less for me to explain. As gently as possible, Pops delivered the news.

"They've got a seventy-two-hour hold for questioning on you, son. Until they drop that hold, there's nothing a lawyer can do. Sorry, but my hands are tied. They can hold you the entire time, then charge you. No telling what they'll set bail at."

"In other words, I may be here until Monday when court opens?"

"No way! No matter what the bail is set at, me and your compadre, Smoody, are determined to get you out of that hellhole as soon as we can. I'll keep checking downtown. But until they drop that fuckin' hold, there's not much I can do."

"Thanks, Pops," I said, "As far as the cash is concerned, I've probably got five thousand in my account. So don't let the money hang you up."

"I wouldn't do that." He laughed. "Keep your fingers crossed, though, and don't go kicking anybody in the face till you're out of jail."

"Sure, Pops. I guarantee you, I'll wait till then."

The clear probability that I'd be forced to stay the full length of the hold was something I couldn't shake. Imagining Donner dropping the hold was not as easy as expecting him to call me down for another chat. But something told me that if he had any more questions for me, he wouldn't have transferred me to County. The hold for questioning was just another way of sticking it to me.

Later that evening, I was led from Cellblock 9500 to another tier and a four-man cell. My cellmates were two congenial men in their late twenties and an older, graying man who spent most of his time sleeping or bemoaning the fate that had allowed him to be arrested three times for driving under the influence of alcohol. One of the younger men, T.J., had gotten caught passing fraudulent checks after years of profiting by the same tactics. Though he showed no signs of remorse for his crimes, he continually occupied himself by consulting the New Testament.

When we were back in our cell, after Friday's dinner march, T.J. asked, "What's with all of this Rastaman stuff, anyway?"

"Just a matter of belief," I said.

"Yeah, but beliefs have to have some facts to back them."

"True," I granted. "However, most people mistake what they believe for what they know."

"Yeah, but it says right here in the Bible that the only path to the Father is through the Son, Jesus Christ. Don't you believe in the Bible?"

"I think it's a great reference point," I said, rolling on

my back to give my sore ribs a rest. "But as far as I'm concerned, there were many prophets who lived and walked this earth—and there'll be more to come."

"Like Muhammad was one?"

"Yes, like Muhammad, like Buddha, like Zoroaster."

"Zoro . . . who?"

"Zoroaster." I pronounced the name slowly. "He lived hundreds of years before Jesus. His teachings were the cornerstone for Christianity and the Nation of Islam. He spoke of an age-long war between good and evil. Basically, he preached three tenets: good thoughts, good words, good deeds."

"Very basic!" he scoffed.

"For his day and age," I countered, "he was saying a mouthful." I paused. "And more recently there was Ethiopia's Ras Tafari, who was later crowned with the title Haile Selassie I. His message was that as long as racism and prejudice exist in any form, there will be war, no peace on earth, no marriage or unification of God and the people."

"Hmmm," he mused.

"But no matter whether you call the Supreme One Elohim, Allah, or God, He's still listening. Probably saying something like, 'I don't care what name you use, just make sure you call me.' "

"All that sounds good," T.J. finally said skeptically, "but I'm sticking with the Good Book."

"Then do it. Do what you believe in," I said. "Follow your beliefs, whatever they are, if you expect them to matter. For me, when I pray or give thanks, I use the name Jah."

My pessimism concerning an early release proved correct. It wasn't until late Saturday afternoon that I heard my name announced among the list of people being released. I'd dreamed the same sequence many times before. Only this time, it wasn't a wishful fantasy—my name had actually been called. Another six hours were spent retrieving personal property, along with other timeless phases of release from the system's belly.

Finally, I was walking past the last door with bars. With dry trails of blood still caked to the front of my clothes, I must have looked like someone heading in the wrong direction.

Expecting to walk quietly into the evening might, I was taken aback when I saw a couple of news crews lingering in the lobby. At first sight of me, they rushed my way. I looked for Pops, but instead there was Collette Carter, asking a question and thrusting a microphone at me.

"Mr. Priester, exactly how long have you been incarcerated, and for what reason were you arrested?"

Smoody used his thick shoulders to muscle a path to me. "Leave him alone," he was shouting at everyone. "Back off and leave him alone!"

He forged his way to my side, and with one quick look assessed the shape I was in—hungry, weak, beaten, and barely able to walk. He put my arm around his shoulders and led me through the lights, cameras, and questions—pushing aside anyone who got in the way. I heard Collette's voice rising distinctly above the racket.

"Was the deceased girl more than just a fare—perhaps a girlfriend, a lover?"

"Ignore her," Smoody said.

We pushed through their blockade and out into the invigoratingly fresh, wind-swept January night. I took a deep breath.

Smoody's '67 indigo-blue Cadillac—driven by one of his friends—swept to the curb. With bright lights still shadowing us, cameras still rolling, and asinine questions still being fired, the Caddy pulled away, Smoody and me in the back.

"Make sure no one follows us," Smoody said to

John-John, a thin man with a pock-marked face, behind the wheel. "But don't do anything to get us pulled over, either!"

" 'Nuff said, cap!"

We pulled away at a good clip, hanging a left toward Macy Street. As we passed a host of bail bond shacklike offices and huge billboards advertising them, Smoody spoke. "Welcome back to the real world."

"Thanks! You don't know how much I owe you."

"Thank me and Pops," he said, reaching inside his coat to pull out a flask. "The lawyer he got talked to the D.A. and got the bail they set reduced from fifty thousand to ten thousand."

"I thought he was going to pick me up."

"We decided to take a few extra precautions." He took a long swig from the flask. "Lucky thing we did, too. Considering the eager bandwagon that just greeted you!"

He saw me flinch as we rode over a big street bump. "Pretty bad, huh?"

"Yeah, but I'm feeling better than I felt three days ago."

He held the flask out toward me, "I know you been dry a long time. But anybody could understand you taking a swallow for medicinal purposes only."

Reflections from the amber streetlights of the Macy Street underpass seemed to dance and sparkle on every contour of the silver-plated flask, which appeared suspended in time. I could almost taste the quick-fire of its contents.

"No," I finally said. "But thanks, anyway."

He shrugged, then said, "No harm in offering." After another swig, he began to fill me in. "Got to finally talk with the famed Pops you always be talkin' about. And what we decided is, somebody wants you bad. Your house turned upside down! The cab blown to holy hell! It's easy to see somebody wants you laying low. Or if need be, dead!" He lowered his head and shook it slowly from side to side as the hum of the tires filled the silence. "Until somebody finds out who that is, or at least till you can walk right, you need a safe place to stay."

"Like an insane asylum?"

"No, man." He laughed and gingerly embraced my shoulder. "It ain't me or you that's fucked up. It's the violent and silent majority out there, brother. That's why we've got to look out for each other, 'cause nobody else will."

He grabbed a plastic bag from the front seat and handed it to me. Inside were two brand-new pairs of wash-and wear slacks, a couple of pullovers, underwear, socks, toiletries, and a robe.

Aster, the Ethiopian woman who I had seen in Smoody's the night before I got busted, had agreed to put me up for a few days until I was in better shape.

"How'd you convince her to do that?" I asked skeptically.

"I just told her that you're special people, a person who cares." He smiled sagely. "And sometimes caring gets you into trouble."

"And she bought that?" I laughed, even though it hurt.

"I'm serious." His tone was low. "Remember how we met?"

"That was nothing."

"It was something to me! What average cabdriver, or anybody for that matter, gonna see some nigger lookin' like a bum on the wrong side of town, sayin' he's been mugged, and trust 'im? Believe 'im? Offer 'im a ride?" He answered himself. "Not many! If any!"

Like a revelation, I realized how isolated and adrift my life had become, and how precious friendship is. For where would I have been without pragmatic Pops and sentimental Smoody? I'm sure the humility I felt was expressed in my voice.

"If you think that she really doesn't mind, I do need to sort things out."

As we rolled away from downtown, up Sunset, I learned more about the messages and happenings of the last three days.

My van, Silver Shadow, was parked in Smoody's garage, no longer impounded. My landlady was furious and demanded that I repair all of the damage done to her property, posthaste. She agreed to allow me two weeks' grace time, threatening me with an eviction notice if I didn't comply.

Lastly, and most importantly, I learned that Shorty's funeral was the next day.

Inside Griffith Park, off Los Feliz, we stopped while Smoody slipped out of the car and took a piss. Satisfied that we hadn't been followed, he jumped back in the car and gave new directions, and we made a left on Red Oak following the sharp ascent of a tight, curving road that ran the rim of the western end of the park.

All of the neighboring homes were built on sizable lots surrounded by thick-trunked, wide-armed live oak and wispy, nearly anorexic eucalyptus. Most of the dwellings were of the Spanish hacienda or English Tudor styles, popular in the forties and fifties. However, Aster's house stood out from the others.

It was a modern grayish-blue stucco job, trimmed with an occasional red decorative border. It rose three stories high and had just a few streamlined stained-glass windows facing the street. With its ninety-degree, straight-edged lines, the house embodied contradiction, appearing like a misplaced business structure rather than the semi-secluded private residence it was.

Smoody helped me to climb the pink tiled stairway, up to a warmly lit alcove and the front door, and he rang the chimes.

Chapter Eight

At my urgent request, Aster turned the powerful jets to low, then gratefully to off. Floating in the liquefied heat of the Jacuzzi was enough reward in itself, especially after telling myself that I was in heaven during the shower I took.

Besides, the pressurized jets stirring the one-hundred-and-ten-degree water were a little too much for the aches of my body to endure. It was like being in the ring with a half-dozen lightweights, all jabbing only me.

Clouds of steam rose up into the open night air. The sweat on my face defied the chilly overcast sky. Off the back veranda, I could look out into the stillness of the forest that surrounded a crest in the nearby hills of the park. There were no other houses in sight, and all was black and still except for the glowing light from the Jacuzzi.

Aster slipped back into the water beside me. We were both naked. The lighted pink, blue, and yellow bottom waved the colors of our skin against its background like flags unfolding against the sky.

I closed my eyes.

A coyote's long, mournful cry lifted up from the valley below us. The sound vibrated and echoed in its loneliness. It came again—this time farther away. A few night birds chirping and the slight rustling of leaves filled the void.

"I'm glad that you had no trouble abiding by my rules," Aster said in a soft, soothing voice, as though our conversation had not been broken. "Some people are so uptight about their bodies. But to get into a Jacuzzi in a bathing suit would be like listening to your favorite music with earplugs. Besides, being self-conscious about your body isn't going to magically change it. May as well like what you have, I say."

I thought, Very easy for you to say.

Instead of speaking, I exhaled a deep, extended breath that I had just swallowed. Then I sighed a great whoosh of air in exaltation.

"Thank you, Jah!"

Yet, comfortable as I was, it was impossible not to be supremely aware of Aster's sculptured beauty. Seeing the glossy silkiness of her rich and dark rosy skin, shimmering so near, made me feel a little uneasy, because all of her actions were so natural that it would be hard to read anything she did, or any special movement, as flirtatious or sexually suggestive. She had the kind of tall, firm figure that I knew could—even when fully clothed—inspire a lot of hungry scrutinization. Women probably took careful notice as well, some with admiration, others with boiling envy. But all of them would undoubtedly prefer to see Aster keep her clothes on.

"What is there to hide?" I finally spoke.

"Exactly!" she said, her eyes lighting up playfully. "But don't get too comfortable yet. This is only step one. The doctor has more in store."

She climbed out of the Jacuzzi and dried herself on the redwood deck with her back to me. "Five more minutes," she said, slipping into a robe and leaving me, disappearing from the veranda.

Once I was back inside the house, Bianca, a young

but matronly shaped Salvadoran woman who worked for Aster, brought me some fresh-made vegetable soup. When I was done, she took my empty cup and led me to a sauna large enough for six adults.

"Twenty minutes," she said, speaking in Spanish, sliding the door shut.

I was savoring the dry heat, the solitude, and the luxury of having food in my gullet after so many days of passing up County food, when the door again slid open.

"Tiempo."

"Already," I said, amazed at the swift passing of time.

With Bianca's assistance, I walked to the bathroom for a quick shower. Then she helped me lie down on a chiropracticlike table that faced the same barren hills that I'd seen from the veranda. Bianca excused herself, saying that Aster would be with me soon.

The room was lit by several dozen scented candles that flickered and danced their light off the religious icons that covered the walls.

I smelled Aster's jasmine fragrance as she entered. She fumbled momentarily with a cassette tape, loading it into a player.

Drumbeats, flutes, and chants played at a low volume.

"Music from home," she said gliding up to me. "If it's too loud, say so."

"Too loud for what?" I laughed.

"Well, well." She returned my laughter. "Seems as though you're feeling a lot better already. But what I'm talking about is a therapeutic massage, to promote relaxation and a night of well-deserved rest."

"I know, I know," I said, still finding it hard to believe that indeed all that Smoody had told me was true. For he had said that she was a student in the arts of healing who put herself completely into a spiritual grace when administering the arts.

He had added, "You'll feel like your namesake, King Solomon, before the night's out."

"This ointment has all kinds of healing properties," she said as she laid a cold, wet hand on me. I shuddered as though I had been brushed with an iceberg.

"Good." She sighed. "Gently, I'm going to rub you down with this. I won't use any pressure because I can see that your body is much too bruised and tender for that."

She spread the solution across my back and shoulders. My nose picked up the scent of eucalyptus and camphor.

"Very good," she said, beginning to work at the base of my skull. "When I first saw you, I wondered what your creative interest was."

"That's not surprising. Everybody always assumes that I'm a musician."

"Stereotypical. With me, they hear what country I'm from, and naturally I'm supposed to be starving."

"Doesn't look like that's the case."

"It never has been that way for me or my family."

A groan escaped my lips.

"Sorry," she said. "I was getting too rough. Excuse."

"That's okay," I managed to say, still biting on my lip as the salient solution soaked into my raw skin.

"But I didn't think musician, not after I'd studied you. I would have guessed you to be more a man of letters, a poet—quote unquote—of sorts."

"You'd have been straining, but partially right."

"How's that?"

"I used to fancy myself a poet, a long time ago."

"Once a poet, always a poet," she retorted quickly. "Why did you stop, though?"

It took a long time for me to answer.

"Just felt that I was spending too much time trying to think of what to say rather than just living."

"Can you recall anything you've written?" she asked.

The eucalyptus smell immediately prompted me to think of the last poem I'd taken time to jot down, some two years earlier.

Aster had me turn over. "Can you remember the inspiration?" she asked, covering my midsection with a towel.

"Sure." I sighed. "My cab. I had been driving a lot of nights at the time. It was the rainy season, like now. And one night, I happened to look up at one of the mountainsides in the distance. It was shaped like a woman lying down. The lights were like her jewelry. And the poem came to me."

"What do you call it?" she asked. Finishing with my lower half, she moved to my belly and chest.

" 'Lost Angel.' "

"Let's hear it," she whispered.

I took a deep breath, then went for it.

"I search her. I investigate her, the folds of her dress. She lies there. A half-smile, a wink—no further to touch than the most luscious of her folds—spread out. All four hundred and sixty-eight square miles sensitized."

She smiled. I went on.

"Night lights wink and she expresses herself best. A little wine makes her tickle. And she winks, red lights, yellows, greens, amber streams, gold-plated footsteps, dreams relit and kindled by perhaps the faintest moon.

"I see her now. She's resting. Her pulse soothed by the music. Her breathing less congested.

"Now she sparkles. She illusionalizes. She invites but never promises. She waves fragrance, eucalyptus and burnt lead. But she never snores. And it would be a mistake to equate her deep sighs with sleep."

There was a long silence, then Aster said, "That's beautiful." She finished applying the solution. "Very beautiful."

I followed her to another room that had a bed with its covers pulled down.

"It's late," she said. "Get some rest, and I'll see you in the morning."

I lay down on the firm mattress as she closed the door behind her. Remembering the phone calls I'd intended to make, I decided to put them off, and soon drifted into a peaceful sleep.

The next morning, I was surprised by how much better I felt. Still stiff, but feeling surprisingly rejuvenated, I got out of bed and found a note from Aster telling me to make myself at home.

There was a large serving bowl of fresh sliced fruit in the refrigerator. I had two helpings as I enjoyed the solitude and spaciousness of the expensive but sparsely furnished house. Modern paintings, by a variety of artists, were hung on practically every wall, yet there was ample empty floorspace in each room, accented with potted palms, hanging ferns, and vases with fresh-cut flowers. Everything was scrubbed and polished to a high gleam.

In the dining room, where I ate, a fishbowl sat on a marblelike pedestal near a morning-lit window. One lone goldfish swam in its clear water.

I listened to the tapes of my messages which Smoody had handed over to me the night before. Most of them were from the same callers—Ramona, my landlady, and my mother.

Neither Ramona nor my mother answered their lines. I left a message on Ramona's machine and promised myself that I would contact my mother as soon as possible. It had been four days since she had tried to reach me, and I'm sure she was beginning to worry, because not returning her calls was something that was unlike me.

Dialing my landlady, I hoped that she, too, might be

unavailable. No such luck. We talked, or should I say she talked, nonstop for thirty minutes, repeating the same terms that she had relayed through Smoody. I promised that I would repair the damaged floors within two weeks, but then she'd lose her composure and start all over again.

Finally, I shouted, "Okay, I'll fix whatever has to be fixed. Just shut the hell up!" And slammed down the phone.

Bespectacled Randy Blackwell, one of the cab dispatchers, picked me up before noon in a clunker whose doors and fenders were mismatched in their faded colors.

We were sullen and reticent as he drove us south to the city of Carson, where Shorty's funeral was being held. The gray sky emphasized the bleakness that marked the industrial skyline bordering the Harbor Freeway. Factories and warehouses surrounded by towering electrical transformers, oil refinery tanks, and salvage yards of all types dominated the passing scenery.

Funeral weather, I thought to myself.

"What a day to get buried." Randy seemed to take a cue from my thoughts. "One hell of a day!"

My mind was too preoccupied to think of a meaningful response.

Thick black clouds converged, and before we reached our exit, heavy pellets of rain began attacking the windshield. Randy was a bit peeved that smog had gotten to his driver's side windshield wiper.

"Just what I need now!"

We recognized the funeral home by the many Independent cabs parked nearby. Randy and I were among the last to arrive, and the restless crowd was meandering toward the usher and the open door of the red-brick funeral home. Poor air ventilation heightened the crampedness of the old place and the oppressive humidity. We sat near the rear of the assembly. An elderly, frail-bodied organist played an uninspired rendition of "Nearer My Lord to Thee."

The minister strode to his place at the podium. He was a dark, youngish man with thinning gray hair and a stomach that overrode his belt and its wide buckle.

He thanked the organist and turned his attention toward us.

"Death is never an easy fact of life to reconcile ourselves with. But it is a fact of life." He went on to speak about the transient nature of life and the gift of redemption guaranteed to all of humanity by the one and only savior, Jesus.

I closed one ear to him, but the Catholic upbringing that had been so much a part of my early school years began to make me feel an uncomfortable need for fresh air.

Nothing he said was new. The same tired phrases followed one another like a parade of withered soldiers wearing sparkling new uniforms to cover their deformities and wounds. The moans and weeping that arose from around me bore witness to the incongruity of it all.

I remembered the nuns and their unwavering strictness, the wooden rulers cracked across my knuckles, the yardsticks across my bent-over ass, the blackboard where I was forced to write—a hundred times—the Ten Commandments and other expressions of a Deity that I felt alienated from. It wasn't the teachings themselves that left me with the hollow feeling of an outcast, it was their methods of teaching that left me so enraged as to rebel, then live to rebel again and again.

At home, my father, like his father before him, had inspired me to see Jesus as a man of color, unlike Michelangelo's model, his light-haired, light-eyed cousin. My mother, although raised a Baptist, thought that a Catholic school upbringing was the only hope for me receiving a decent education, something she felt Philadelphia's public schools could never offer.

Having difficulty making the adjustment, I was eventually kicked out of Catholic school. But the collective damage was already complete.

Years passed, and I was kicked out of more schools than I could name.

My remembrances were disturbed by the husky voice and intonations of the minister. "When death comes, it is often preceded by awareness of its coming. Not always does it come like a thief in the night. Sickness, old age, and infirmity are some of the signs that help us, the loved ones of the deceased, to ultimately prepare for that most unwelcome of all times."

He lowered his head and wiped at his brows with a starched white handkerchief. Then, slowly, he lifted his hooded gaze to stare out from the podium, seemingly straight into my eyes.

"But Bartholomew Short's death was different. Very different, dear Lord. Different in that he was a man whose untimely demise was like a wrongful sentence meant and deemed for the likes of someone else." He paused, bit his lower lip, and added. "And that, for everyone concerned—family members and friends alike—may seem too big and too bitter a pill for any mouth to swallow."

A chorus of amens purged the air.

"But it is not for us human beings to judge." His voice rose louder. "No! It is not for us. And as we ask our Lord, Jesus Christ to forgive us—hard as it may be sometimes to forgive ourselves and others around us—we, nevertheless, pray for His forgiveness and mercy."

He waited a long beat. The abrupt, sirenlike cry of a child punctuated the silence. The minister raised his hands in a manner of holy subjugation as he ended his eulogy with a question.

"For without forgiveness and mercy, what is the meaning of life, any life?"

We filed past the closed casket as the organist played music that sounded vaguely familiar.

Outside, Randy appeared at my side. I searched out Vera, Shorty's wife, whose black widow's gown was being clung to by one of her two adolescent daughters. They were surrounded by a sympathetic entourage which I was sure, because of physical similarity, included Shorty's parents.

"I have to say something to her," I said, nodding in Vera's direction.

Randy caught my arm. At the same moment, Shorty's wife lifted her dark veiled eyes, and across the crowded brick courtyard, they pierced me with hatred.

"I don't think that would be a good idea," Randy said. "Another time, maybe."

Vera's expression confirmed Randy's advice.

Randy replaced his smog-eaten windshield wiper with the one from the passenger side, and we followed the funeral procession through the seedy, wet streets of Carson.

"She's taking this real hard," Randy said. "Give her a while. I'm sure it ain't a personal thing as much as an emotional one."

"You think time will heal it, huh?"

"Maybe," he answered, eyeing me dubiously. "I know you've been through a lot with all of this shit." He lit a cigarette with a throwaway lighter. "First the girl. Then you being a suspect. Your house, Shorty and L-92 all fucked up. I know it's not your fault. And I'm sure everybody else knows that. But you got to give Vera some time. After all"—he blew out a mouthful of smoke, which clouded the already steamy windows and caused him to lean forward, squinting his eyes, wiping the glass with a palm—"she's a woman who just lost her man."

Rain washed down my side of the window unimpeded, creating ever-changing swirls of light and darkness. At that point, suddenly, Randy, Smoody, Pops, and everyone I could think of seemed infinitely wiser and more prepared for the real world than me. The shambled state my life was in hadn't come about overnight. It was something I had apparently worked to attain.

I tried to remember a time before my self-imposed isolation had become my prison. Before the world that I had withdrawn into had become my cell. The cab, though it had wheels, could never escape the jailer. The books on ancient and African history, the novels of adventure, the dream of being a full-time investigator were only methods of deluding myself into playing it safe in a world of no commitments. Only day-to-day survival—so that I could feed myself and in turn feed my fish. Only now the fish, too, were gone.

The parade of black and gray umbrellas marched as the rain slackened into a misty drizzle. The minister said a prayer to consecrate the ground and bless the body that was about to enter it. The casket was lowered into the hole. Flowers toppled down on it. Then the workmen's shovels began the slow job of covering it with dirt.

All the while, I stood removed from the others, who likewise seemed to move away from me whenever it seemed I might move too close to them.

As the crowd drifted back toward their cars, sobs, rustling feet, and the sound of dirt landing on the casket blended with the soft patter of rain. I could see Randy, ahead of the others, getting into his beat-up car.

I felt a tug at my sleeve. I jumped and turned to meet the quiet, sad eyes of a medium-built, swarthy white man. Despite his trench coat, he looked like a CPA at the wrong funeral.

"Yeah," I snapped. "What do you want?"

"Sorry to startle you," he said, extending a business card. "My name is Benjamin Ross, FBI."

I took the card and scanned it quickly as he continued.

"I'm with a special task force. And we've been given reason to believe that we're on a case which you might be able to help us solve.'

"And what kind of case is that?"

He smiled as though he had expected my skepticism. "One that a friend of yours is also working on."

"A friend, like who?"

"Carter. Kevin Carter," he said. "He mentioned that you might be helpful to the team."

Chapter Nine

Near downtown Los Angeles just off Alameda, we pulled along a row of nondescript warehouses that ran parallel to a line of old railroad tracks.

The door to one of the warehouses lifted open to Ben Ross's remote control command. We drove inside and parked beside Kevin's Le Mans. Ross got out quickly, opening the passenger door for me even before the garage door had completely shut. I followed him up a short flight of stairs to a door overlooking the loading dock. It opened into a large, well-lit strategy room, filled with several manned computer workstations. One wall held a big enough arsenal of weapons to supply a small army.

"This way," Ross directed, leading me toward a glass-enclosed section, the one secluded room on the floor.

"God!" Kevin said when he saw my healing but still scarred face. "Don't tell me who."

"You know who: that fuck Donner."

He looked awkward, unable to respond with anything appropriate. Instead, he shook his head and sighed, then turned to introduce the head man, Agent Ted Delaney, a pale bear of a man. Rising from his desk, Delaney greeted me.

"We know you've been through a rough ordeal," the bear said. "Why don't you have a seat, anywhere. Take a load off your feet."

I chose a recliner for its softness and climbed into it. Kevin handed me a cup of hot water and a tea bag.

"I quit Thursday morning," Kevin said. "They held an inquiry. Got everybody's story. They liked Donner and Nash's much better, though. So my captain was threatening me with suspension when I lost my cool and totally blew it. I ended up throwing my badge and gun on his desk and walking out."

"Sorry to hear that," I said.

"Don't be sorry," he said. "I guess it had to be."

"Ever see this man before?" Delaney asked, flopping a stack of photographs in my lap.

They were all shots of the same man.

He looked like an albino circus midget with hair by Carpeteria. He had wild bushy eyebrows and was almost always seen in sunglasses. He had a pudgy flat nose and a severe overbite. When his eyes were visible, they were so light that they were hardly noticeable behind the small slits of his eyelids.

"Never," I said almost immediately. "Not the kind of face I'd soon forget."

"Here's a partial file on his activities for the last twenty years." Nimble and lightfooted, Ross came from across the room and handed me a thick bound book. "If you want more, there's plenty on the shelves."

I flipped the pages, scanning the details, studying the accompanying photographs.

"The freakish little chap's name is Trevor Nathaniel Underwood," Delaney remarked as an adjunct to my reading. "Code name, the Dwarf, born into British aristocracy forty-four years ago. His family's wealth could only be guessed at, but I'd say it's beyond substantial. He inherited quite a sum of cash and property at age twenty-one. However, it only took him a few years to create enough controversy for his family to disown him. Drugs, womanizing. Anything big bucks could buy, he lavished in," Delaney shook his massive head, staring up at the ceiling. "But beyond his sordid affairs, he finally committed the unpardonable by British aristocratic ethics—he sold every acre of land held in his name."

As he talked, I read on about Trevor "The Dwarf" Underwood's suspected links to crimes in such major American cities as New York, New Orleans, and Dallas.

Ted Delaney continued, spitting each word out like a man trying to rid his mouth of a bad taste.

"Rumor goes, even after he'd screwed up as grand as he did, his doting parents set up a healthy trust fund for him. However, for their protection from further embarrassment, they had the foresight to include one major clause that reads that Trevor, their dearest son, should never again set foot on English soil. Ever since, he's been like a cancerous tumor to us here in the good ole U.S. of A. Every time we're ready to move in on him, he vanishes. And given his—shall we say camera shy nature, he's hard to track. He lives the life of a recluse, never venturing too far outside of whatever palatial domain he occupies."

"What makes you think he's operating out of L.A.?" I asked,

"A pattern." Delaney lit his barrellike pipe, "Drugs, prostitution, kiddie porn are like engraved invitations to him. And L.A.'s got plenty of that and more. Now doesn't it?"

He blew a few rings of smoke and sat down on the side of his desk.

"All this weasel needs is the scent of smut and he finds some way to muscle in and capitalize, usually into existing businesses." He coughed, then cleared his throat. "He has this habit of placing his henchmen together in odd pairs. Ex-cops and criminals working side by side in two-man teams." He nodded in my direction, then toward Kevin. "Like the pair you guys uncovered. It all fits the scenario we're primed to look for."

While he relit his pipe, Ross added, "He's eluded us for a long time, but if we could just nail him now . . ." He trailed off, then finished his thought. "It would be some consolation. Because, believe me, this asshole's left a long trail of blood and gore behind him. Possible witnesses, the unfaithful, used-up cronies. Anyone who doesn't fit his plans ends up dead."

The photographs I glanced through confirmed his words. There were lots of coroner's shots, and even more eight-by-ten on-the-scene shots of bloody corpses in a variety of ghastly poses. I was engrossed in a particularly tragic one. The victim could not have been more than ten years old.

A queasy feeling enveloped me, turning my stomach.

"He could quite possibly be behind the death of the Collingsworth kid," Delaney said, his words seeming to echo my very thoughts. "It was her case which first alerted us to pulling Kevin aside. When he quit the force, it seemed like the act of an honest man. Because the Dwarf's not above having active law enforcement agents on his payroll. Therefore, we have to be extremely careful about every move we make." He laughed hoarsely. "Discretion has truly become our middle name."

"He's a king scuzbag!" Kevin interjected. "And we get the chance to fold his tent for good."

"How?" I wanted to know.

"That's what the four of us and the rest of the entire team out there has to figure out," Delaney said. "How."

He offered me a salary of six hundred a week, with one week retroactive and available immediately.

"But first things first," Delaney said. "You've got to get healthy before you'll be any good to anyone, including yourself." He went on to suggest that I should recuperate at some remote safe house and return when I was in better physical condition. I declined the offer.

"I'm happy with where I'm staying."

"We're not asking you to join us for the few bucks we're allotted or for the mere honor," Ross said diplomatically making his presence known by taking my empty cup. "There's a sizable reward involved, too."

"Well," I said. "We should all be able to collect on that soon enough." I turned to Kevin. "Have you checked that stolen BMW for traces of whoever was behind the wheel?"

Kevin sighed and dropped his head, and before he lifted it to speak, Delaney answered my question.

"We went down with the proper authorization to inspect the vehicle," he said. "But, not too surprisingly, it had disappeared. Whoosh! Gone, with whatever evidence it contained."

"Fuckin' shit!" I said. "Just when I was beginning to feel optimistic."

"Like Delaney was saying," Ross said calmly, "Underwood probably has help from inside the system. One word that the car could've toppled his empire was enough to guarantee that we'll never see it again. Ever."

After a lengthy silence, I threw my hands up in exasperation. "Besides conjecture and theory, what you're telling me is, you don't have anything to go on. Not even enough to pull those two bastards—who probably killed the little girl—in for questioning."

"No," Ben Ross finally answered, "not enough to keep them behind bars for more than a few hours. Although we do have them under surveillance."

"And that's the best you can do?"

"For right now, yes," Delaney said. "That's the best we can do."

"Not unless," Kevin said, staring straight at me, "we can get some dope on this Collingsworth guy." He winked. "Your tip checked out. One hundred thousand dollars was what he withdrew while you were tailing him." He smiled. "So maybe this Dwarf guy's into murder for hire now, and Collingsworth bought a ticket to have his own daughter knocked off."

"Could be." Delaney rubbed his hands together.

"I hate to muddy up your theories," I said. "But it don't jibe with what I know." I told them about my sunrise meeting with the lawyer at Malaga Cove. "That little confession on Collingworth's part just about exonerates him from anything more than paying blackmail," I concluded. "If he were a part of their act, I couldn't see him making me privy to any of that information. Though I still find something awful fishy about the guy."

It was quiet in the room, except for the buzz of activity from the outer room.

"So," I finally said, "Looks like you guys are as far in the dark as me."

"All we have is a half-ass plan." Delaney sighed, his big shoulders sagging.

"Why don't you run it by me."

"We'll study it more," he said distantly, as though his mind was preoccupied with other thoughts. "Then maybe we'll propose it to you when you're healthy enough to decide."

"Tell me now," I said. "It may speed up my recovery."

The three of them looked at one another, then Delaney shrugged and spoke. "Our only hope is you."

"How's that?"

"We're hoping you can flush the two thugs out," Kevin said, "and in turn, have them lead us to Underwood.

"Ohhh." A nervous laugh slipped past my lips. "Ohhh."

"You see." Ross took the lead. "Seems you've struck a sensitive nerve with them."

Delaney stood up and began to pace his big body around the room. "Our thinking goes like this," he said. "We put you into another cab, back on the road. We have it wired to the hilt for sound and cover you with an army if necessary. And if the Dwarf, or whoever it is, still wants you dead, we'll be there when they try."

"And," Ross added, "hopefully, we get to bury the bastard."

In the impending silence, they waited for my reaction.

"Where do I sign?"

Ross gave me a tour of the facilities, introducing me to the entire staff. Lastly, he showed me the basement, which surprisingly contained a full-length shooting range.

Later that evening Kevin gave me a ride to Aster's. I called her to make sure she was home before we set out from the warehouse. Along the way, he stopped at a 7-Eleven and picked up a six-pack of Coors. Again, we were rolling down Temple Street.

"Grab a cold one," he said, popping the top on one of the cans and helping himself to a good guzzle.

"I gave it up, remember? I told you about it a couple of years ago."

He looked at me as though he were seeing me for the first time, "That long, huh? My hat's off to you, Sol."

He turned his radio on, tuning to the classic rock station.

"Could we talk without the sounds for a while?" I asked.

"Sure." He smiled, clicking off the radio and rolling up his window to shut out the hissing sounds of the slick streets. "Has been a lot of changes for both of us, huh?"

"Too many." I grunted. "But are you really okay about some of them? I mean, not being with the department anymore?"

"It'll take some getting used to," he said after a moment of thought. "I've been at it for sixteen years. And maybe you've guessed right—I'm not used to a lot of changes." He laughed. "Jesus, I thought I'd seen it all. Everything had become pretty much routine. I never even stopped to think what it would be like to do something else."

"Well, it looks like whether we like it or not, we've both got the opportunity to do something else."

He laughed heartily and lifted a can of beer as a salute. "So, like they say, 'here's to the best of times!' "

"The best of times, from now on!" I clicked my gold ring against his half-empty can.

As soon as I arrived at Aster's, she insisted that I have my "daily therapy" as she called it.

I did the Jacuzzi, the sauna. She spread a blanket on the living room floor and gave me a much deeper massage than she had on the previous night. Without the music this time, she applied the same oils but dug much deeper with her fingers, bearing all of her weight down on me, coaching me to breathe correctly.

"Let me hear you. Yes. In. Yes. Deeper." She sucked her lungs full of air. "Now, let it out. Let it go."

Her hands were stronger than I would have imagined, and their touch brought on alternate feelings of pain and release. She'd find a sensitive spot, and her long fingers would work with it until it succumbed to her will. Then she'd search, find another painful muscle or joint and have it surrender to the healthy bliss of . . . release.

Slowly, for what seemed like hours, she worked her way down my back and then up my front.

"You heal fast," she said, finally finished.

She told me to get dressed, she had a surprise for me.

The surprise turned out to be a good spread of take-out Chinese food, spring eggrolls, sweet-and-sour shrimp, fried rice, and hot and spicy vegetables. During the meal, Aster sipped a white, sparkling wine with her food as she talked about Ethiopia and her family.

Her father had been a leading businessman and military officer serving under Haile Selassie as a general. When that government was beseiged in a takeover, he was imprisoned and later executed. At the time, Aster was attending a private school in Germany. Her older brother, a journalist whose views differed from those of the new government, attempted to return home a few months after her father's death was announced. Like many other students, he was arrested as a dissident the moment he unboarded his flight. No further reports could verify whether he was still alive or dead.

"It was a very frightening time," she said. "Many of the students who returned had no idea what kind of reception they'd receive. Many of them were taken into custody by people whom they had gone to school with—people whom they considered friends."

She went on to tell me that, though we did not look alike, I reminded her of her brother.

"How's that?"

"He was a quiet, thoughtful, serious person," she said. "But when he did open his mouth, you listened."

"How long since you've been home?"

"It's been too many years to count."

"Ever think of going back?"

"Every day." She smiled. "But going could never top my memories."

She finished the wine in her glass, wiped at the tears forming in the corners of her eyes, and excused herself from the table, saying, "I haven't talked so openly in quite a while."

Later, she took me on a complete tour of the house.

"I was saving this for when you were healthy enough to climb steps," she said as we reached the top floor, where her studio was. "I just didn't think it would be so soon."

"I guess you're a better healer than you thought."

Her work area consisted of at least five hundred square feet. It had skylights on four sides and was filled with large finished and unfinished paintings.

"I'll show it to you again in the daylight," she promised. "The colors are much more vibrant then."

It was hard to believe that the colors could be more lively than they were. All of the huge canvases followed the same theme. Windswept skies meeting tropical, tree-lined shores. Native huts busy with the activity of the inhabitants. Canoes and rafts of men fishing with nets and spears. Women cooked over open fires, some wove baskets or rugs. Ceremonies that included dance were alive with everything except movement and the sound of the music coming from the instruments that she captured in the hands of the players. Each was a depiction of daily life as it might have been some hundred years ago.

Serene. Peaceful. Uncluttered.

"I minored in anthropology, so the dress and artifacts are authenticated."

We talked as I gave each work a thorough viewing.

"I started doing commercial work to supplement my artistic efforts," she said. "Then, about four years ago, my own creations began to be appreciated far more than I ever expected." She flashed her eyes in disbelief. "Now I can't turn them out fast enough. All of these, some forty paintings, are what I've kept myself busy with for the last five months. When they're exhibited next month in Spain, they'll go like there's no tomorrow."

"I can see why," I said, drawn to a particular piece that showed a young man following his father, who was aiming his spear at an antelope in some nearby brush. "Speaks of a much simpler time."

"A time that is gone forever," she said whimsically. I continued to study the background of lush jungle and misty, rising mountainscapes. While the hunter weighed his spear, the son mimicked him with a tree limb.

"This reminds me of a photograph I saw in a book called *The Family of Man*," I said. "A similar feeling."

"That's where I got the idea." She laughed. "A different rendition. Same thought. As the saying goes, All great minds think alike."

I heard her words, yet the destruction of my house and the books, like *The Family of Man* and others that had become part of a garbage heap, reappeared to me. The bare walls of the wrecked place seemed a perfect home to rebuild around the painting I held.

"How much would this go for?" I asked tentatively.

"It would bring about six thousand dollars."

"Phew!" I said. "No wonder you can afford to live in a place like this."

"Do you still like it?" she asked in a teasing way. "As much?"

"Certainly," I said, noticing more fine details as I set it down. "I just can't afford it." I smiled.

"Yes, you can."

"What?"

"Please, take it." She picked up the painting and pushed it into my hands. "I feel I'm giving it all away anyway. This time it will be to someone I know really deserves it. And one day when you can afford to, you can pay me for it."

I wanted to say much more, but "Thank you" was the best I could offer. "Thank you." I said it again.

We sat in front of the fireplace, looking at snapshots that she had taken on recent vacations. Shots of the Greek Islands, Australia, Hawaii. The hot spots. The scenic shots were worth looking at. But I felt a tinge of jealously whenever I saw her in group shots. Unreasonable as the desire was, I wanted to have been there.

After turning the last page, she returned with some Martinelli's Sparkling Cider for me and more wine for herself. On the thickly woven Berber rug, she slid closer to me.

"I've been talking so much." She snuggled closer. "I haven't even taken the time to ask how your day has been."

I sipped my cider in its long-stemmed glass, remembering my promise of silence to the task force that I'd so recently joined.

"Pretty good," I said, going on to lie. "A friend is lending me money to get started in a new cab."

"Oh, you must be excited," she said with an air of sarcasm.

"It's my business!" I said. "Common, perhaps, but until further notice, it's me!"

"I didn't mean to hit a sensitive nerve," she said after a while. "You just seem capable of so much more."

"It's just a matter of degree." I said. "Like your paintings. I long for a simple kind of life. I work for me. The cab provides that for me. Until something better comes, it's me."

She laughed and rolled on her back, spilling most of her drink. "You must . . ." She gathered her voice. "I mean, I must sound like some kind of snob." She inched even closer, her eyes staring into mine. "If so, I don't mean to."

"I understand." I lightly stroked her forehead.

"Do you?" She shifted uncomfortably but kept her gaze focused.

"Right now," I said, "you seem like someone who's afraid of intimacy."

"You're terrible," she said. "Am I that obvious?"

"Maybe it's not you or me." I smiled. "Maybe it's just the vino."

She glance down at her glass, "You mean, if I hadn't had a drink, you wouldn't look so attractive."

"That depends. 'Cause you always look supergood to me."

Her eyes began to well up with tears. I drew her close to me and kissed her gently on the lips. She returned my kiss, then pushed me away with a sudden jolt and sat upright.

"You," she said. Her eyes seemed crossed as she spoke, "You're just too much. It's like you're forbidden. If I were a year or two younger, I don't know if I'd have the power to resist you."

She threw her glass at the wall of the fireplace. Before it could shatter, she was up, disappearing into the oval darkness of a wide hallway.

I rose to follow her but thought better of it.

Spying a wall clock lit by the blaze from the fireplace, I noticed that it was after midnight. We'd talked far longer than seemed possible.

Unable to fathom Aster's sudden change of attitude, I found my way to the same bedroom where I'd slept the previous night. As I had found it before, the bed was cold and empty.

I was dozing off, confused and befuddled, when the door opening sent an awakening breeze through the room. I sat up on an elbow to see her coming toward me.

She was draped in a sheer white nightdress that fluttered in her wake. Before I could react, she was at my side, pressing a finger against my lips.

"Shhh!"

I wrapped my arms around what easily could have been an apparition, but made solid contact with the softness of sheer cloth and wanting flesh.

"Ohhh, Aster," I murmured.

She touched my lips again, and then placed a single finger against her own mouth.

"Shhh," she said. "Please, don't say anything."

She kissed me softly, playfully above one eye.

In a single motion, the negligee was gone. Her silky skin incited a surge of electricity within as she slid her warm body across mine.

Our lips met.

"Aster . . ."

"Shhh!" she said, lifting herself slightly from our embrace.

"Not a word," she repeated. "Hum if you want to, but don't say a word."

Chapter Ten

Aster was in my thoughts through all of the tedious things I had to accomplish on Monday. Memories of the previous night, and anticipation of the night to come, had me appreciating the day more than otherwise would have been possible.

The skies were washed clean and the landscape was alive with greenery, unlike the brown, burnt-out look of the dry season. It was like spring had suddenly decided that it was no longer January.

Everything seemed blessed and sweetened by my feelings for Aster. The sensations we'd experienced were still close enough that I could not discount them as mere fantasy and wishful thinking. She actually existed, and there was so much I hungrily looked forward to saying and sharing with her.

Our lovemaking had been like returning home after a long absence. My mind, like a canvas on which each new touch from her created a plethora of unbounded energy, at last was released. Visions of Africa, with all of its glories and mysteries, seemed contained in her body—the body that I held so closely, clutching it as if it were a phantom that might suddenly evaporate. Each touch, each taste held elements of a strange familiarity.

Earlier that morning, I had caught a cab to Smoody's

Blue Note, where I picked up Silver Shadow. From there, I headed downtown to the Criminal Courts Building to face my arraignment on the charges that Lieutenant Donner had brought against me. Seeing him and his partner Nash sitting in the courtroom halls during a recess was the biggest outrage of the day. His little yellow teeth showed themselves as he smiled at me with sadistic pleasure.

I asked the public defender assigned by the court why Donner was there. "I thought this was just the time for me to make my plea."

"It is," the young attorney assured me. "He must be here on another case."

"How unfortunate," I said, hating to look in the pudgy man's direction but doing so nevertheless.

The judge recorded my plea of not guilty and assigned me a court date—two weeks from the day.

"We'll see you back here, Mr. Priester," she said, reciting and entering the new date on my forms. "That will be all. Next case."

I made a stop at my bank in Silver Lake, deposited the check that Delaney of the task force had advanced to me, and withdrew enough cash to pay Smoody back the dough he used for bailing me out of jail.

It was late afternoon when I stopped into the Hollywood Boulevard club. Smoody was upstairs. The girl working the bar told me he'd said I should come up to the apartment.

"Rastaman!" he said, giving me one of his patented bear hugs.

"Brother man."

"Had lunch?" he asked after we had chatted for a few minutes.

He warmed up a meal of fried squid and rice with some French bread toasted with a garlic spread.

"Some girl, that Aster," he commented, "wouldn't you say?"

"For sure!" I said.

"I figured just being around a woman as beautiful, physically and spiritually, as she is would do wonders for you and your healing process. In the New Age circles, she's considered the best."

"Even better than you?"

"Even better than me," he admitted exercising the fingers on both of his hands.

I didn't think that I should reveal the nature of the relationship that Aster and I had established, so I decided to alter the course of the conversation.

"Fact is, I'm going to have mixed feelings about moving out when my place is finally fixed up again."

"Moving out?" He looked perplexed. "When's that?"

"As soon as possible." I said. "I've got to go on with what's left of my life."

I gave him the same falsified story that I'd served up to Aster—a friend was loaning me money to invest in another cab.

"Thought you'd try something else," he said, shredding a piece of toast. "Something different."

"Like what?" I shrugged. "Other than owning my own investigation agency, there's nothing else I could picture myself doing." I grunted a disgusted laugh. "That's what I was saving for—to start an agency. Amazing how much money a person can save in two years if they give up any facsimile of a social life."

"Especially if it includes giving up the sauce and the ganja." He chuckled.

"Especially then," I agreed. "Anyway, for me, it's back to the streets, chalking up more rides on the meter."

"To each his own," he said, throwing his hands up in the air. "What do I know? Like I always say, I'm just a drummer, doing the best I can."

"Oh, yeah," I said. Remembering the bundle of bills

in my jacket pocket, I plopped it down in the middle of the kitchen table. "Thanks again, partner."

He nodded, scraping his plate clean.

"Don't you want to count it?" I joked, pointing at the wad of bills.

"Funny," he said flatly as he got up to serve himself another helping. "Real funny. I don't know if you're still interested," he said, once he was seated again, "but John-John may have hooked up a connection with a supplier who deals in false I.D."

"No shit!" I exclaimed, feeling my pulse quicken. "Who?"

"Right now, it's just rumor—from a good source, though. But little brother's trying to set up a meeting for later in the week. Could be the same source that supplied the voice-boxer with hers."

"Good!" I rubbed my hands together with a napkin, crumpled it, and tossed it in the trash. "As soon as you hear anything more, give me a call, right away."

"You surprise me," he said with a halfhearted laugh, leaning back in his seat. "You're still intent on pursuing this mess, huh?"

"Why should I have changed all of a sudden?"

"I don't know." He shook his head wearily. "Seems as though you're just begging for more trouble, as though you haven't already had enough shit dumped on you." He whistled a short, shrill note and wiped food from his graying beard. "Sounds like you're an accident waiting to happen."

I felt tempted to tell him about the task force and my affiliation with them, and how my involvement had become more than just some obscure personal vendetta. Instead, I said something that I hoped would sound convincing.

"I am a P.I. Sometimes danger goes with the turf."

I picked up a cassette of my messages and used his

phone to confirm an appointment with a building contractor to estimate the damage done to my apartment.

It was nearly sunset when Tony, the contractor, left.

Fifty percent of the floorboards were in need of replacement. The price he quoted me was a thousand dollars more than I had remaining in my bank account. Because he was a long-time neighbor, I trusted his honesty, and I had no desire to shop around for a better deal. So I signed the work order and promised to be on hand to let him in on Wednesday morning.

"We're talking four or five days before I'd be anywhere near done," the lanky workman said, chewing on a wad of tobacco. "But I'll finish up as fast as I can. I know you probably want to move back in as soon possible."

"Right," I said absently, writing out a check for half of the tab. "Whatever time it takes to do it will be all right."

After he'd gone, I sat down on the blanket-covered couch, facing the setting sun.

Knowing what to expect had not lessened the pain I'd felt when I had stepped inside the place. Tony had been parked in his company truck waiting when I arrived, so we entered together. Holding my emotions in check required a lot of restraint, but it was hard to look at the aftermath without immeasurable anguish as well as the ever-present painful flashes of the place as it had once been.

The empty aquarium seemed oddly out of place, an eerie reminder of the roller-coaster ride I'd become a passenger on. I vowed to see the aquarium alive with a new collection. Little by little, I was determined once again to have the place return to being a home—though I had no idea how long that would take. But already I could imagine the painting that Aster had given me hanging above the fireplace which now looked so life-lessly dark and forgotten.

"Not for long." I said as I turned my gaze, admiring the last fading rays of sunlight that colored the horizon beyond the lake and the nearby hills that faced it.

I was brought back to the present by my ringing phone. Sitting near the middle of the empty, warped floor, it rang louder than I'd ever recalled.

"About time," my mother's familiar voice intoned disparagingly. "I was wondering if the earth had opened up and swallowed you."

It was never easy to make up a tale that my mother would believe. But I did my best. Wanting to protect her from the sickening truth, I said that I had been called out of town on business.

"Someplace where they don't have phones, I suppose."

"There's no excuse," I finally told her. "Just forget-fulness on my part."

We talked a little longer, but the conversation was strained with unnecessary politeness. I apologized again and promised to call her soon—knowing that she didn't believe one word of the rosy picture of contentment I tried to convey.

When I hung up, rather than get bummed out, I picked up the phone and made a few calls that were meant to get things rolling.

First I contacted Randy at the dispatcher's desk.

"Find me a cab," I said. "I want to get on the road again."

"Solid, man!" he said. "That's the best news I've heard in a while, Sol. And I was just beginning to worry about you, too."

"Don't do that. Just find somebody that wants to sell. The newer the better. Preferably something with no more than twenty thousand miles on it."

"Why don't you just go ahead and buy new?"

"That would take too long. I'm not interested in detailing a customized job. All I want to do is get rolling—like yesterday!"

"Roger, my good friend," he said, rattling his words off as he shifted into his fastest pace. "I'll check into it and have Courtney do the same. We'll see what we can come up with. Call me in the morning, at home, after ten. Got orders piling up. Over and out!"

As soon as I got a dial tone, I called Agent Delaney at the warehouse headquarters.

"Delaney," he said, after the switchboard operator got through to him. "How can I help you?"

"Solomon Priester here, Ted."

"Good to hear from you. What's the word?"

"I've put the hunt on for a new cab. As soon as I find one, I'm ready to roll."

"Good, Sol. Glad to hear that." His cheerful voice was laced with a faint degree of concern. "But are you sure you're physically up to the demands that you might"—he sought the right expression—"encounter on a job like this?"

"I've had a miraculous cure," I assured him. "And I'm as ready as I'll ever be."

Delaney seemed pleased with my response, and we agreed to talk more the next day.

Aster answered on the second ring.

"Could you be ready to go out to dinner in thirty minutes?"

"Curious you should ask," she said. "I'm ready now."

I stopped at a florist and picked up a bouquet of flowers—Hawaiian orchids bunched with African violets of a lavender hue, together with an occasional stem of horsetails, seemed the best choice.

After we had decided on sushi, I knew exactly the right spot to dine.

Seated at Ten Sho, a Japanese restaurant in Glendale,

I told Obie and his wife, Yoko, to feed us until we surrendered. Rather than sit at the sushi bar as I usually did, I relished the privacy of one of their back booths.

Obie knew my favorites. Tuna, mackerel, salmon, and eel were at the top of the list. He followed that with shrimp, crab roll, and a broiled cod which he prepared for us—on the house.

Aster ordered another sake.

I sipped ice tea, remembering when I thought that the giddiness I experienced at sushi bars was the results of the hot sake. Later, I was to realize that a good sushi man, like Obie, could produce a mental high by the selections and order of the food he presented. The lift could still be felt the following morning if you were wise enough to abstain from the immediate influence of the sake.

I mentioned my revelation to Aster as matter-of-factly as possible—trying not to sound sermonic.

"That's interesting," she said. "I'll have to try that sometime."

She bit into her crab and cucumber roll.

"When Smoody told me that you didn't smoke or drink, for a minute I thought it was his way of making a joke."

Our eyes met in the dim light of the booth.

She shrugged and smiled. "I did. That's what I thought."

We laughed.

"I know," I said. "It's kind of hard for me to believe it sometimes."

"What's that?"

Much as I didn't want to get into it, I told her about Jocelyn, generalizing as much as possible, leaving out the part about her demise. Then I realized that it sounded as though my problem with drinking too much had been the sole reason for our breakup. But somehow, I felt the truth was too much for either one of us to handle at that moment.

Perhaps later, I thought.

"She's an actress?"

"Yes," I answered. "A pretty good one, too."

"Do you have a picture of her?"

"Not on me," I said, then after a long pause asked, "Why?"

"I just wondered what she looked like," she said nonchalantly. "That's all."

I could see Jocelyn's image as clearly as if she were sitting across from me. The fair skin, high cheekbones, dimples that showed themselves with her almost perpetual smile. The way Aster grinned, I surmised that in some metaphysical way she had gotten a glimpse of my mental picture of Jocelyn.

Yoko interrupted our thoughts, gracing us with the final touch, two orders of ikura crowned with the yolks from quail's eggs.

"I always save this for last."

"Fish eggs." She held a piece up for inspection. "I never had the guts for this before."

"Try it!" I said, dipping a piece in the soy sauce and horseradish concoction that I'd mixed. "It'll top the whole meal."

I bit into the hand-rolled wrapped eggs. The small gelatinous capsules burst as I crushed them with my teeth and rolled their potent, olive-oil-thick flavor around the roof of my mouth.

"Hmmm! Now that's eating," I said.

Aster took a tentative bite. She obviously liked the taste because she quickly stuffed the rest of the crumbling roll into her mouth.

"Not bad," she said, as though she were trying to convince herself of what she was saying. "Not too bad."

After chewing and deliberating for a moment or two, she reached for her second piece.

I thanked Obie and Yoko for an excellent meal and tipped them gratefully.

"How did you find that place?" Aster asked on the way back to the van. "I don't even know where I am."

"I live near here," I explained, "and word about good sushi gets around fast."

Following her suggestion, I gave her a tour of Silver Lake—a short hop from the restaurant. Like others I had met—some of them Los Angeles natives—Aster was getting her first exposure to the hidden-away nature of Silver Lake, located only a few miles from the towering skyline of the city's major business district. We cruised around the lake. The fact that it is a fenced-in concrete reservoir didn't take away from its glory. Twice we cruised around the two-and-a-half-mile grassy perimeter while a full moon danced on the surface of the water.

Avoiding my street like a cancer, I climbed the hills to a spot known as view-of-the-lake. I cut the engine off, and then turned down the volume of the tape that was playing.

We got out and walked.

The stars were incredibly visible and the lights from the houses across the lake sparkled like they were competing for awards with the grandeur of the heavens above. The brisk wind carried the pleasant aroma of burning wood escaping from chimneys.

I gave Aster my jacket. She put both arms around my waist, and I pulled her close to me as we climbed a steep, winding road.

"I hope I wasn't being too inquisitive earlier," she said. "Prying is a habit of mine that I try to control."

"I have the same habit," I said.

She giggled, snuggling closer to me. "But I'm still confused."

"About what?" I asked, almost wanting to stop so that I could see her eyes rather than have her walk stride for stride beside me. "What's confusing you?"

"Jocelyn."

"How's that?" I asked, bracing myself for the worst. "What's she got to do with anything?"

"An actress." She laughed, trying to contain the humor that rocked her ribs. "I just can't imagine you being in love with an actress."

"So she's an actress," I declared. "What's wrong with that?"

She stopped walking, dropped her hands beside her, and looked up at me, blinking her eyes and shaking her head as though I would never be able to understand what she was about to say.

"Isn't that a kind of superficial occupation?" She made a mock courteous bow. "For them, where does acting leave off, and real life begin? Or is it just about looks and saying the proper thing at the proper time?" An explosion of disbelief gushed from her. "Somehow, you come across to me like someone who would much more favor spontaneity and free form than some—"

"Don't go any further," I warned. "Whatever my relationship was with Jocelyn—it's over. And whatever my reasons were for loving her, no one else could begin to understand."

She lowered her head, and the wind stirred her hair, covering her eyes. Then she rushed me, wrapping her arms tightly around my body, planting cold kisses along my face and neck.

Soon enough, I returned the kisses.

"There's one thing you need to know about me," she said as we made our way back to the van. "I don't believe in sharing my man."

Back in the van, she asked, "Can we sit for a while?"

"Sure," I said.

"I'm sorry for the way I spoke back there," she said. "But there's a lot that you don't know about me."

"How will I know unless you tell me?"

She told me about the last meaningful relationship that she had had. She had been living in New York at the time, employed as a resident artist for a firm that handled big commercial accounts. Almost immediately, she began dating one of the company's executives. He was a well-educated black man from Boston, twelve years her senior. For the first few months, he had been all that she could have expected.

"He was very romantic," she said in a hollow voice. "Always knew exactly what to say, when to show up and when to stay away."

But it wasn't too long before she realized that she had been just another conquest for him, just another notch on the bedpost.

"I tried to put up with his flings, as he called them." She turned her head toward the peacefulness of the night. "But I could never get used to the feeling of being treated like secondhand goods." She sighed. "His promises of fidelity were no more than empty words, meant only to appease me until the next time his horny nature got the best of him."

It wasn't until she moved West that she broke off the relationship.

"He thought he was the cat's meow," she said softly. "And all I wanted was to be loved by someone who loves me more than anyone. I can't be just a part of someone's harem."

I held her close and kissed her gently on the forehead.

"I've been avoiding commitments since then," she went on. "You're the first in more than a year. And I guess it's kind of scary. But I don't mean to be distrustful. I just can't seem to get rid of the past."

"That explains a lot," I said. "Now I have a confession to make."

I spilled out the truth about Jocelyn.

"Sad as that story is," she said, after exploring all of the ramifications of what I had revealed to her, "it's kind of funny that you couldn't have told me the truth from the beginning instead of being so—"

"Some things are hard to talk about without cluttering the air."

"I know, I know," she sighed. "But it's good. We've come a long way. Haven't we?"

We looked into each other's eyes, and suddenly nothing but our closeness seemed to matter. We held each other tight and soon found ourselves laughing as all the built-up tensions subsided and washed away.

"Let's go home," she said, "and celebrate our honesty."

Chapter Eleven

It wasn't until Friday evening that I was able to hit the streets as an Indepedent Taxi driver. K-21 was a Chevy Caprice with only seventeen thousand miles on her, but the last owner had neglected her badly.

Four hundred dollars in body work was able to conceal the old dents and scratches. The tires had never been rotated, so new ones were required. A friend of Smoody's was happy with the twenty bucks I'd given him for shampooing the interior. With that and a few other amenities, like a tune-up, an alignment, and new brakes, K-21 felt like new. At least new enough for Delaney's boys in the warehouse to overhaul and equip her with their micro-audio technology.

They installed four mikes—in case four people happened to be talking at the same time, they could adjust the volume so that a tongue licking the corner of a mouth could be isolated and identified amid a heated argument.

"What if five people happen to be talking?" I asked, just to give the tech boys something to think about.

The system could be activated by a foot switch. A similar gadget turned on a speaker that allowed headquarters and the rest of the roving team to communicate with me. Also, a little chip, no larger than a quarter, was attached near the base of the antenna. With that one gizmo, I'd show up on a radar screen that could track me for more than thirty-two miles.

Under the dashboard, near the steering column, was a spring that when pulled would drop a .357 automatic revolver with twenty-four rounds down into my waiting hand.

"What, no grenade launchers?" I asked, getting at least one smile from the three-man team showing me the ropes.

Finally, they installed a neat system that allowed the driver to control special inside locks for all the windows and doors, so that all the passengers could be instantly trapped.

I had had several breifings with Kevin, and with Agents Delaney and Ross. We ran through "What if this and what if that?" Questions like: What if Collingsworth knows more than he had revealed to me? If so, what was he hiding? Were Lieutenant Pete Donner and his partner, Joe Nash, working from the inside for the notorious Underwood? And was the Dwarf truly connected with any of the subterfuge surrounding the death of Jennifer? What happened to Bryan Mann, and could he possibly have been her executioner? If not, was he somehow involved? Then also, how did the tape of the threatening calls that Jennifer had received at the 976 line fit into the equation?

Those were some of the questions that we batted around continually.

During the briefings, we also created a code language to confuse anyone that might stumble upon our frequency or, more likely, be in the act of monitoring it.

The government footed the bill for my time, the cost of the cab, and its restoration. That in itself was vindication of sorts, but I also knew that deep down, I wanted nothing short of full revenge. Having the chance to work with the task force was something that

I also saw as fate's way of telling me that my pains and my prayers were not in vain.

Another storm system was being forecast, but the skies were still clear except for a few patchy clouds on the run. The new tires purred as only new tires can, and the wind that rushed through the window felt warm with anticipation.

I joined a pack of cars and empty cabs heading west on Sunset, caught in a snarling parade of Friday-night lookie-lous.

Most of the time, I engaged in banter with headquarters or with my two chaperones, Kevin in one unit, and Ben Ross driving the other car, accompanied by another agent named Earl Grant.

Our working theory was that I would continue driving and investigating the death of Jennifer Collingsworth as though I were acting as a lone entity. The coup de grace, we were sure, would follow.

As Delaney put it, "If you should happen to ruffle the wrong feathers, they'll either try to further incriminate you or"—he shrugged—"eliminate you. But either way they open themselves up to exposure. Which is all we really want."

I took a few radio calls from the cab dispatcher, Randy, who never seemed to take a night off. They were all short runs of the same kind—from Hollywood apartments to Hollywood restaurants, clubs, or bars. All of the rides averaged less than two miles apiece. With the consumption of time that it took to get through traffic to pick up the fares, it was hardly an equitable situation. Fortunately, the meter was not as significant a factor as it had once been.

"What the heck you doing L-92? I mean, K-21," Randy corrected himself. "Never known you to play the thick of things on a weekend night."

"Reminding myself of the first night out," I lied. "But really, I'm expecting a date." I kissed the mike.

"Right here in the neighborhood, so I'm your anchor if you need me."

"You sure is, man," he sighed off, laughing. "That you are!"

"You's a anchor, man," Kevin kidded. "All right, anchor man!"

"I bet you never had a night of driving a cab like this," Ross said. "Like 'Candid Camera,' huh?"

At 9:19 P.M. I parked near a popular expensive Italian restaurant on Melrose. I was running a little behind schedule for my so-called date. As I parked and left K-21, I was glad I wasn't wired for sound outside of the cab.

The maitre d' escorted me through the quiet din of the main dining room, adorned in a baroque decor. A few heads shifted like they had never seen a natty man before, yet a sophisticated I've-seen-it-all attitude prevailed.

I was led down a hall lined with wide alcoves of spacious booths.

Collette Carter didn't seem peeved by my tardiness. In fact, she almost took the maitre d's job in her anxiousness to see that I was seated with a place setting and glass of ice water in front of me.

"Can I get you something from the bar?" a waitress asked, just as Collette and I were wearing thin on greetings.

"The water's plenty," I answered.

"They've got great food here," Collete said, looking quite different than I had seen her before. "I was waiting for you before I ordered."

I tried to decipher the change that I saw in her as I browsed through the four-page menu. With her hair worn loose, instead in a French twist, her entire demeanor seemed more relaxed, less threatening than when she held a mike in her hand. She appeared younger now, like someone who was embarking on a new career, still eager-eyed and armed with a youthful kind of idealism.

"Order anything you like," she said casually. "I told the studio that this was a business meeting. If I don't come back with a stack of receipts, they're bound to think I've been sleeping on the job."

"We wouldn't want them to think that." I winked, still trying to find an entree for less than twenty dollars.

I ordered a salad for myself and veal parmigiano for Collette. Other than the one drink with an olive that she had been nursing when I got there, she didn't order from the bar. She looked as sober as me, alert and patient.

While we waited for our meals to be served, I found out that she was a LSU communications graduate who had to work extremely hard to eradicate her Cajun accent before being finally accepted in her profession.

Our dishes arrived, and she seemed to be waiting for me to give her a list of my accomplishments. I let her wait for a while, then said, "I'm just a Philly boy who doesn't like seeing or knowing people who get killed."

She put her empty fork down delicately on the side of her plate. She clutched both hands together and cracked her slender, short-limbed fingers while puckering her mouth, as though she'd just bitten into a rotten lemon.

"I just get a strange feeling that you're judging me by some standard that I don't know anything about," she said. "I may report the news, but I don't commit the crimes. So if you're looking for someone to blame, look elsewhere."

"There's no need for you to let my attitude make you paranoid," I said. "But you should remember that this whole deal isn't some incident that I happened to read or hear about on the news. It's a series of events that are wrecking my life. So it's real hard for me to look at the situation objectively."

She picked up her fork again. "I can appreciate that." Confronting me with a very businesslike appraisal, she asked, "So obviously you have some further updates that you feel are newsworthy?"

"Precisely," I said, pushing my half-emptied plate aside. "I'm working for a source, which I can't disclose. But it's our educated belief that when the person behind this girl Kim's death is finally nailed, it'll surely make front-page headlines. And then you'll have an exclusive jump on the other networks."

Collette was quiet for a long time. Then she finally spoke. "That's it?"

"Just about," I replied. "I just know that you seemed awfully anxious to interview me before, and I apologize for not having been emotionally prepared at the time, but I do intend to break this case wide open." I sat back in my chair. "And if you're willing you can help me do that by seeing that it's public knowledge that I'm on the case."

She finished a small sip of her drink, then took her time finding and lighting a Sherman cigarette.

"What you're telling me sounds quite interesting," she said after exhaling a puff of smoke. "But so far, I only have your word that you know any more about this case than I do."

"Believe me, I do."

"Like what?" she challenged.

"This could all be part of some big conspiracy which has affected a lot more people than the girl who died."

"Aha!" she said with a cagey smile. "The girl. It's good that you brought her up again. It leads me to a question that I've asked you before."

"What's that?"

"Her name." Her eyes narrowed. "Her real name. Do you know it?"

"Yes," I said, realizing that it was a fact which I had to admit. "Do you?"

"What do you think?"

"Jennifer," I said. "Jennifer Adrian Collingsworth. But," I added, "that's off the record."

"Well." Her eyes lit up. "Maybe now we're getting somewhere."

"Before you get your hopes up, that's about all I can confide at this time."

"And on the basis of that little tidbit of information—which I was already fully aware of—I'm supposed to go along with this idea of yours for some kind of an exclusive interview." She laughed and snubbed out her half-smoked cigarette. "They'd laugh me straight out of the newsroom if I went in there with that suggestion—based on what I've heard so far."

"Well," I countered, "what did you expect when you agreed to talk to me tonight?"

"I'm not sure," she said with a raised eyebrow. "Let's say I came with an open mind." She checked her watch. "Now I'm running out of time."

There were a lot of things that I almost said impulsively, but instead I studied her as she sat there so serenely indifferent.

"When I initially tried contacting you," she said, pulling her wallet from her purse, "you were news. However, that's no longer the case."

"We'll see about that," I said, rising.

Exiting, I realized I should have expected her to react as she had. There was something about her that irked me. Therefore, I had foreseen difficulty. And as much as I wanted to, I was unable to play the required role— the diplomat.

We hadn't expected my first night out to be filled with the thrills of a high-wire act. In fact, we kept calling it a test run, hoping only to stir up the quiet waters.

I tried contacting Karen, the roommate. When her phone rang unanswered, my entourage and I struck out for the San Fernando Valley beer bar where I had last found her working.

"We got a clean, sharp read on you," a voice from headquarters reported, following the blinking red light that the chip near the antenna created on their radar screen. "Got you heading west on the snake," he said, using our code name for the 101 Freeway.

"All systems look go," the same voice said.

"Yeah," I said. "Now all we need is an opponent."

"Want one of us to go inside with you, to watch your back?" Ross offered.

"Not if I'm supposed to be acting alone."

The Mixer was overflowing with Friday-night revelers, and a small crowd spilled out onto the street. I made my way through them with the attitude of someone who knew where he was going. Two broad, muscular backs blocked my entrance.

"Excuse me," I said, inching my way into the bar.

There was a plump barmaid doing her best to pour out the beer and wine for a demanding crowd. I stood in line, waiting for an opportunity to question her. Before too long, I got my chance. I had to shout above the live country-western band that was performing on a tiny stage.

"Will Karen be in tonight?"

Because of the band's volume and the raucous sounds of the packed house, I had to shout my question again. The barmaid finally understood and shook her mop of a head negatively and spoke with vehemence.

"She don't work here no more!"

"Know where I can find her?" I asked as she bent closer to hear me.

The band's number came to an abrupt ending, and the barmaid's overly loud and animated response rang clear.

"I don't give a shit where she is, Jack! She was supposed to be subbing for me and nearly cost me my job by not showing up but once!"

"If you happen to see her," I said, "give her this." I handed her a taxi card with K-21 penciled in. "I need to talk with her," I lied. "She owes me some money."

The cocky barmaid thought twice, then tucked the card away in a garter belt. "I don't expect to see her again, but if I do, I'll gladly give her the message," she said with all the warmth of an angry wrestler. "Now get out of the way so my customers can get some service."

"Thanks for the hospitality," I mumbled, leaving as the country band picked up the beat to an Elvis tune, "Little Sister."

I was met outside the entrance by the same two scruffy rednecks whom I'd nudged by earlier. Three of their cohorts gathered on their flanks.

As their undisputed spokesman, the biggest, burliest one of them moved toward me like he was frothing at the mouth from too much beer and blind hatred.

"What the fuck's your problem, bearhead?"

"Just looking for a friend," I casually answered. "Now I'm outta here."

"Looks to us like you were giving the girl in there a hard time," another guy, shaped like a fireplug, blurted out, using the same drunken speech pattern as his sidekick. "And that don't sit too well with us."

"Just trying to find somebody," I said, letting the biggest guy with the long, unruly hair move closer. "Not looking for trouble."

"Well," their leader said. "You found it, anyway. 'Cause you on the wrong side of town to begin with."

"I go where I want."

"That so," the big man in my face said, throwing a windup right.

Pivoting slightly, I let his fist sail by, missing my head by a fraction of an inch. I grabbed his passing wrist with one hand and cracked his elbow with the other. The sound of a bone snapping came just before his squeal of pain. I kneed him in the rump, and he crumpled to the ground, crashing his head on the sidewalk with a whimpering groan.

The fireplug looked dazed for a second, then seemed to blow himself up, swelling his fury for the charge.

"Fucka!" he cried out, doing a double take at his friend heaped on the ground. "You—"

But, before he could take a step, I whipped my Cobra out, cocking the hammer. I aimed at the place where his brains would be if he had any.

"I'll blow whatever's between your eyes all over the valley," I said. "Just one more step and you can say goodbye."

The rest of the gang dispersed with haste. We were left, fireplug and me, face to face. The sound of his moaning partner came from the ground.

"You win this time," he lamely admitted, staring down the barrel of my gun. "I ain't no fool."

"That's debatable," I said, backing away and reholstering my piece.

The guy on the ground turned an anguished face up to me, rising wobbily with a hand held over the gash in his head. "If it wasn't for that gun, you'd be a deadmeat prick!"

"If it wasn't for the gun," I said, "I'd have broken your neck instead of your arm."

At a quick pace, I made my way back to K-21.

Kevin cruised by, concerned. In the glare of oncoming traffic, I showed my teeth in a broad smile to indicate that everything was under control. No need for him to break cover.

Though it seemed like a futile and wasted gesture, I continued taking calls from Randy, perpetuating the myth that I was just another cabdriver who moonlighted as a private investigator.

I played the part until 3 A.M.

I switched cars, picking up Silver Shadow, and with my posse behind me, I drove in circles until I felt that it was safe to head for Aster's house. Once there, I parked the van beside her white Corvette inside her three-car garage.

Using the key which Aster had recently given me, I let myself in the house. Though I had been sharing her bed, seeing her sleeping peacefully, I chose to crash in the room that had been initially granted to me.

Before dozing off, I replayed the events of the day.

I shuddered at the errors of judgment which I had made with Collette Carter. Given a chance, I would have played my cards differently.

But, I vowed, tomorrow is another day.

Chapter Twelve

At 8:30 Saturday morning, I stirred myself fully awake. Aster had left a long note for me, saying, among other things, that she had gone shopping. The sexually suggestive note also reminded me about a gallery opening that she wanted me to attend with her that evening.

I ate some toast, drank some juice, and headed out in Silver Shadow to keep my appointment with Kay, in Hermosa Beach.

Kay had been listed in Jennifer's address book by her first name alone. A cross reference check proved that the listing belonged to a Cheryl Stouffer. The last name spurred a wealth of curiosity for all of us connected with the investigation. Stouffer was the last name in the alias that had appeared on Jennifer Collingsworth's phony I.D. Upon further investigation, we discovered that Cheryl's daughter, Kaylyn Kimberly, had been a former classmate of Jennifer's.

Twice I'd called the number.

The first time I reached a woman, probably her mother, who told me that Kay wasn't in. "Who should I tell her called?" she asked.

"Donnie," I answered, trying to sound young and white.

"Donnie? Is there a number where she can reach you?"

"I'll just call back later," I said, hurriedly hanging up the line at the task force headquarters.

The next day, from a pay phone, I had better luck. Kay answered. I was straightforward, asking if she was aware of Jennifer's death. A photograph and story in a newspaper had informed her of the tragedy. I offered condolences, then went on to tell her that I was investigating the murder. I asked if she could shed some light on Jennifer's past history. She had been tentative and reluctant, but soon yielded to my insistence, agreeing to meet with me.

The streets and freeways had dried from the predawn rain, and traffic was flowing moderately. With one stop, I filled the tank with gas and picked up a morning *Times*.

Ten minutes early, I pulled up and parked in front of the laundromat Kay had directed me to. I leafed through the paper and worked on a crossword puzzle until she arrived twenty minutes later.

Like Jennifer, she was thin, fragile-looking, and had similar keen features. Her long, reddish-blond hair was worn loose, falling across her shoulders, halfway down her back. She wore a cardigan sweater with the sleeves pulled up, baggy khaki shorts, and a pair of hiking boots.

Out of the van, I introduced myself, helping her unload a pile of laundry from the old yellow Honda that she drove. Light freckles showed on her cheeks, and behind the tortoise-shell glasses she wore, her eyes were a lively emerald-green.

Together we found enough washers to accommodate her. While she loaded the machines, I waited outside in the fresh air of the quiet street.

"Let's take a walk," she said, when she finally joined

me. "I'm in the mood for some Häagen-Dazs. There's a little market not too far away." She indicated the direction with a nod, explaining, "Ice cream's my reward for braving laundry day."

She chatted freely while we strolled along a grassy island that divided the avenue which ran parallel to the ocean, a few blocks away.

With little or no prompting, she told me about being close to Jennifer for many years. They had lived on the same street and been classmates from the first grade until their second year of junior high school.

"She was my closest friend," she said wistfully, stuffing her tiny hands into the pockets of her oversize sweater.

Without breaking pace, she went on, her head bowed. "Then my family started having problems. Marital and financial." She sucked in a deep breath. "That's when me and my mom got a little apartment up this way. But even after I moved, Jennifer and I swore that we wouldn't let the distance come between us."

"Did it?"

"Not right away," she said. "But finally, I guess, we did drift apart."

"What do you remember most about her?"

"So much," she said, sounding almost exasperated by the thought. "She was just a good friend. Somebody who you could always talk to." The corners of her eyes crinkled with the flash of a smile. Then she bit her lower lip, adding, "She was always sensitive to other people's feelings." She paused. "It's like she told me once, 'You can't change people, so you may as well like them as they are.' "

"Very astute," I remarked.

"That's just the way she was," Kay said with a shrug. "I think her love for books and poetry had a lot to do with the way she saw the world."

"She liked poetry, huh?"

"Not liked!" she corrected me. "She loved it. Especially William Blake." Her voice was filled with grief, but she forced herself on. "She read everything he wrote and used to have posters of his drawings and sketches on every wall in her room."

"Did you share her love of poetry?"

"How could I not?" she said with a fractured laugh. "We were like sisters. In fact, we used to pretend that we were sometimes when we met new guys at the mall or the beach."

"Do you think that's why she used your last name when she decided to find a new identity?"

"That's how I explain it to myself," she said softly.

"It's a common practice," I enlightened her. "People looking for new names have a tendency to borrow from friends."

We reached the market.

On the way back, she tried to answer my questions while still enjoying the ice cream that she scooped up with a wooden spoon.

"Why did she leave home?"

She shook her head in the salt wind, then smoothed her hair back across her shoulders. "I've asked myself that question a million times. I mean, who wouldn't prefer living in Palos Verdes?" she asked with a mock air of aristocracy. Then she went on. "I'd move back in a minute. Then I wouldn't have to be trying to finish high school while working at a Burger King weekends and nights. Doing my own laundry."

We walked in silence for a while, then I said, "It is kind of confusing, her reason for leaving home."

"It is," she said adamantly. "I'm just sure that she never would have run away if her mother was still alive."

I urged her to continue.

"Her mom was great! I guess she remembered what it was like to be a child. She had a lot of patience with us," she said, with a slight bounce in her step. "That's where Jennifer got her love of poetry. Mrs. Collingsworth had the biggest private library around. And she loved to read to us. For as long as we wanted. Any book we picked."

"How did Jennifer feel about her dad?"

"I don't know what she thought about him, because she hardly ever mentioned him. To me, he was like most dads—never around. Just someone who pays the bills. I mean, I rarely ever saw him or gave him much thought, until . . ." Suddenly, she perked up. "Until that one night . . ."

She stopped herself in mid-sentence.

"What night was that?"

She appeared flustered, having difficulty gathering her thoughts. "Let's sit down," she finally suggested.

I sat with her, sharing a sunny spot beside a tree.

"When Jennifer ran away from home, she spent two nights with me. 'I'll never go home again!' was all she kept saying, over and over." Kay shook her head. "I kept asking her why. But she said it was too horrible to talk about. 'What about your dad?' More than once, I asked her. But she just clammed up."

"How long ago was this?"

"The summer before last, right after the school term ended," she answered. "She kept going on about traveling on the road with some guy she met in a rock band. I even asked her to talk to my mom about staying with us, but she didn't want any part of it, like all she wanted was to get as far away as possible. She had enough credit cards to get by, she said."

Kay received one postcard from Sioux City, Iowa, another from somewhere in Minnesota, and then the communications had ceased.

"If I had known." Kay began to sniffle. "I would have been there for her, somehow. The same as I know she would have been there for me if the situation had been reversed."

She pulled a bandana from a rear pocket and wiped at her eyes, which were becoming red and puffy with tears.

"Don't blame yourself, Kay," I told her, patting her on the shoulder. "You're not a fortune-teller."

"I thought I was through with the crying routine," she said. "That's all I did when I read the news."

Later, as we neared the laundromat, she began to ask me questions, wanting a thorough account of what Jennifer's life had been like prior to her death.

"No real hard clues, as of yet," I lied, purposely avoiding the grim details of what her friend's life had become. "I suspect that she'd been living in the Hollywood area for over a year."

"And she didn't even call me once!" Unable to mask her hurt, she sniffled and fought back more tears.

"When I called Mr. Collingsworth," she said as we stood in front of the laundromat, "to find out if the picture I saw in the paper was really Jennifer's, he never called back. My mother even tried. We told each other that he might be taking the news real hard. But if it was her, we expected to find out when they sent a funeral notice. But none came."

"Do you think Jennifer may have believed that her father was responsible for her mother's death?"

"No." Her expression was one of extreme disbelief. "What makes you ask that?"

"Just a wild hunch."

"Her mother died years ago, when I was still living near them. Sure, Jennifer took it hard, but that wasn't the change that sent her over the edge."

Then she asked something which I thought was extremely peculiar at the time. "Could you show me some identification," she asked awkwardly. "To make sure that you are for real?"

I complied.

"Fine," she said, handing my identification and badge back to me. "Hold on. I have something to loan you. Even though it might not be of much help."

She rushed to her Honda and retrieved a backpack from the rear seat. From inside, she pulled out a red, faded old book.

"Some of the things that she used to write," she said, handing it to me. "She left it with me that last night."

Unsuccessfully, I tried reaching Collingsworth at his home even though I had no preplanned idea of how I would play my hand. His snooty housekeeper informed me that he was out of town and wasn't expected back until Wednesday.

It was almost noon when I reached the task force headquarters on the border of downtown Los Angeles.

I walked into his office as Delaney was yawning and rubbing at the stubble on his usually clean-shaven face.

"Don't you ever go home," I asked, pulling up a seat.

"For the last year"—the big man stood up and stretched—"home to me is nothing more than some empty hotel room."

He sent out for sandwiches, but I didn't have much of an appetite, finishing only half of what I'd ordered.

While Delaney stuffed himself, we debriefed each other.

The surveillance on Preston Reynolds and Armando Sanchez had uncovered no further indication that they were doing anything more than running a legal body-guard service. Their lines were all tapped, but they were either very cautious or fully aware of the tap.

"Perhaps," I offered, "we should think about me taking a ride over to their office and have a personal confrontation."

"We better wait." Delaney shot my suggestion down

quickly. "Once they start feeling comfortable that they're off the hook, they may break routine and lead us straight to our man."

He wolfed down his lunch, not leaving a crumb, and reached in his drawer for his pipe tobacco.

"Besides." He belched, filling his pipe. "You're supposed to be acting alone. If you go up to their place by yourself, it could be like walking unarmed into a lion's den."

"Not neccesarily," I disagreed. "I don't think they're dumb enough to bloody up their own office. But it certainly would light a fire under them, get something sizzling," I added. "That might prove more advantageous than counting on our garbage detail," I said, making a reference to Delaney's policy of searching trash filched from exclusive neighborhoods on the chance that Underwood's fingerprints might be found on some drug paraphernalia or on an empty bottle of champagne or caviar.

"Some of our time-consuming methods may seem unproductive at first," Delaney said pragmatically, "but that's the nature of gathering information from a wide source. It all seems pointless until that magic moment when everything comes together."

We were still debating the issue when Kevin Carter reported in, after following up the tip Smoody's friend John-John had supplied us with.

"Looks good," he said. "We followed the man who's running the false I.D. operation back from his meeting with your friend John-John." He smiled in my direction. "So we know where he lives. We can either bust in on him or wait for him to deliver the goods and compare them to a copy we have of the phony license the little girl was carrying. If the workmanship is the same, we may be able to squeeze some useful information out of him. Find out if he's part of the Dwarf's ring."

"Good work," Delaney congratulated Kevin and me,

"but we don't want to force our hand. We'll wait until John-John gets his order."

I started to disagree, but instead I remained quiet.

Knowing that I needed more practice with the automatic that had been installed in K-21, Kevin and I spent half an hour in the basement's shooting range. Firing the automatic, I had a tendency to shoot high with the first few rounds.

"Let me try it?" Kevin asked.

He showed the same uncanny ability with the automatic that he displayed with a single-shot pistol. Every round he fired hit the center of the torso-shaped target as though the bullets had eyes. The target was riddled to shreds.

Later, I found a semi-quiet corner in the main room and began reading the book of essays and poems that Jennifer had written. It was tough to read the idealistic thoughts of someone who had recently died so savagely.

Shortly after I'd read most of the entries, I excused myself to keep my date with Aster.

"Much as I hate to do it," I joked, "I may have to spend to rest of the evening in a social mode."

"When will your floors be ready?" Kevin asked. "So you can move back to your place."

"Hopefully, Monday. They keep running into more problems every day," I said. "See you in the morning unless something comes up."

"Sure you don't want someone to tag along behind you?" Delaney asked. "We've got the manpower."

"I think that as long as you know where Preston and Armando are, I'll be safe."

Delaney looked as though he was about to say something, but I was gone before he had a chance.

* * *

I left the cab parked at the headquarters garage, prefering the quiet anonymity of Silver Shadow. I stopped at a cleaner's and picked up some clothes that had been ready for weeks, forgotten.

Just before sunset, we set out for the party.

Aster drove her Corvette, dressed immaculately in a long golden evening gown that highlighted her rich complexion.

The gallery was located on Wilshire Boulevard in Beverly Hills. As fine as Aster looked, her driving left a lot to be desired. Several times she raced against yellow lights, crossing intersections long after it was permissible.

She was in a very talkative mood.

"Lawrence had another gallery in downtown New York," she said, speaking of her friend who was throwing the party. "He had a poor location though, and ended up having to close down and file for bankruptcy. But you have to admire his determination. He found another backer, and no one could ask for a finer location than he has now."

I sat on the edge of my seat as she shifted gears, changing lanes almost constantly. As she went on, I couldn't help thinking that she was speaking so glowingly about her friend because she hoped that I might be taking notes.

"That's what it takes," she said emphatically. "Once you set a goal, you can't let any obstacles sidetrack you. Or you invite nothing but failure."

"Does he have any of your work on show?" I asked, wanting to change the subject.

"I lent him three pieces to help him along," she said.

There were about thirty or forty people milling in small groups when we arrived at the gallery. Introducing me to some of her friends, Aster described me as a sensational and unique poet who liked to drive cabs.

Leaving her in the middle of a discussion about the value of Andy Warhol's contributions to the world of art, I browsed around by myself. It was easy to spot Aster's work among the others. The rest of the paintings were amateurish compared to her craftsmanship.

Returning from the loft, I met Aster rushing toward me, leading a tall man with light-colored hair and a clean-cut, boyish face.

"This is him," Aster said. "My friend Sol."

We shook hands.

"Sol, this is Lawrence Jacobs, our host."

"Nice place," I said. "Today's day one, huh?"

"Actually, we opened a few days ago, but today's the day I chose to have all of my friends stop by so that I could get a chance to see the place alive with people." He smiled.

"You'll get plenty of customers who will come back, again and again," Aster lifted her full drink in its plastic cup, "Because," she said, patting him on the arm, "if anybody deserves success, it's you." She gave him a kiss on the cheek. "You've certainly earned it."

Lawrence blushed and said, "I just think of myself as a merchant whose love for art saves him from selling shoes or used cars for a living."

"Don't belittle yourself," Aster admonished. "You give a lot of artists a chance they might not otherwise have." She shook a finger at him. "That in itself makes you my hero."

Lawrence accepted the compliment graciously and thanked Aster before turning to me. "I hear you're a poet?"

"Of sorts," I answered as a matronly woman slid up beside Lawrence, seeking his attention, pleasing me with her timely interruption.

Lawrence excused himself.

Aster and I danced to the taped music, enjoying the act of upstaging everyone else.

Soon after, while I was filling up on hors d'oeuvres, Aster announced that she was ready to leave.

She carried a full drink with her, sipping it as we walked along the boulevard to find the spot where she'd parked. An ambulance blazed by, nearly colliding with a limousine crossing an intersection.

When we reached her Corvette, she handed her cup to me while she searched her purse for the keys.

"Mind if I drive?" I asked, adding, "I've never driven one of these."

"Go for it." She tossed me the keys. "That way I can finish my refreshments."

Our relationship had been surprisingly calm since the night that we had confided so much to each other. Yet I noticed that she had abstained from drinking during that same period of time. I was wondering if that had been coincidental or a direct correlation.

I headed down Wilshire Boulevard.

"You like to drive?" she asked, slurring the words together in a husky voice. "Don't you?"

"Right," I said, enjoying the feel of the powerful engine. "It's something I do well."

"You must meet a bunch of interesting people," she went on. "Driving—so much!"

"Some," I allowed, swinging a left on Doheny. "It's a job." I shrugged. "Like Popeye says, 'I yam what I yam!' "

She laughed, reclining her seat to the maximum. "You didn't like me telling my friends that you were a poet, did you?"

"You can tell 'em what you want. Whatever pleases you."

"But you really care," she said in a sing-song voice. "I know you didn't like it."

"Then why'd you do it?" I asked, facing her at a red light. "Are you ashamed of what I do?"

"No," she answered after a pause. "I just don't understand how you could be so satisfied."

"Like I've told you before, I work for myself. And as soon as I can, I'll have my own investigation service. Then, again, I'll be working for me, my own boss."

She finished her drink and tossed the empty cup on the floor. "Don't get me wrong, Sol. I'm not against you." She caressed my thigh. "I love you. And that means I care about you."

"I love you, too," I returned her caress. "But I yam what I yam."

She seemed to accept that and I turned the radio on as we cruised east on Beverly Boulevard, avoiding the heavier traffic to the north. KACE supplied the mellow sounds. Soon I noticed that Aster had fallen asleep. She straightened up in her seat as rain began to spot the windshield.

"We're almost there," I assured her, turning the wipers on.

"Good," she said, barely audible. "Maybe I drank too much."

After arriving at her house, we went straight into the huge master bedroom and began undressing each other slowly.

The sound of the rain's constant patter on the skylight gave rhythm to our movements.

"Ever fall in love with someone you met in your cab?" she asked while I was slipping her panties off.

"No," I answered honestly. "Never."

I entered her . . . and gave way to an ecstasy of silky smoothness.

She dropped her arms from clutching my sweating neck, flopping them heavily at her side.

"You're trying to break my heart, aren't you?" She sighed, thrashing her head about on the pillow.

"Never," I said, trying to find her lips through the matted thickness of our entwined hair. "Never, Aster. Never!"

"Yes," she whispered, whining low. "You want to break my heart."

"No, that's not true. I love you too much, Aster. I love you too much!"

"Stop," she begged in a high-pitched voice. "Please, stop."

With a few strokes more, I reached an intensive climax.

Later, with the fireplace snapping brightly, I relaxed alone in the comfort of the sparsely decorated living room on a plush couch which was centered in the middle of the room.

I had the large-screen TV on while I scanned the Cable Guide for something worth watching. It was only a few minutes after 10 P.M. and I was hoping that I hadn't missed the beginning of a good movie. However, my search proved futile. Every movie being shown for the rest of the night was a feature that I had either seen or avoided.

As a last option, I turned up the volume of a special featuring stand-up comics. I got a few good belly laughs from a black comedian whom I'd seen in person, more than once. But the next couple of acts almost made me want to stop watching TV forever. I decided to grab a glass of juice and give the show a few more minutes.

The sound of the next comedian's voice reached my ears as far away as the kitchen. Immediately, a scathing sense of familiarity struck me with its sound.

Hurriedly, I got back to the screen to catch the face behind the voice.

He was the collegiate type, slim, about thirty, and red-haired. His skin had so many freckles that no amount of makeup could hide them. And although his light blue eyes and European heritage were obvious, his whole act was based on speaking with a lisp as he mimicked blacks.

"So I goes in front of the judge," he said, gripping a hand between his legs. "And I says, your honor, Ise a bizznessman, you see!" He gripped himself firmer, humping his hips. "And I knows, your honor, that you must got some kind of special for bizznessmans like myself. You know, the bizznessman's special!"

I turned up the sound, not realizing that Aster had entered the room. I had listened to his voice enough times on the infamous tape that Karen had given me to be able to recognize it in my sleep.

When Aster stroked my neck, I almost jumped up from the couch.

"What are you watching?" she asked with a disgusted look on her face.

"Shhh! Shhh!" I said as the emcee retook the stage while the comic bowed to applause.

"Let me hear this!" I hushed Aster again.

"Thank you," the old emcee said. "You're such a wonderful audience that I'm sure this guy would like to take you home with him," he squawked. "Give him a big round hand, ladies and gentlemen! A young, new talent, discovered right here! Richie "Red" Raymonds!"

I flicked the set off, slumping back into the cushions of the couch, unable to rid my mind of the voice—a voice which echoed with the blatant, rawboned threats that were contained on the tape.

"What's wrong?" Aster sat down beside me, pulling her robe closed. "You look strange."

"That guy." I had to take a big gulp before I could go further. "The one we just saw." I pointed toward the darkened screen. "Him . . ."

"The old guy?"

"No," I said, raising my voice before I'd realized it. "The other one . . ."

"What about him?" Aster remained calm.

"The girl," I said, not knowing how much to say and what to leave out. "The fare I had. The one who died, Jennifer. This guy might be behind it."

"How?" she asked, after studying me in silence.

"I can't explain it all," I said, rising. "It's important, though. I've got to go."

As I walked away, I could feel—almost see—her stiffen with wounded pride, anger, and indignation. But I was trusting that she was strong enough to listen to needed explanations later.

Chapter Thirteen

A hard rain fell as I started making the rounds of the comedy clubs. I called task force headquarters to alert them to the new trail that I was on.

Though Delaney recommended that I trade Silver Shadow for K-21, I opted to save time by staying behind the wheel of the van. I used my C.B. to communicate with my backup team of agents Ben Ross and Earl Grant, and Kevin.

Delaney put a man on the phone, calling clubs to see if he could help track Red down.

The TV special that I had been watching was taped at The Improv. I sped along Melrose Avenue, making it my first stop.

Paying the cover, I watched a couple of performances from the bar, where a Seven-Up cost as much as a mixed drink.

Soon one of the performers, a roly-poly guy who had just come off stage, headed toward the men's restroom. I followed, finding him standing over a urinal, lighting up a huge cigar.

I occupied a stall near him, and though his act had been totally unimpressive, I warmed up to him by saying I thought he had a lot of talent.

"Thanks." He smiled gratefully, then admitted, "My

timing could have been better. Most of the stuff I was doing was new."

"Yeah," I allowed, "it must take time," and without wasting a beat, I asked, "Know a guy named Red Raymonds?"

"Sure," he said with his head arched back, puffing on his smoke. "I run into him on the circuit all the time."

"Know where I might catch up with him tonight?"

"He could be anywhere," he answered. Looking at his watch, he noted, "Close to midnight—there's a hundred and one spots between here and Canoga Park, sir," he slurred the last word. "And he could be anywhere between here and there. Good luck," he shouted as the door was swinging shut.

An hour later, having stopped at The Comedy Store and The Laugh Factory, I had still made no headway in tracking down Raymonds, and neither had Delaney's man on the phone.

With each minute that slipped by, time became a greater factor. Fortunately, the rain had ceased and traffic was less erratic, therefore I hoped to be able to hit a few more of the clubs before closing time.

In a search for privacy, we changed C.B. channels often, but I kept my backup informed and aware of my position and thoughts.

"I'm going to give The Punchline Palace a quick once-over," I reported, rolling down the steep decline of La Cienega Boulevard. "It's on Third," I said, announcing the block number.

"We read you," Earl Grant's baritone confirmation crackled through the van's C.B. speaker. "We'll be lookin' over your shoulder. Over and out!"

After parking, I walked up to two yuppie types who were standing under the awning in front of the club. One of them was winding up the delivery of a punchline.

"So," he said, "the old rummy turns back to the

whore and says, 'I don't know what you're talking about but I been spitting blood for two blocks!"

When they finished their squalling laughter, I asked if either one of them knew where I could find Red.

"You a friend of his?" the joker asked dubiously.

"Kind of," I answered. "Looking to interest him in some new jokes."

The joke teller laughed. "I hope you got cheap prices."

"Then you do know him?"

"Yeah, everybody knows Red," the other guy said. "You're in luck." He smiled. "He's up the street, parked on the other side." He pointed. "In that old white station wagon."

I knocked on the steamy window of the driver's side. Vaguely, I could make out the silhouettes of two people seated in the front. The window slid down slowly. A wave of pungent ganja smoke crept out and assailed my senses. He was wearing the same loud red blazer that he had worn for the TV tape. The girl beside him looked under age and caught after curfew.

Raymonds smiled crookedly to mask his anxiety and confusion. "What's up bro?" he finally asked in his off-stage voice. "Do I know you?"

"We've haven't met yet," I answered, squatting down beside his window. Eye to eye, I said, "But I've seen your act, and I wanted to talk about some possible engagements."

"Now you talkin' square bizzness." He went into his act, and just as quickly, he switched out of it. "Why don't you jump in?"

He reached behind him to unlock the rear door.

"Looks too stuffy in there for me," I said. "Can't we talk out here?"

He excused himself from the girl and left her to wait in the parked car.

"Follow me this way," he said, tonguing a fat, unlit joint stuck in the corner of his mouth.

We crossed the wet street, jumping across a stream near the curb, and walked about fifty feet toward the club.

Unexpectedly, Raymonds veered left and stepped into an alleyway. He leaned against a wall with one hand extended, legs crossed, saying, "My office."

"It'll do."

"So," he said, lighting the joint with a match, putting his foot up on an overturned garbage can. "You're an agent?"

He took a big puff, getting the spliff to glow and burn evenly.

"Get this," he said, with his onstage persona. "I offered the girl in the car a hit on this joint and she said, 'No, it makes me paranoid.' So I told her"—making his face into a fierce grimace, shouting—" 'That's why I smoke it! I get tired of being so self-assured all the goddamned time!' "

Almost falling over the trash can, he doubled over with laughter, coughing and gagging on a lungful of smoke.

"Don't you think that might have scared her?"

He straightened himself up from his crouch, extending the joint to me.

"Just having some fun," he said. "No need to look so serious."

"Was it fun calling up on a 976 number trying to scare the hell out of a little girl named Kim?"

The joint slipped from his fingers as his arm flopped heavily down to his side.

"Was that fun, too?" I asked again.

"I don't know what the fuck you're talking about," he said, backing away from me. "I thought you wanted to talk about work."

With one quick step, I grabbed him by the collar. He

whimpered as I lifted him. Slamming his back against a graffiti-covered wall, I stuck his head under the direct, gushing flow of a rain spout. His eyes seemed ready to bulge out as the water filled his mouth.

I shouted, mimicking his taped threats, "I'm going to roast your ass! Yeah, that's right! Roasted pig's ass!"

When he began to cease struggling, I let him drop to the ground. He rolled to his knees and elbows, coughing, spitting vile water, and losing his dinner.

"Look," he said, when he was finally able to address me. "I don't know what you're talking about. Why me?"

I flashed my badge. "We can continue this discussion with you under arrest." I smiled down at him. "I've still got the tape. So try telling a judge that it's not your voice. Maybe you can add that to your comedy routine."

"Okay, okay," he said, wiping grime from his face. "I do know about those calls."

"Now we're getting somewhere," I said, helping him from the ground. "Talk to me!"

What he told me made sense.

Bryan Mann had paid Red to make the calls when Jennifer was at her 976 post.

"He said," Red recalled, "he'd give me an extra hundred if I could get her to quit." He appeared sincerely remorseful when adding, "I had no idea that anyone would get in trouble."

"Why did he want her to quit so bad?"

"He said he didn't like the idea of his girl working on the phone helping a whole bunch of guys get their rocks off."

"You think that was his real reason?" I asked, helping Red to rearrange his wet, rumpled clothes.

"That's what he told me, and I had no reason to doubt him," he said with a helpless shrug. "I just called myself making a couple of extra bucks. Nothing else, honest."

After we walked from the alley, I pulled two fresh twenties from my wallet. "Where can I find Bryan?" I waved the bills under his nose.

"He's crashing at my pad," Red said, quickly defending himself by adding, "He needed a place to go. Gave me ten bucks."

"And, as usual, you needed the money." I sighed, sliding the bills into Red's hand. "Where's your place?"

He gave me a Bronson Avenue address and was about to walk away when I warned him, "Stay away from home for an hour or so and pray that Bryan's really there, or I'll be back looking for you for as long as it takes."

I found the house, a two-story job converted into units. It was set in the middle of a rapidly decaying block of similar homes.

As expected, the front door was locked, but rather than knock or ring, I slipped around to the side of the darkened house. I found the kitchen window cracked. Pushing it up further, I climbed inside.

Through the cluttered, unlit rooms, I followed my ears until the sound of someone's snoring grew louder.

I flicked the overhead light on, but Bryan was so deep in sleep that he hardly budged.

He had shaved the mustache and beard that Karen had described him as having—no doubt to avoid being picked up for questioning.

Sitting down on the side of the bed, I leaned a forearm across his chest and shouted his name. He woke with a start and squealed as though it was his last breath. Seeing me and feeling the pressure of my weight on him, he panicked, screaming and pleading.

"Please don't kill me. Please don't kill me."

I put a pillow over his face and spoke to him calmly.

"I just have a few question for you, Bryan. Nod if you can hear me."

The pillow moved with a positive reply.

"I'm going to take this pillow from your head," I went on, "and you're going to sit up in the bed, and, like gentlemen, we are going to have a little chat. Right?"

His head quivered the right response, and I withdrew the pillow. Jolting upright, he gasped hungrily for air. His eyes seemed to grow wider with each intake of breath.

"Who are you?" he finally stammered.

"Somebody looking for answers."

He pulled a blanket up around his neck, retreating timidly into the furthest corner of the bed.

"Why are you here?" His voice trembled.

"Because I just got finished talking to a friend of yours, and he thought that you'd be more helpful."

"What friend?"

"Red, the comic."

His eyes darted like those of a cornered mouse.

"Why did you pay him to scare Jennifer?"

"Says who?" He tried a play at indignation but his sincerity fell short. "Why do you think I would do—"

"Cut the act," I said, leaning closer. "I'm the one with the questions. Not you!"

After giving Bryan a moment to let the reality of his options sink in, I asked, "Why did you pay him to do it?"

"It's a long story," he said, clutching his fingers, almost in the form of prayer. He whined, "But I am really sorry about how things turned out."

"Talk to me. And maybe we can sort things out," I promised. I shook an intimidating finger at him. "But you better come across straight or I'll stop listening, and then I'll start twisting and milking the real deal out of you."

I allowed him to get up from the bed and slip into some clothes to cover his frail body.

"You're the cabdriver?" he asked, buttoning his shirt. "The one that was on the news?"

"That's me," I said. "Now let's get down to business."

We moved into the living room and sat down. Bryan began talking, and pieces to the puzzle that I'd been wrestling with began to take on a harsh clarity.

While still living at home, Jennifer had become aware that her father's interest in her had begun to simmer with sexual overtones.

One night, in a drunken stupor, he came into her bedroom naked. She rushed from the room, trying to lock herself in the bathroom. He burst in before she could lock the door. While scuffling with her, Collingsworth fell, cracking and slashing his head against the bathtub. Blood ran freely from the open wound.

Jennifer gathered a few belongings, and not knowing whether her father was alive or dead, she fled the house.

"She traveled around for a while, then ended up back here, and I met her through Karen," Bryan said, avoiding my eyes. "And we hit it off, right away."

After Jennifer had confided in him about the incident with her father, Bryan began to see huge dollar signs.

"I thought it was rotten," he said. "What he tried to do to her. And, one day, I suggested that we make him pay for it."

"Blackmail!"

"I didn't think of it like that," he said, balling up his fist. "More like justifiable revenge for all the shit he put her through. All the freak things that happened to her on the road. It was all his fault!"

"Blackmail's blackmail!"

"That's kind of what she said," Bryan admitted. "But there we were, fighting day and night just to make ends meet. It just didn't seem fair with him sitting up in his castle in the sky—like nothing happened!"

"So when she wouldn't go along with you, you called Red in—to nudge her over the edge."

"Yeah." He sighed as though talk exhausted him. "I kept telling her that the phone job could be dangerous, and I was just trying to make her see that. See how a little financial independence could free us."

"A lot of good it did!"

"Yeah," he blurted out. "But I didn't kill her."

"Then why'd you go on the lam?"

He told me that he had run into some trouble back in Detroit where he was from.

"Bad checks," he said, "stuff like that." He licked the corners of his mouth, speaking in a low voice. "So rather than stick around to do time, I jumped bail."

I was silent for a long time, letting the facts he'd revealed congeal.

"Something doesn't make sense, though," I finally said. "When I saw her running across Sunset, she was clinging to a manila folder like her very life depended on what was in it."

Bryan's eyes got big, flashing fright. He tried to regroup. "I wonder what that was about?"

"You know!" I declared. "You know! And now's not the time to start holding back on me."

"I've told you everything I know." He squirmed in his seat. "What would I gain by lying to you?"

Quickly, I crossed the room, grabbed him by his scrawny neck, and shouted, "I told you I wanted the truth!"

I pulled my Cobra out and pressed the cold barrel to the side of his frightened head.

"There are two guys," I said between gritted teeth. "One named Armando Sanchez and the other named Preston Reynolds. I think that they killed Jennifer. And I think that they would love to get their hands on you."

"Why?" he cried in a shaky voice. "I didn't do anything."

I pressed the barrel of the gun hard into his temple, cocking the hammer, saying, "I could pull the trigger and not kill you. Just sort of graze your skull, knock you out. Then I call the two guys we been talking about, and tell them where they can find you."

"No, please." He began to cry. "Don't do it, please. I'll talk."

As I'd surmised, Bryan knew who Armando and Preston were.

They were couriers for the company that owned the phone service.

Once a week they would stop by, bringing the paychecks for Bryan to give to the other employees, and they would take readings and accounts on the volume of calls that had come in during the week to the various lines.

"They'd kick me out for about twenty or thirty minutes and use my office," he said. "When I would come back after they left, there was always the strong smell of pot in the air." He went on, "Just one look at them and you could tell that they were probably into a lot of dirty business."

They would always call just before they made a visit.

Still hot on the idea of blackmailing someone, Bryan had started snooping. He taped a recorder to the bottom of his desk and would leave it to record the couriers' conversations.

"They'd call to say they were on their way, and when I heard their footsteps coming down the hall, I'd turn the machine on."

More than a dozen times before he was fired, Bryan had recorded their conversations.

"Just as I expected." He shook his head, grimly twisting his mouth. "They were into a lot of shit!"

"Like what?"

"Drugs, prostitution," he said blandly. "That much I expected, but these guys were into deeper crap than that."

"Go on."

"They were into taking whatever they wanted. I mean, one time I heard them talking about some guy who had an X-rated movie theater that they wanted. To get him to sell for practically nothing, they kidnapped his girlfriend." He took a deep, hurried breath, looking on the verge of spilling more tears. "And they laughed about the way they raped and tortured her."

He had written down the personal and business names that he overheard before erasing the tape each time.

"Then I was told they didn't need me anymore," he said. "They fired me." He spat the words out. Then he grew calmer, saying, "I realized maybe I had left some of the lists in a drawer."

"So you asked Jennifer to get the notes so that you could blackmail them instead of her father, huh?"

"No," he said with unquestionable conviction. "I knew these guys were far too bad for an amateur like me to be tangling with. Collingsworth was one thing, but these guys are something else. I just didn't want them to find something like that written in my handwriting, in my folder, in my old desk."

He had an extra key to the office, which he gave to Jennifer. The rest was history.

"You're sure they were just couriers working for somebody else?"

"Yeah! They were just soldiers." He smiled slightly. "Hardcore soldiers, but pawns, nevertheless."

"They mention who they might be working for?"

"Waterhead." His smile broadened. "They always called him Waterhead, and laughed. Like it was a joke, something they couldn't say to his face."

A picture of the big-headed dwarf and a flash memory of some of his victim's corpses surged with the adrenaline pumping inside my head.

"Look." I broke the silence. "I'm working with a special task force, and what you've just told me may be the straw that breaks the camel's back."

"So what are you saying?" he asked, tightening the corners of his mouth, tensing on the edge of his seat.

"Don't worry," I told him. "You could be a hero tomorrow."

"Hey, man, who said I wanted to be a hero?" He shrugged. "You can use any of the information I told you, but I'm not anxious to talk to any cops."

"Bryan, if you help us out here, whatever the little beef in Detroit was about, we'll get it dropped. The fish that we're after is bigger than Moby Dick and any of the small shit from your past."

"All right," he said, after some thought. "You want to go right now?"

"Right now," I insisted.

"Let me grab a coat," he said, rising. "Probably cold out."

"Sure," I said, so busy compiling the information I'd just received that I didn't notice the brass lamp swinging toward my head.

I was still feeling groggy and disoriented when we fanned into the street.

Ross, Grant, and Kevin had become suspicious after two hours of waiting for me to emerge from the house.

After knocking and receiving no answer, they had forced their way into the house.

Bryan had hit me with the lamp more than once before leaving me unconscious and escaping out the back door.

"We'll scour the neighborhood," Ross said. "If he's still on the street, we'll find him."

I was heading toward my van when Kevin caught me

by the arm. His pale green eyes were on my bruised forehead.

"Maybe you should call it a night," he suggested, giving me a brotherly pat on the shoulder. "Go get some more of that good physical therapy, and some well-earned rest."

"Thanks, but no. We've got to find him," I said, pulling away. "He knows too much."

Chapter Fourteen

It was early Monday afternoon when I pulled K-21 into the parking lot of Gabrielle's Tropical Fish Store on Sunset, located a stone's throw west of Silver Lake Boulevard.

The rusted bell attached to the door rang as I entered.

"Sol," Gabrielle said, dropping the plastic bag of feed that she was ringing up on the cash register.

The withered old woman customer went back to Gabrielle's overstocked shelves of ripened goods when Gabrielle abandoned her to rush around the counter's edge and give me a vigorous hug.

"Don't worry your sweet little head a bit," she said, giving me a friendly peck on the cheek. "Pops told me all about what happened."

"Yeah," I said. "It hasn't been easy."

She released her warm grasp, saying, "Don't worry, though. I've got your last order put away. And I've got some beautiful Polynesian angelfish that I won't sell to anybody. They're waiting just for you."

"Thank you, Mom," I said, disengaging myself from her wide body. "Is Pops here?"

"In back. You can go in," she said, turning from me, shouting, "Bert, it's Sol." She smiled, explaining, "Pops's not feeling too well. The flu's got him down."

I'd talked to Pops a few times, but I hadn't seen him since that morning that Donner and Nash had knocked on my door.

He had his feet propped up on an old couch, watching a horse racing report. The dark, unventilated room was filled with the odor of Vicks and rubbing alcohol, and the strong stench of cigarette smoke and stale, crushed butts.

"Dammit," Pops was yelling at the TV screen. "Pull it out! Pull it out." His voice trailed off as the race ended. He threw the remote control that he had been gripping with a vengeance. It crashed to the floor, disconnecting and darkening the TV screen. "Bastards!"

I sat down in a wooden rocker, facing him. Oblivious to me, he continued ranting.

"The fuckers," he said. "Why do they do this to me?"

"You lost?" I ventured.

"No." Pops fumed. "I just didn't bet enough on the winner."

He reached for an opened pack of his filter-tipped cheroots that were sitting on a stack of LP movie soundtracks, and went into a coughing spasm.

"Looks like you better start taking better care of yourself," I said. "Maybe you should be home in bed."

"Think this flu is bad?" he said. Rolling up a pant leg, he showed me his left knee, which was darkly discolored and severely swollen. "Take a gander at this."

"How the hell'd you do that?" I asked, turning my head from the sight. "Geez!"

"Twisted it getting out of the tub yesterday," he explained, rerolling his pants down. "Whatever you do, Sol," he said with a melancholy air, "don't live long enough to get old.

"I don't think you have to worry about that, Pops."

Setting up the pieces on his chessboard, Pops won the right to the white men. Knowing that my defense was poor against a queen's gambit, he opened with the dreaded tactic, smiling sagaciously, puffing on his cheroot.

My heart and thoughts weren't really into the game, and after his attack crumbled my defense, he called "Check" on me with an increasingly annoying knight. Realizing that there was no way for me to do anything but lose, I reined in my frustrations, tipping over my king with a finger, conceding defeat as it clattered on the board.

"You win!"

"What is it?" Pops began prying me open with his rheumy old eyes. "You must have something else besides chess on your mind to play so poorly."

"There's some heavy-duty shit going down," I broke down and told him, "and things I'm supposed to keep confidential—I can't anymore."

He waited for me to continue.

"The girl's case—Jennifer," I said. "I'm still on it."

He looked surprised, then said, "Getting paid, I hope."

"Yeah." I half-smiled. "Getting paid."

"Scale?"

"No," I said, hating to admit it. "Salary."

He shook his head, disappointed. Lighting a cheroot, he leaned back and lifted his bad leg up on the couch, waiting for me to continue.

I told him about the federal task force contacting me to join their team. As sequentially as possible, I told him about how our investigations had crossed paths, the Dwarf being the common denominator.

From that point in the story, Pops closed his eyes as though he were in on the chase, breathing heavier as I retold my lengthy conversation with Bryan. Then I broke the bad news to him.

"Not only did he get away from me, but Daryl Welch—alias Bryan Mann—was fished out of the Los

Angeles River yesterday afternoon. Shot twice in the head by a .22."

Pops rubbed his thinning hair back with a scrawny forearm, sighing as though in pain, then cursed. "Dammit! Dammit!" He sat up, moving the bad leg quicker than he wanted to. "Don't you have any stories with happy endings?"

While he caressed the thigh of his hurt leg, I went on, "Now I know that Sanchez and Reynolds killed her."

"Only, without the boyfriend, you don't have an ounce of proof." Pops's raspy voice sounded even grittier when combined with the flu. "Unless, that is, you can get Collingsworth to finger them for blackmail."

"No such luck," I said. "We pursued that angle. Collingsworth made some big withdrawals, depleting his liquid assets. Now he's supposedly in Japan on business. The only question is: Will he ever come back?"

"No wonder you look so depressed." He shook his head sadly. "Running out of leads can do that."

"True. But I've still got two big ones, ripe for plucking."

"Oh, now I see," Pops said wearily. "I know what you're thinking."

"What's that?"

"Ramming it down their throats! Convincing this Delaney and his crew that they'd be making a mistake by not letting you do a face to face with the two muscles." He squashed his butt, snapped the plastic tip off, and stuck it back into his mouth. "I knew you had something heavy going on inside of your head to make you try to look so relaxed when you first came in here."

"Yeah," I said, "and you've got it right, 'cause I'm just about ready to explode." I stood up and began to pace around the tiny room that was like a crammed bachelor apartment, complete with a Murphy bed. "Their methods are stuff like: calculating the distribution of his favorite foods, garbage details, analyzing the Dwarf's relationship to everything but the high tides! I mean, you wouldn't believe some of the studies that keep these guys going twenty-four hours a day."

"And you think that they're just jacking off while you here—"

"You said it," I interrupted him. "As far as I'm concerned, that's exactly what they're doing—knowing what we do!"

"Maybe," Pops said, clearing his throat. "Maybe they just know what it's like to get a case kicked out of court for lack of evidence, and they want to make sure that when they hit this guy it'll be with something that can't help but stick."

"Maybe," I conceded, sitting back down. "Maybe I'm just getting too jumpy. It's like I don't know who to trust."

"That's understandable." Pops winked shrewdly. "But no need to get all bent out of shape." He stopped, stroking his chin, eyes toward the ceiling. "'Member when I first met you?"

I nodded.

"You were so anxious when I hopped in your cab. And all I was doing was tailing this dame for some cuckold who wanted to find out who she was giving the nooky to." He smiled as though his bad leg was no longer a part of him. "So I gave you my card, and you came by the office I had on Alvarado. Again it hit me, This guy's a little too eager, but I said to myself something like, What the hell—give him a try."

"And I still haven't changed in six years, huh?"

"A little." Pops stuck a hand out like a shaky balancing beam. *"Un poco,"* he allowed, "but sometimes, *un poco* ain't enough."

"So you think I should just bite my tongue and play things their way, by the book?"

He studied me awhile, then asked. "Ever read a story called 'The Zen Art of Burglary'?"

"No." I leaned back in the rocker. "Is it a long story?"

"No," Pops countered. "It's a real short-short story." He coughed and spit some phlegm into a handkerchief. "Wanna hear it?"

"Yeah. Why not?"

"Good," Pops said, sticking a new cheroot in his mouth, but not lighting it. "It was written about a thousand years ago."

The story told of a young man whose father was a burglar. Seeing that his father was getting old, the young man asked the burglar to teach him his trade. The old man took his son to a very rich house and picked the lock. Inside, the father found a brand-new suit, and had the boy try it on. The son was admiring himself in a mirror when the old man slipped out of the house, locking his son inside. Then he knocked on the door until everyone in the house was awake and alerted.

"Thief! Thief!" the father screamed.

The son was forced to use his wits, and after many harrowing experiences he made it home and confronted his father.

"Why did you do that to me?" he asked.

The old man replied, "You asked me to teach you how to be a burglar. Now you know."

Neither one of us laughed, but Pops smiled, satisfied, and lit his smoke before going on. "Different professions require different personalities. For a gumshoe, impulsiveness has to be spoon-fed a lot of patience. But nothing anyone can tell you should be regarded more than your own intuition."

I pondered his words in silence, then asked. "So, no suggestions, huh?"

"It's your case." He shrugged. "Right?"

* * *

Back in K-21, I got on the radio to headquarters and to the tandem backing me to tell them that I was once again rolling.

Hearing about Bryan's death had put an immediate damper on my enthusiasm. While his body had not been found until Sunday afternoon, the coroner had speculated that he had been murdered earlier that same morning, then dumped into a six-foot deep section of the concrete-bedded river. The estimated time of his death suggested that he had lived for only a few hours after we had our talk at Red's house. Unlike the story that he had told me, he was wanted in Florida and Oklahoma for several counts of grand theft and embezzlement, which explained his reluctance to talk with any authorities.

But, as much as I had learned from Bryan, there were questions that continued to crop up that only he could answer. I was firm in the belief that Sanchez and Reynolds were responsible for Jennifer's murder. Since a constant round-the-clock watch was on them, I also knew that they could not have killed Bryan. Perhaps they had ordered his execution, but accounts of their movements exonerated them as suspects.

I imagined the possible scenes: Jennifer went to retrieve the lists that Bryan had left in his desk; Sanchez and Reynolds came upon the scene; Jennifer fled; they followed. Yet how did that link them to the information that led them to make a blackmail call on Collingsworth? Could Bryan's manila folder also have contained proof concerning Collingsworth's attempted rape of Jennifer?

Collingsworth himself had mentioned written accusations as part of the threat that Sanchez and Reynolds had leveled at him. But the lawyer, when we talked on the beach, had professed a certainty that the two brutes seemed unaware that the murdered girl had any relationship to him. While I knew that someone, or maybe everyone, was lying, it didn't help me feel that I was getting any closer to the truth.

The only hard facts that remained were that Bryan could talk no more, and Collingsworth had apparently absconded with every cent he could gather before his blackmailers could drain him dry. Though his office and household help continued to claim that he'd return to town on Wednesday, I had enough doubts to bet my life otherwise.

Rolling down Vermont, I saw a businessman raise his briefcase to hail me. I ignored him in favor of a think-tank kind of privacy.

I had expected Pops to be his pragmatic self, advising me to be cautious and patient rather than volatile and impulsive. Yet he had uncommonly taken the middle road, uncommitted.

Suddenly, I flashed on a childhood incident that had laid the foundation for many of my later actions. In third grade, I had been the continual target of a school-yard bully. My mother had talked to the Catholic school's principal with no results. She had then confronted the boy's mother, who had promised a change. But nothing kept the bully from intimidating me.

When my father, who avoided the ordinary details of my everyday life, heard about the problem, he took me aside.

"I had the same thing happen to me," he said, gritting his teeth with the unwelcome memory. "One day, I decided that the next time I saw him, I wouldn't wait to see what he would do; I'd punch him square in his fat face. And believe me, I did kick his ass real good. That was the last problem I had with him. In fact, we even became friends."

Taking his advice, I threw the first punch. Though I still got the shit kicked out of me, it was the last time that the bully made me his target.

* * *

Making a right on Wilshire, I got on the horn to headquarters.

"I need to talk to Delaney," I said with frank determination. "Get him on the line quick."

Unexpectedly, Delaney spoke in a calm, even manner. "Been thinking about our ongoing conversation," he said before I could make my proposal. "Suppose you're right, are you really ready to deal with the shit that might come down?"

"Try me."

"Okay, go make a call on them." He sighed heavily. "But you've got to represent yourself as the lone maverick we agreed on."

"Understood."

"One of them, sometimes both, close up office in about thirty minutes. So go for it, Sol."

Making a screeching U-turn, I headed east with my heart beating faster, turning right on Crenshaw.

"We've got your back, buddy," Kevin announced. "Push it, bro."

I hung a left on Olympic and found a parking spot near their mid-Wilshire office.

Fifteen minutes passed slowly as I paced up and down in front of their office entrance, marked by a large advertisement for car phones. All the while, visions of Bryan's body found so near Aster's house haunted me with second thoughts. If I'd had a cigarette handy, I'd have smoked it.

The sun was dipping below the horizon when I spotted their brand-new Mercedes pulling from the side of the building that housed their office. The rush-hour glut of traffic caused them to stop at the curb.

Rushing headlong, I pounded on the hood of their car, shouting, "Get out, you lowlife sons-of-bitches. Get out!"

Shocked, both of them looked at each other, startled

and bedeviled as I continued to rant and pound on the hood. Sanchez, who was driving, mustered his sensibilities first, jumping from the car, showing signs of recognizing who I was.

"What the fuck you doin'?"

"Calling you out, punk. That's what I'm doing!"

"You crazy, man?" Reynolds sneered, climbing out of his seat. "What the hell's wrong with you?"

"You," I screamed. "You two are what's wrong with me!"

Sanchez looked around at the passersby who slowed to observe the disturbance.

"If you've got a problem, it may be your last," he threatened, casting an eye at the damage I'd caused to the highly polished hood.

"Fuck you!" I said, pointing a finger toward his head like it was a loaded gun. "I'm going to bust your ass! And there ain't nothing you can do to stop me!"

They looked at each other, undecided.

I danced around, playing to the crowd that was beginning to form. "You guys belong in jail, and I'm the one that's going to make sure you get there fast."

Sanchez turned his head back toward the dents I'd created, almost helpless in his attempt to contain his fury.

"You killed her," I went on. "The two of you killed Kim, or Jennifer, whatever you called her."

They both stood frozen, tense, lamely unable to advance a concerted charge. I backed away a few steps, turning my back to them. Then I spun around, adding. "And there's no place to hide, 'cause not only do I know why you killed her, I know who you're working for." I shouted even louder, "His time is up, and so is yours!"

Standing like statues in awe, they allowed me to walk away.

Chapter Fifteen

Tuesday morning, I moved back into my rented house on the hill. I called my landlady to come over to inspect the new floors. Although her schedule wouldn't allow her to stop by until the next day, she did sound pleased that I'd taken care of my responsibility.

I dialed Aster's number, but Bianca, her housekeeper, informed me in broken English that she was busy in her studio, working. I promised to call later.

Though I had talked to Aster twice on the phone since the night I'd walked out in search of the comic Red, I'd been too busy to see her. The fear that I might be being followed also kept me from visiting her. The foldout bed in my van, parked in the garage at the task force headquarters, had become my only place of rest and sleep.

When I thought of her, I felt like kicking myself. There she was, everything I had ever vaguely dreamed of in a woman. Yet I had been unable to be truthful with her, and the memories, the longings for our loving embraces haunted the very depths of my soul. Every touch, every caress and stroke had been like an awakening, like being reunited with my own—though far removed—African heritage, a direct journey back to the motherland, back to the Garden of Eden.

At another time in my life, I would have forsaken any and all personal goals for the privilege of fulfilling and enriching our relationship.

Instead, I felt trapped.

However, I knew there was no room for retreat. Upon returning to my cab following my confrontation with Sanchez and Reynolds, I had sat unable to drive for several minutes. Both of my legs had danced spasmodically to the beast of repressed, yet unrestrainable, fear.

Interrupting my thoughts, the phone rang.

"Priester," I answered.

"Hi." Aster's voice was vibrant, positive. "What's going on?"

"Oh," I said, taken aback. "Just moving in."

"Been thinking about you all day," she said with a willowy, sullen sigh, "wanting to talk to you."

Awkwardly, we rattled off meaningless talk, then we agreed to get together that evening.

"I know a nice joint," I said, suggesting that we meet at a place on the shore, near Malibu, "if that's not too far away."

The sun was half-hidden by the Pacific as we walked hand in hand. Neither one of us had been hungry enough to forego talking before our meal.

Leading the way down a rocky path toward the beach, she had lost her footing. While I assisted her, she wrapped her arms around me, planting a passionate kiss on my lips. I squeezed her tightly to me. She tilted her head back, sucking in the ocean breeze with a wistful breath.

"You don't know how nice it is to see you again," she said, before breaking our lovers' hold, skipping down the rocky path in front of me. "Last one to the beach is a dirty scoundrel," she cried, racing ahead.

A quarter of a mile later, the sun had set behind the

breaking waves, leaving only a faint trail of its brilliance to light the crimson clouds blowing inland from the horizon.

"There's a lot I need to explain," I finally said.

"You don't have to," she assured me, "unless you want to."

"It's necessary."

"You're a bigamist," she teased. "And I'm your latest prey."

"No. It's nothing like that."

Perched on a large rock, facing a black sandy slope, I told her all, violating my confidentiality agreement with the task force. I left out nothing, ending with the challenge that I'd laid at the doorstep of Sanchez and Reynolds.

"That's why I haven't been up to the house," I offered. "And why I asked for this clandestine meeting."

"Is that why you have your hair tied, too?" she asked, making reference to the scarf wrapped atop my head, concealing my locks.

"I didn't think you would mind," I said, running a hand across the purple scarf that covered my head, knowing that she didn't believe in Haile Selassie's elevation to the throne as all-encompassing prophet; yet, nevertheless, for some reason, she liked the symbolic statement that my locks represented. "Makes me look Indian, huh?"

"Hardly." She laughed.

We enjoyed our dinner, seated at a table that allowed us to view the new moon and its reflection rippling across the fluorescent waves.

A trio played, highlighted by the pianist's vocalization of "Tobacco Road."

"So when do you think I'll be able to see you again?" Aster asked while we waited for our dessert.

"I'm not sure," I answered, lost in a reverie of

thought. "You have to remember, right now I may not be the safest person in the world to be around."

After walking Aster to her car, I revved up K-21, tore the scarf from my head to let my locks fall free, and tuned into the dispatcher's channel for leads. With the heaviness of the evening traffic, it took a long thirty minutes to finally swing a left on Sunset, heading away from the shore.

The next few hours were like any normal driving shift; I got one long ride from Bel Air to Hancock Park, and then I picked up a couple of short hops.

I was certain that at some point the Dwarf would send someone to deal with me. An enveloping air of anticipation hovered inside my head like a dark storm cloud.

Just before 9 P.M., my pager sounded. Immediately, I recognized the phone number on the digital display as Ramona's. I called her from a nearby pay phone.

"Been so long," she said with her familiar, unique accent. "Twice last week I tried to reach you for a ride, but you've been like the invisible man out there."

"It's been hectic," I explained. "Going out tonight?"

She and Raul had a job for a private party in Century City. She asked me if I could fit her into my schedule.

Outside of her Bunker Hill apartment, I blew the horn three short blasts, and she came down carrying Raul in his cage.

"Think I've fallen in love again," she said as we cruised west on the Santa Monica Freeway.

"I thought you looked different," I said, as a way of saying something. "The glow in the cheeks, I guess."

She smiled, almost blushing. "He's a lot older than me, but he's so gentle. He treats me like a queen."

"You deserve it."

"We're going to Hawaii next week for ten whole days." She shook her long, jet-black hair back as she lit a cigarette. "And believe me, I could use a change of pace. All this rain's depressing."

"That's funny," I said, laughing. "You're starting to sound like a California native. If it rains once in six months, everybody complains."

Before I dropped her off on the Avenue of the Stars, she intimated that she might decide to stay in Hawaii if her new love life showed any signs of waning.

"I've already lived here longer than I intended," she rationalized. "Besides, I have a good girlfriend that lives on Maui. For years she's been trying to talk me into retiring and going into partnership with her in a souvenir shop that she has near the beach."

She gave me a wet kiss after I handed Raul's cage to her.

"If I don't get to see you again," I said sincerely, "it's been great."

"Even if I don't come back," she said before heading toward the high-rise behind us. "I'll stay in touch."

I tried reaching Jennifer's roommate, Karen, to no avail. Like so many times before, the line rang and rang. Her disappearance added more questions to the dilemma that had me spinning in circles. Of all the suspects, people I'd questioned, she seemed the most adept at lying, the most unflappable. But, though I doubted she would offer any further clues, she was at the top of the list of people I would have liked to explore some theories with. Though the little yellow house was under surveillance, her whereabouts were unknown.

I recalled that toothy smile she'd given me when I made the observation that she was using Jennifer's roach clip to hold her joint. Her explanation that Jennifer had given it to her didn't ring the least bit true then, any more than it did now. I knew the same roach clip had been in the plastic bag with the address book which I'd uncovered that Tuesday morning, a mere two weeks ago.

How my life had changed since then.

"Got a plan," I announced to my backup, breaking a silence that had been prefered for security reasons. "Let's track Red. See what he knows about running Karen down."

The music from his apartment sailed far down the street. I entered the lame-looking party and soon found Red, chopping up some rock cocaine in the bathroom.

After chasing three of his friends away, we were alone, with Red seated on the commode.

"You caught me at a bad time," he admitted.

"How can I find Jennifer's roommate?" I wasted no time getting to the reason I'd come. "Karen. Where is she?"

"I don't know. Or I'd tell you," he said, innocently bemused. "What's she got to do with anything?"

Something about his demeanor let me know that he was completely unaware of his friend Bryan Mann's fate. Impulsively, I informed him.

While he gagged, spilling the contents of the mirror holding the rocks, I lied, "Yeah! His balls were found stuck in his mouth!"

"I only knew Bryan from around the clubs," Red said, abruptly rising from the commode with a violent stance. "So why don't you leave me the fuck alone!"

When I climbed back into the van, my adrenaline was pumping at such a level that I would have driven even if I had no purpose.

Randy was at his post, dispatching leads.

"Got a 543," he repeated twice, then said, "near 543."

"K-21," I announced into the mike, "near 543."

"Where are you?" Randy asked.

I gave my location, approximately two miles away from the taxi stand. A garrulous voice broke through as Randy was beginning to give me the address.

"Hey, man," the voice growled, "I'm right around the corner from there."

"Then speak up," Randy went into a brief on policy. "Should have spoke up when I called near."

"Give it to him," I recommended.

"If you're going to be nearby, K-21," Randy said, as a matter of diplomacy, "I'll flag you something good later."

"Just cruising," I said, easing back into the driver's seat, ready for either a short or a long haul. "You got my number."

Soon there was a call for an apartment building at the top of Ivar that I'd grown accustomed to finding. Leaving my flashers on, I doubled-parked like a host of other cars with no parking spaces left to fill. Following the steps that led through a palm- and camellia-lined walkway, I looked for apartment number nine. I located it in the rear corner of the complex and knocked.

Abruptly, the door swung open. I found myself facing a .45 at close range.

"Welcome," Reynolds said with a deadly smile.

Before I could react, Sanchez, the ex-cop, grabbed me, yanking me inside the empty apartment, and slammed the door forcibly shut.

"Hands up!" Sanchez ordered as he frisked me, relieving me of my piece, warning, "Don't even blink an eye!"

Staring down the barrel of the gun held by Reynolds, I obeyed.

"Okay! Come on!" Sanchez barked, once he had double-checked me for weapons. "One false move and you die right here!"

They ushered me out of the vacant apartment by the

rear door, into a driveway where a four-wheel-drive Trailblazer was parked.

"Get in the back!" Sanchez yelled as Reynolds pushed me roughly, facedown, into the tight confines behind the front seats. "Down on the floor!"

As Sanchez, driving, screeched away, Reynolds kept his gun aimed at me. Up a hilly path, Sanchez blazed a bumpy trail. Soon I felt the smoothness of asphalt beneath the tires, knowing that we were speeding toward Franklin, a block east of the street where I had parked K-21, the focal point for my backup.

"Nice surprise, huh?" Reynolds sneered. "All by your lonesome, too."

"You may be able to get rid of me." I finally found my voice. "But your day's coming."

"To hear you tell it, cuz." Reynolds laughed wickedly.

"You killed her and you'll pay because I'm not the only one who knows."

It was Sanchez's turn to laugh, "You don't know as much as you think, dickhead. But you are about to find out."

"We blackmailed the father for some extra spending change," Reynolds bragged. "Yeah! But we didn't kill her or know that she was the lawyer's daughter when we grabbed her, either."

"Sure," I said. "Tell me anything."

"It's true," Sanchez interjected. "Our boss called in Casey the Cowboy to get rid of the girl. But it'll all make sense soon, I promise. 'Cause you've got the surprise of your life coming."

"Your last surprise," Reynolds said emphatically. "The biggest and the last!"

From the floor, I could only guess at our whereabouts and the general direction that we were heading. I knew that by the time my backup became aware that something was wrong, it would be too late for them to make heads or tails out of anything.

As though reading my thoughts, Sanchez spoke, "Don't look for any help. 'Cause there ain't none to be had."

Against the night skyline, I spotted a large cement silo which told me that we were passing Highland and Fountain, a neighborhood filled with production studios, soundstages, and prop houses.

We stopped, with the engine still running. Sanchez jumped out while Reynolds kept his gun trained on me. Sanchez hopped back into the driver's seat and pulled into a dark, empty parking lot.

"You leave the gate open?" Reynolds asked.

Sanchez nodded, "That's the plan, pard."

Inside a darkened soundstage, Sanchez flicked on some lights. We were in a section that displayed a medieval castle.

"Make yourself at home," Reynolds said, sticking his piece into his waistband. "We shouldn't have too long a wait."

I sat on one of the lower levels at the foot of a kingly throne, facing the studio lights that all but hid my captors from me. Squinting into the glare, I asked, "Is this where the big surprise comes?"

"Be patient," Sanchez said in a patronizing way. "The longer it takes for him to get here, the longer you get to go on breathing."

"Him?" I pondered aloud. "You mean Waterhead?"

Though I could only vaguely see them in the surrounding flare of light, I could sense them tighten up at the mention of the moniker they had stuck on their boss.

"Just shut the fuck up!" Sanchez's voice finally exploded. "You'll get all the answers you want, and more, in a minute."

Suddenly, all the lights went out.

I dived for cover. Spitting red flames from their guns punctured the darkness. Curses rang with the echoes of gunfire. Adding to the confusion, the front door burst open.

The silhouettes of armed men slithered into the deeper shadows.

"FBI," Earl Grant's voice announced. "Drop your guns—we've got you surrounded."

Sanchez and Reynolds turned their fire toward their newfound enemies. The fractured sound of bullets landing and ricocheting surrounded me.

Through the darkness, I could make out Reynolds heading toward the mouth of a hallway that showed illumination from a skylight. Ducking low, beneath the hail of lead, I followed him.

He raced down the long concrete hall, turning once to fire two quick shots at me pursuing him. I dived to the floor, covering my head as the shots whizzed by.

When I looked up, the hall was empty. Back on my feet, I reached the hall's end. An open door led to the street on the opposite side of the building from which we'd entered.

Quickly, I spotted Reynolds fleeing along the barren sidewalk. Hearing my footsteps behind him, he turned again, aiming. The click of his empty gun seemed intensely magnified.

In futile desperation and anger, he hurled the useless weapon toward me. As he turned to run, I tackled him.

Getting to my feet before he did, I reached out to restrain him. Instead, I got a well-placed kick in my chest that flattened me.

Baring his teeth, he stood over me, lifting a garbage can, ready to heave it.

"Hold it!" Kevin cried, some thirty yards behind me. "Drop it! Or I'll shoot!"

Reynolds looked delirious, the can raised above his head.

Kevin's shot rang out. Reynolds tossed the can with a wounded grunt.

Blocking the full force of the blow, I climbed to my feet again.

Reynolds, screaming psychotically and holding the side of his bleeding head, darted into the street.

A white compact car screeched while attempting to brake, but it was too late. With a sickening thud it collided with the man, tossing the body into the air.

Like a slow-motion replay, I saw the body spin head over heels above the car. Then it landed with a final crunch and splat in the middle of the street.

Reaching the gruesomely contorted body a few beats before Kevin, I checked for a pulse.

"Anything?" Kevin asked anxiously, standing over me.

"Nothing," I said, dropping the limp arm back to the ground.

The driver of the white compact, a young Chicano, stepped from his car, trotting toward us with alarm written all over his face.

The sound of distant sirens grew louder.

"How about Sanchez?" I asked Kevin, standing up.

"No luck with him, either," he said, shoulders sagging wearily, reholstering his gun. "He wouldn't give up. We had to plug him full of holes."

"Dammit!" I cursed. "What lousy fuckin' luck!"

"At least you're alive." He paused. "That should count for something."

Chapter Sixteen

Saturday, a few days after Armando Sanchez and Preston Reynolds bit the dust, Agent Delaney insisted that I take a day off.

I contacted Pops, who was equally insistent that I accompany him to Hollywood Park to enjoy a day in the sunshine with the prospect of winning some money by betting on the ponies.

While Pops drove to the racetrack, my mind began to wander. It was bad enough that my chief suspects would no longer be able to answer questions or stand trial for the murder of Jennifer; they had also laid new perplexities at my feet. What was the promised big surprise that they had had in store for me? I had been their captive, unable to foster any more threats against them, so, therefore, they had no reason to toy with me, to lie—unless there was something that I was overlooking. Yet they had been unequivocally certain that my information was lacking and off base. Then there was their absolute assurance that they were innocent of murdering Jennifer.

"Our boss called in Casey the Cowboy to get rid of the girl." The words reechoed firmly.

And while they had not denied kidnapping and possibly torturing her, they refused to accept the responsibility for finishing her off. Like it was inconsequential, a moot point, a way of suggesting my ignorance of the actual facts.

At the task force headquarters, an air of apathy seemed to plague everyone, including the younger men whose only job was to monitor information. Everyone went about their tasks like a football team lining up for the last play of a game, behind by an insurmountable number of points.

After all, Karen, the roommate, was still at large. And Collingsworth's office personnel were insisting that his return, though late, was imminent. Also, the lead on the man who made bogus I.D. had proved unrelated. According to Kevin, the workmanship was of an inferior quality to that of the false I.D. that had been found in Jennifer's purse.

"I only got a peek at it," he said, "but it was almost the genuine article that she was carrying. Unlike this crap," he said of the work commissioned by Smoody's friend John-John.

It was one of those warm Southern California days, the temperature above eighty degrees. The bright colors and fanfare of the racetrack seemed enhanced, as though waiting for just such a day.

"Useful Ruler is a longshot to win," Pops said, studying the race forms before the fifth heat, leaning on an aluminum walking cane, "but he's my bet to show."

We were watching the horses trot out of the stables for the limited crowd's inspection. I had been admiring one of the best bets, a chestnut filly who held her head proudly, almost seeming to wink at me.

"I'm kind of drawn toward Double X."

"Even if she wins," Pops said, "it's less than two to one odds. The challenge is to figure on the longshots with the higher odds."

Determined to prove him wrong, I went with Double X for twenty dollars. She finished a late fourth while Pops's bet won big.

Aware that I was still moping about the what-could-have-beens, Pops suggested that we bet on one more race, then head for home. "I got my picks on the books already, so no need for me to play double jeopardy."

Being a passenger is never easy for me. Unlike Aster, Pops drove his ten-year-old Buick like it was minus two pistons, cautious to a fault.

"So you didn't win anything," he said. "Sometimes I don't, either, but going is still a celebration. Like life, same message. You win, you lose, sometimes you draw. So you play the game again."

"Either that or give up," I said too harshly.

"Yeah," he agreed, uncommonly turning his head from the road to look at me. "Giving up is always an option."

Intellectually, I knew that after my last meeting with Andre the Giant and Tarzan of the Apes, I should be kissing the ground and thanking the stars that I was still alive. However, my overall feelings were those of inadequacy and supreme anxiousness.

Luckily, Kevin had taken the notion to do some nearby reconnaissance. It was fortunate that he had made Andre and Tarzan in the Trailblazer crossing Franklin. Following them, he had alerted the other members of the team. They had checked out the empty apartment, then joined Kevin, who was trailing us to the soundstage.

"You take what you have"—Pops was finishing a thought—"and make the best of it."

"Back to basics, huh?"

"In every respect," he said calmly, with a shrug. "In every respect."

Pops dropped me off at my place on the hill. There was round-the-clock protection still being supplied by the task force. Although, with the dead ends we'd come upon, I wondered if it was necessary.

On my blanket-covered couch, I stretched out for some meditation. Notwithstanding the damage, destruction, and loss of possessions at my apartment, its emptiness now created an almost healing quality. The space was occupied only by the couch, the empty aquarium, the painting that Aster had given me, and a portable radio-cassette player that I'd picked up to keep me company.

The moment the door had swung open at the apartment on Ivar, the moment that Preston Reynolds had said "Welcome," the mystery of who had wrecked my apartment had been solved. His voice had been the same as the one that had gloatingly taunted me when I'd discovered my ransacked house.

"Thought we'd leave your phone live so we could welcome y'all home." I could still hear the words.

Now that he and his partner, Sanchez, were dead, it was as though the memories of pain connected with my losses felt somewhat assuaged.

Even so, knowing what I did only compounded the unknown. Namely: If they had planted a bomb in my cab, why take the time and the risk to mess up my place before or later? Unless someone else had planted the bomb?

Watching the sunset from my blanket-covered couch, I kept replaying scenes from my last experience with Waterhead's two musclemen.

While we were waiting at the soundstage for our mysterious guest to join us, I kept having the eerie premonition that I would immediately recognize whoever it was that they were expecting. As much as I had been conscious of my impending demise, curiosity had still been an uppermost factor. Who would walk through the door?

* * *

Something got me to thinking about my dad.

A crystal-clear picture emerged of a time long ago: It was Christmas Eve, and together, my father and I had worked diligently to repair the TV for a neighborhood woman with five children, who was noted for moving whenever the rent was too far behind.

I remembered the way she thanked him when he refused to accept the coins she was offering.

"You keep that and take this home to the kids," he told her.

She thanked him like he was a king.

Because of the holidays, we closed shop earlier than usual. Uncommonly, the sun was still hanging half-mast.

"Come here, son," my father said, guiding me back to his private room. There he had a small work desk, cluttered with electronic parts. Behind him were more shelves stacked with instructional manuals, receipts, and more dusty parts.

"It's about that time," he said. "We sit down here together."

From behind a thick red book, he pulled out a pint of Gordon's Gin. Because I had only tasted a few sips of wine on the corner with the boys, the short, clear bottle appeared enticing.

He poured a shot glass for us both.

"*Salud,*" he said as we clicked our glasses together. "You're growing up!"

Later, I remembered a talk about friendship.

"Don't put too much stock in friends," he lectured, saying something like, "The guys that you call friends today, by the time you're my age, half their names, you won't even be able to remember."

He went on, castigating friendship, saying things that would cause me many sleepless nights. I wanted to tell him that he was wrong about friendship. I also wanted to show him that he was wrong—friendships could last.

"Holiday season, any time of year, you can't depend on nobody but you! 'Cause your best friend could be your worst enemy."

I was slipping into sleep when the phone rang. Wondering who it might be, I answered after the third ring.

"Priester here."

"Mr. Priester," Aster teased, "is that you?"

"Who do you think it is?"

"A man that has been avoiding me for too long."

I laughed. "Never."

"So you say, but what are you doing tonight?"

"Hmmm! No plans, really. But I still think that—"

"But"—she cut me off—"negates everything that precedes it."

"You're a real wit tonight, huh?" I chuckled. "Why, what do you have on the agenda?"

"Oh, I don't know." She stretched each word out for a beat. "Probably just stop by my favorite dive."

"Think I know the spot."

"If you can tear yourself away from playing Dick Tracy for a minute or two, you know where I'll be," she said.

It was 11:33 when I couldn't take it anymore.

"I'm rolling," I said, alerting headquarters from K-21. "Too restless to sit home. Going to do some socializing."

"Thought you were trying to sneak out for a minute." Kevin's voice sputtered across the static interference caused by the hilly landscape. "Talk to us, Homes!"

"Trying to make sure that all good things don't come to an end," I explained. "Just a personal thing," I said, "but at least we'll be moving."

"To where?"

"To six square," I said, using a code that denoted the radius surrounding Smoody's Blue Note.

"Reading you clear. Reading you clear," Earl Grant's baritone voice chimed. "I was falling asleep back there at the house anyhow. But if you really call yourself a brother, you'd let me hang out for some of the good times, too. Call me cousin."

"Okay, cousin," I relented. "I'll take the back door. You take the front. Five minutes apart. I go first."

Aster and I spotted each other the moment I entered through the back. Up on her feet with incredible speed, she wrapped herself around me before I could get much past the threshold.

The place was more crowded than I'd ever seen it.

A reggae group called Jah Thunder was mashing up some heavy sounds. As they began a new song, Aster led me to the dance floor. We didn't stay in the spotlight long before the floor was filled around us.

"Let's not play the cousins," I whispered to Earl Grant as I passed him, leaving the dance floor, sweating. "Just watch my back."

During a musicians' break, Aster and I cuddled in the corner of a booth, trying to block out the noise and interruptions around us.

"Do you know how long it's been since I've done any serious work?" she asked.

"How long?"

"Not since I met you," she said, twirling a straw around in her mixed drink. "Luckily, I've got three weeks until my deadline."

"That's not really the kind of news I was hoping to hear."

"Well, believe me," she said, placing her drink down hard on the Formica-topped table, "I didn't plan it this way."

"Neither did I," I assured her, wishing that we were alone, to talk, to be closer. "But it did happen!"

"Didn't it?" She sighed, holding me tighter. "Didn't it?"

Quickly, the hours slipped by, and soon, Smoody's bartender announced last call.

We left Aster's car parked in back of the club, and she joined me in K-21. Before I could start the engine, she wrapped her arms around me. In the chill, we groped and kissed desirously.

"Since your place is so well-protected, why don't we go there," Aster suggested.

"There's nothing there but a couch and the painting you gave me."

"What else do we need?"

After making hungry love, we sat staring out at the star-studded sky while the glow from the fireplace danced on the empty walls and ceiling.

"The opening of my one woman show is right around the corner. Why don't you go with me? We could get there earlier than I planned." she asked bluntly. "You'd love it! Madrid is so beautiful this time of year."

"Sounds interesting," I said, without much enthusiasm.

Her eyes lit up, "Then let's go." She seemed ready to bound up and rush off to the airport.

"I don't know," I stammered, retreating to the far end of the couch, turning the tape which had just ended to the other side. "I've got some business here that's not complete."

"You mean the Dick Tracy stuff?"

"Yeah." I stretched my arms and yawned. "The Dick Tracy stuff."

"Look at you," she said, running her soft fingertips across my furrowed brow, encircling the knot that Bryan had inflicted with the brass lamp. "You said yourself, not more than a few hours ago, you're probably heading down a dead-end street with this case, anyway."

"Yeah." I stroked my chin pensively, not liking the direction that the conversation was taking, "but it's still an open case which—"

"Shhh!" She pressed a finger to her lips. "Just listen for a minute. That's all I ask."

"Okay, I'm listening, Aster."

"Good," she said as I rested my head on the back of the couch. "Do you remember the shape that you were in when Smoody brought you to my house—your first day out of jail?"

"How could I forget?"

"And I helped you to get better. Didn't I? I nursed you."

"True . . ."

"Shhh!" she quieted me. "I'm not finished." She stood up, wrapped in a blanket, and began to pace back and forth in front of the wide window, her arms folded near her waist. "It took a lot of energy out of me, a lot of faith and strength. How much, you could never guess. But seeing you healthy again was a great reward."

She stopped speaking, fixedly gazing from the window. I almost spoke, but knew that I should remain silent.

"Then," she went on, in a soft, faraway voice, "I fell in love. And that's made quite a difference in how I feel about everything."

Deeply, I sighed, restraining the desire to go to her, to comfort her in my arms.

"With all of the money I have"—she turned back to me, smiling—"we could live like a king and queen, because I don't see anything for us here. I mean," she said, her face contorted, pained, "how many times will I have to look at your body all battered and bruised, and find the power enough to heal you? How many more times? Again and again?"

She sat down beside me, taking both of my hands in hers. "What do you have here, Solomon, besides bad times and horrid memories?"

I've got my cab, I thought of saying. My cab, and the dream of running an investigation service. All of that, and an unsolved murder case.

I finally spoke. "There's still the question of who killed the girl."

She threw her hands up, exasperated, and stood again. "You said yourself that there was little or no chance that you could tie anyone to her death, now that those two animals are history."

"There's a chance," I said. "Maybe only a slight one. But there's a chance."

"How?"

"I don't know how yet. I just know I've got to try and do my best."

"You're such a stubborn man." She shook her head, dropping her eyes for a second. "What am I going to do with you?"

"Give me a couple of weeks. That should give us both time."

"Suppose I can't wait?"

"Two weeks isn't asking a lot, is it?"

"I'll have to think about that," she said, finding her dress and purse. "Right now, though, I need some sleep. Please, take me back to my car."

After driving Aster to her car behind Smoody's, I sat beside her as she warmed the Corvette's engine.

"Can't you see how unreasonable you're being?" I asked. "I can't just leave the task force and everything behind and run off like some Gypsy with no ties."

"You can do anything you want, Solomon." Her voice was cold and distant as she stared straight ahead as though I no longer existed.

"Right, Aster!" I stepped out of the car and slammed the door as hard as I could.

She roared away.

Stereo music sifted through an open window near the rear entrance of Smoody's. I knocked at the door. Smoody cautiously asked who it was before opening the door to let me inside.

Even though it was after 4 A.M., members of the reggae group who had performed earlier were still packing up their equipment. One of them, sitting beside me at the bar, took a long toke on an enormous joint and offered it to me.

"Hey, Ras, take a hit on the ganja, man," he said. "Then maybe you won't look like the world just ended."

"No," Smoody said, walking up behind me. "Sol gave up smoking."

"Aha!" The other Rastaman laughed. "A Rastaman who doesn't smoke—now that's a true rarity. But bra, the smoke is a link with everything natural."

"What the hell, pass it to me," I said, reaching his way before he could give it to someone else.

I took a small, timid hit. That was enough to almost choke me. Everyone laughed and encouraged me to take another drag. I did, this time holding all the smoke inside. The rush was immediate. It filled me with a sense of euphoria that I hadn't felt in ages, making me wonder why I had ever said no to the weed.

"How about that shot on the house that you've been offering me for so long," I asked Smoody.

It was well after twelve noon on Sunday when I finally awoke with an excruciating hangover. At first, nothing made sense. My memory was foggy, and it took a while before I could recall how I had got in the shape I was in.

Then I remembered smoking the herb and finishing

off nearly a fifth of rum that Smoody had left on the bartop before he retired to go upstairs to his wife. I still couldn't remember how I had gotten home.

The pounding inside my head increased dramatically as I looked outside into the near-blinding light of day. K-21 was parked in its usual spot, and Silver Shadow was there as well. I could only assume that I had somehow managed to drive home.

My mouth was dry and tasted foul. I went into the bathroom to brush my teeth, but my reflection in the mirror halted me. My eyes were bloodshot, and my skin seemed to have lost all of its sheen.

Unable to cope with the sight, I stumbled back to the couch and pulled a blanket over my head—wishing I was dead.

Chapter Seventeen

Monday morning, I kept my appointment in court. The two weeks had slipped by so quickly that I had made no preparations for my defense. So I had the public defender ask for another two-week continuance.

Fortunately, while I was waiting, Lieutenant Pete Donner was nowhere to be seen. I was saved the anxiety of seeing him while wondering if it had been him and Nash who had set the bomb in my cab, hoping to cover the fact that they were on the Dwarf's payroll.

Back at the task force headquarters, I sat down once more with the book of essays and poems that Jennifer had written. The last entry I clearly understood now, thanks to my talk with Bryan.

Eye of Evil

Each touch
That once nutured
Screams in torment
Demanding far too much.

It happens when eyes
That once smiled with love

*Turn to beastly tiger talons
No longer peaceful like a dove.*

While some of her other writings posed universal questions, none struck such a haunting note. Indeed, the night that she had left home, leaving her father bleeding on the bathroom tiles, she must have wondered—what happens now?

I reread more.

A feeling of helplessness began to harness me, much as it had probably engulfed Jennifer continually during her year-and-a-half odyssey of living on the streets.

An hour later, I was back on the streets myself, in K-21.

Having moved to the front of the line at the downtown Hilton, I discovered that I was thinking like any normal cabdriver, hoping for a long ride on the meter. Coming toward me was a middle-aged couple following the doorman, wheeling a full load of luggage. Just then, someone from headquarters signaled an alert.

No doubt I appeared peculiar, leaving the ride for a rival company's driver, tires squealing away from the curb.

"Talk to me," I announced to headquarters.

"The long-lost roommate," Delaney said over the airwaves, "is back at point A."

"I'm on my way." I spoke while completing an illegal left turn, thankful that the installed microphones didn't have to be hand-held. "If she tries to leave, have one of the boys stall her. If she puts up a fight, for God's sake, arrest her."

Hearing the sound of my roaring engine, Delaney spoke. "Don't drive so fast that you get pulled over for speeding."

My watch read 3:30. During rush hour, the freeways were out of the question, so I opted to run south—away from my destination—to pick up Olympic. Racing west,

I used every trick I possessed to not get bogged in the ever-changing bottlenecks.

Swerving into oncoming lanes when necessary, I made it to Beverly Hills in record time.

Once there, things slowed. Eventually, I turned right on Beverly Glen, caught in the glut of a bumper-to-bumper snake line of cars wiggling through the tight curves of the canyon road, climbing to the crest of Mulholland.

The sun had dipped low, blazing red and violet tones, shadowing the valley. Yet, in less than an hour after talking with Agent Delaney, I pulled in front of the little yellow house.

I jumped from the cab, spotting the stakeout team, giving them a nod as I made my way to the house.

All of the lights in the house were lit. Trying the knob on the front door, I found it locked. Rather than knock, I went around to the back door. As I'd hoped, it was open.

Karen's muttered cursing and the sound of closet doors and drawers being slammed came from down the hall. She was trying to close an overstuffed suitcase when she looked up to see me leaning against the door-jamb.

"Can I help?" I smiled.

Grabbing at her heart, she sank heavily down on the bed, overturning the suitcase. The contents fell into a pile on the floor with the suitcase crowning it.

"You nearly scared the shit out of me," she said, letting out a big gush of air.

"Why?"

Quickly, she got to her feet, picking up the suitcase and other belongings. "Who wouldn't be scared with all of the shit that's going down."

"What shit, Karen?" I asked, stepping inside the room.

Piling clothes back into the suitcase, she looked up

with a superior expression on her face. "I guess you haven't heard what happened to Bryan, have you?"

"No. What happened to him?"

"They killed him," she shouted, hands knotted. "And if you could read the papers, you wouldn't be standing here harassing me."

"I just came by to ask you a few more questions."

"How did you get in?" Her eyes darted toward the front of the house.

"The back door was open," I casually explained. "You should try locking it."

"You could have knocked." She zipped the bulging bag shut, leaving out what wouldn't fit. "That's what most people do when they go visiting."

"I was afraid that you might run if you saw me."

"Run?" She turned her full attention toward me. "Why would I need to run from you?"

"One reason would be," I said, smiling, "you knew Bryan's real name. Otherwise, how else would you have connected him with the story in the papers?"

She fumed in her own stew of fury, agitated and indignant.

"So what!"

Snatching the suitcase, she tried storming past me. Gripping one of her slinky shoulders, I tossed her frail form down on the bed.

"You're a sneaky little bitch, aren't you?" I snarled. "But you ain't going nowhere until I say so."

"What the hell do you want from me?" She sat up on the side of the bed, pulling her skirt down, covering her see-through panties. She asked, with a sniffle, biting her fingers, "What do you want?"

I stood over her. "Anything but the bullshit that you've been feeding me since we met."

"I said what do you want?" She glared up at me.

"You said, 'They killed Bryan,' " I spoke calmly. "Who?"

"I don't know." She began bawling. "Whoever killed Jennifer, I guess."

"Fine." I sighed. "Let's go downtown. There's a law enforcement detail that in time can probably do a better job of making you see the light."

She clutched her hands together. "Now who's bullshitting who?"

"It's true," I assured her. "This case is a lot bigger than you think. Either you're involved or you'll talk and tell us the truth about what little you do know. And if not, considering that you're an illegal alien, you get a free ride home."

Finally, she began to talk.

Bryan was on Jennifer all the time, trying to get her to agree to blackmail her father. But nothing he said convinced her. So he started looking for other game. When he found out about the sleazy deals that the owner of the phone lines, Waterhead, was into, he thought about collecting hush money.

"And . . ."

"He got scared by the weight he knew he was up against," she said, "so he went back to putting pressure on Jennifer."

She stood up again, making a sign that she was ready to take her luggage on the road.

"And you knew this all the time?"

"I thought Bryan was a silly person," she said, squinching her purple-painted lips, "but I loved him anyway."

"Aha!" I said, calculating quickly, "and he promised to dump Jennifer, once he had the money."

Dropping her head, she mumbled, "I didn't encourage him, though."

"You didn't try to stop him, either."

"No." She bit on her fingers again. "But who could have expected what happened?"

"No one, I guess . . ."

"Are we finished now?" She made ready to leave. "Can I go?"

I took her right hand in mine, examining it for what I had suspected from a distance. Calluses were thick on the backs of her fingers.

"Bryan liked his girls rail-thin, huh?"

She snatched her hand from me. "I wish they'd locked you up forever."

"So you set me up that night you lied about leaving money under the doormat for Bryan, didn't you?"

"You bet your ass!" she screeched.

I grabbed her hand again, running a thumb across the callused skin before she ripped the hand away from me. "Odds are, you'll be dead before me. Your esophagus has probably already been ruptured beyond repair." I walked away, saying over a shoulder, "Bulimia kills. Hopefully, in your case, it'll be soon."

As I walked toward the front door, she attacked me like a wildcat. Easily, I pushed her away.

"Get the fuck out!" she shouted at the top of her lungs. "Go away! You asshole!"

Halfway out the front door, I turned. "Thank you for that tape you gave me. Without it, I would've never been able to track Bryan down."

"Well," she screamed from the door, "good for you! But I'm not going to feel guilty about that. Because giving you the tape and setting you up for the cops was Bryan's stupid idea, anyhow. Not mine!"

Pulling away in K-21, I felt extremely frustrated.

The conversation with Karen had unsettled me. I told myself it was because of my inability to grasp something that I could hold on to.

"Captain P, here," I said, giving my code name, "leaving the scene of the crime."

"Reading you," Earl Grant chimed.

"Tell the guys watching the house to tail the bitch," I said. "I want to know where she goes from here."

"We've got her," Delaney's dry voice came across the speaker. "We've bugged her car. She'll be on the same screen with you."

While I felt disdain for Karen, I knew that she was no more than an extension of what Jennifer might have become. The first time I'd seen her rolling a joint, there had been something about her fingers that lingered in my subconscious, begging to be recalled. Suddenly, that night, it all unfolded when she began biting her fingers.

Watching a news report some time ago, I'd heard a warning to parents that spelled out signs for detecting behavior linked to purging. Calluses on fingers from forced regurgitations was a prime hint, which, at the time, I'd found hard to imagine. But, nevertheless, Karen had proved the theory valid the moment she'd snatched her hand away from me.

While I could feel sorry for her, it didn't take up a lot of my time.

Cruising the main artery of Ventura Boulevard, I found myself thinking of Aster and looking for a pay phone.

Late Sunday night, she had invited me to her place for a "snack," as she called it. Forgetting about my hangover, I had raced to her house.

She had cooked the meal herself; it was hot and spicy, the way I like food.

"It's as traditional as I can make it here in the States," she informed me. "I had to substitute here and there."

In time, the question of me leaving to go with her to Spain came up.

"Have you made up your mind yet?" she asked flatly.

The food suddenly became too chewy, and I wondered why I was there with her. Before I made a reply, my eyes fell on the lone goldfish swimming in its small oval bowl, its mouth puckered as though blowing kisses, seemingly watching everything that went on at our table.

"Who's going to take care of the fish?" I managed to ask.

She calmly answered, although I don't remember what she said. I was too busy shamefully recalling the previous night when I'd fallen off the wagon.

I pulled to a cabstand near Laurel Canyon, cut the engine, and waited. Neon signs blazed with a variety of colored lights. Boulevard night sounds and the sulphuric smell of the traffic were all about me.

Having taken a drink, I now felt counterfeit.

I tried wiping the guilt and other negative thoughts aside, but I knew that would be even more unhealthy. I knew I had to go through it, even if it meant ripping myself apart in the process. Because it was as though I had awakened some beast inside of me who was trying to convince me to give up, surrender.

I began to question everything about myself, including why I had ever decided to wear my hair in locks. I spun in circles thinking about that.

Nothing in my life was going right. I wondered if I could sink any lower. Basically, I knew that I didn't like myself, and that was the worst possible news.

Then I realized that as perfect as Aster was for me, she was probably far better off with me out of her life.

Impatient, I vacated the cabstand, pulling back into the thick throng of oncoming headlights.

Though I had healed scars and fading bruises to point to, everything else seemed ephemeral. Tangible today, totally out of grasp tomorrow. No easy answers. No satisfaction.

Craving a strong drink, a puff on a potent joint, any

distraction, I made a wicked cut toward the curb, stopping at a pay phone.

Aster's line was busy.

Back in the cab, I tuned in to the taxi dispatcher. "K-21. Van Nuys."

"K-21." Chuck, the day man, sounded harsh and stern. "K-21, listen up! Read me?"

"Loud and clear."

"Got a rude report on you!"

"A rude report?"

"I didn't stutter. You heard me. A rude report!"

"I'm crude sometimes, Chuck, but beggin' your pardon, I'm never rude."

"Got it on my desk, right here, joker. The Hilton. About 3:30. You left some customers without a ride. Spitting dust in their face like you were some kind of sideshow—"

Having never established a rapport with Chuck, I felt good cutting him off in mid-sentence.

Suddenly, all of the interior lights were flashing.

"Captain P," I identified myself. "What's the deal?"

"Got a probable," the young voice from headquarters said, excitedly repeating, "Got a probable. Got a probable."

Delaney took over the horn. His normal, in control voice was gone. Now he sounded more excited than I thought he was capable of being. "The roommate might be walking into deep shit. Concentrate on following her. Your backup is already on their way."

"Where's she at now?"

"West Hollywood. The Sunset Towers."

Chapter Eighteen

At last, the heap of information contained in the task force computers was feeding me something relevant. Delaney took joy in personally keeping me abreast.

"We ran the Sunset Towers address through our memory bank. Talk about feedback!"

The name of a seventh-floor resident, Grazella Gordon, set a host of alarms ringing. She was known as Madame G in the prostitution trade, noted for covering a wide spectrum of price ranges for her select clientele. A hundred dollars an hour was her minimum price, but she was known to command payments exceeding fifty times that amount for her girls.

"Been building her book for close to twenty years." Agent Ted Delaney raised his voice for emphasis. "In this town, she's the queenpin of her profession. And get this!" he said in a way that made the hair on my back rise. "Until about a year ago, guess who owned the 976 line that Jennifer and Karen worked for?"

"Madame G," I made a stab.

"Bull's-eye!"

Crawling, bumper to bumper, I passed Barham, then the 101 became a parking lot.

"It'll take me twenty minutes or more to get to the

Towers," I announced. "How long ago did Karen go inside?"

"Walked in about ten minutes ago," Delaney answered.

Squeezing by a pickup truck, I negotiated my way into the emergency lane. Gripping the steering wheel even tighter, at sixty-five m.p.h., I flew past the stalled traffic on the Hollywood Freeway. Spotting an opening in the pack, I veered across four lanes onto an exit.

Rolling south on Highland, I took a little-known route that found its narrow ascent curving back into the westerly flow of Franklin.

Years of courteous driving habits were abandoned. Laying on the horn, I intimidated a jogger who had the right of way as I swerved left on Fairfax.

"So." I did some thinking out loud. "If the Dwarf allowed this Madame G to go on living after taking over her business, she must still have some affiliation with him."

"That stands to reason!"

"And he's probably using her as a foil to get his hands on Karen. She's the only person that knows jackshit about what might have really happened to the Collingsworth girl."

"Maybe," Delaney said. "We'll know soon enough."

As I anxiously turned onto Sunset, it seemed that a host of would-be fares stepped back from the curb, sensing the greater mission that I was part of.

"They're leaving," Delaney reported. "They're rolling out now. It's just the two of them, in Madame G's black Lincoln." Then he cautioned, "Don't rush yourself too much. We've got two units; Ross, Grant, and Kevin as backup. Just pick up the rear 'cause they're all heading west."

I switched frequencies, allowing myself to communicate with the tandem in front of me.

"What's this Madame G look like?" I questioned.

"Tall, dark hair, nice figure from the rear," Ross said, "but don't let her turn around on you." He laughed.

"He's not lying on that," Grant added, "unless you like women that look like horses in the face."

Ross and Grant added a few more quips as I settled into the flow of traffic winding by the bright billboard, street, and neon lights of the strip. Presently, the traffic thinned, and I made better time. Soon, I could make out the back lights of Kevin's Le Mans as the traffic unclogged passing through Beverly Hills.

A while later, Agent Ross announced, "They're taking a right on Mandeville Canyon."

"Yeah," Grant said a moment later from the same vehicle as Ross. "Looks like Madame G may have made us, though." His voice went into a whisper. "They're just moving along at a crawl."

"How far behind are you?" Ross asked Kevin, using his code name.

"Right on your heels!" Kevin reported.

"Good," Ross said. "We'll swing past them like nothing's doing. Then you pick up the tail. Last thing we want to do is scare her off. So if it seems as though she gets onto you, let Captain P take if from there."

"Read you!" I said, "I'm just a block in the rear."

"Don't worry, I've turned off my headlights," Kevin said. "They won't shake me."

With Kevin's instructions, I negotiated a maze of turns twisting and winding by immense walled-in estates. As we climbed higher into the hills the estates grew fewer but more palatial.

"They're pulling inside a place that looks the size of the Taj Mahal," Kevin informed us.

Delaney asked for the specific address.

"Don't want to get too close," Kevin said, giving the street name, block number, and approximate address.

I pulled behind him, parking some two hundred feet

from the entrance. The walls of the place were so high that it was impossible to see beyond them.

Carrying an automatic similar to the one in K-21, Kevin jogged up to me, "Let's listen for a report from here."

It didn't take long for the computers to factor in the new information, and Delaney was soon filling us in.

"This could be the final showdown," he said spiritedly. "We're checking out the phone listed there and comparing that with other data. But it looks like this is our big break!"

Less than ten minutes later, Grazella Gordon's Lincoln pulled out of the drive. She was alone, and as she rolled past us, she sped up.

"We're blocking her escape," Ben Ross assured us, after we had alerted headquarters. "We've got her lights approaching now."

Tensely, Kevin and I waited for further word. It wasn't long before Ross's usually dour voice broke over the lines exultantly. "We hit the jackpot!"

Ross explained that after he and Grant stopped Grazella, they identified themselves as agents and asked her a few questions. Immediately, she broke down, confessing all that she knew, glad that she was lending a hand in ending the Dwarf's reign.

"She says she had no idea that he wanted to execute Karen," Ross said, "until she delivered her."

According to Grazella, the place was heavily guarded.

"Hold on to her," Delaney ordered Ross. "And don't anybody make a move until I bring you guys some help. I've got a dozen men ready to roll. Over and out."

Glancing at my watch, I estimated that it would take forty to fifty minutes for Delaney and his support to arrive, no matter how fast they drove.

After a few minutes, Kevin asked, handing me a stick of gum, "Are you thinking what I'm thinking?"

"Like the hell with waiting?"

"Exactly!" he declared. "They'll probably get here in time to bust this dude, but what about the girl?"

"I'm with you," I said, releasing the automatic that was concealed under the dash of K-21.

Stealthily, we made our way, concealed by the shadows of the estate's walls until we reached the formidable barrier of a massive wrought-iron gate. Floodlights illuminated the entrance, revealing a warning that the gate was electrified. We spotted a camera as it turned in our direction. We ducked aside.

"What now?" I turned to Kevin as we crouched in the afforded shadows.

"Not as easy as I thought." He pondered a moment. "But there must be a way." He pointed across his shoulder. "You go back that way. I'll cross the street and go the other way. We'll look for the electrical supply. If we find it, we cut it off and try to climb the wall."

"Gotcha!"

I spun, moving at a fast clip, heading in the direction that we had just come.

"Sol," Kevin called after me. "Be careful."

Along the side wall, the terrain sloped suddenly and steeply. Unseen rocks, loose earth, and thorny bushes made the going difficult. All the while, I focused on finding the mansion's power source. The continual shining of lights within the grounds told me that Kevin was having no better luck than me. I fought through the undergrowth, which seemed to grow thicker with each step. Eventually, I stumbled into view of a chain-link fence that separated the rear.

Ripping one glove off, I timidly touched my bare skin against the fence's ice-coldness. To my relief, it wasn't charged. Climbing heedlessly to the top, I tore my jacket and cut my thigh making my way over the barbed wire, jumping to the other side.

The property in back was level and easier to traverse. Wishing I'd brought my flashlight, I searched for signs of a utility connection.

I was more than halfway along the rear wall when the lights from within suddenly went out as an alarm sounded, wailing incessantly.

"Kev," I said to myself. Then I began looking for a way over the wall that was well over ten feet high.

On the far side of the property, I spotted a tree with a limb that grew near the wall. Quickly, I shimmied up the trunk. Far out on a limb, the nearest junction was a long jump. I dived and clutched the concrete wall. Still holding the automatic, I used it like a climbing pick to brace myself, and soon I pulled myself to the top.

Clambering over to the other side, I landed clumsily in a bed of ivy.

Before I had gotten to my feet, a host of floodlights cut on. As I fought the impulse to cover my eyes, the alarm continued to scream. Momentarily blinded by fear and the harsh glare of the lights, I almost didn't see an armed man racing toward me. Across the vast front lawn, he came full-speed with an automatic blazing.

A spray of bullets perforated the ground, peppering a path within inches of me.

Reflexively, I flattened myself and aimed my automatic, pulling off several rounds. Two shots caught the guard in his chest. He went down backward, his feet climbing in the empty air while his trigger finger froze, sending a volley of slugs into the air.

Suddenly, a blast of automatic fire came from the second floor.

Sprinting toward the side of the mansion, I ran for all I was worth. Dashing across the harshly lit, open ground, I heard shouted curses mingling with the sound of hot lead whizzing by my head. Ducking low, I covered the last bit of ground, diving and scrambling toward the protection of a garden wall.

Safe behind the wall, I checked to see how many rounds I had left in the automatic. There were twelve.

The blaring of the alarm stopped abruptly while the shells flying all about me continued. Chips from the wall rained down in my eyes.

From somewhere within the huge house, the sounds of a woman screaming punctuated the gunfire.

My effort to formulate a plan was cut short when I looked over the wall and saw two charging Dobermans.

They came silently, without a bark or growl, quickly covering the distance between us with long, purposeful strides.

In the face of the assaulting bullets and the charging canines, I leaped the garden wall and raced up the wide steps of a veranda.

I could hear the nails of the dogs scraping against the masonry of the steps, catching up to me. With one look over my shoulder, I saw the glistening of two pairs of long fangs. I charged headlong through the bay windows of a large sitting room, using the automatic as a shield.

Sliding on the floor covered with shards of glass, I quickly rolled on my back. The Dobermans leaped through the opening I'd created. For a mere second they were framed against the brilliance of the security lighting—black and ominous.

I riddled them with a steady stream of bullets.

The hammer fell on an empty chamber several times before I realized that my clip was spent.

I backed further into the darkness, drawing my Cobra from its holster. I trained my ears to the slightest sound within the room. What I heard caused me to toss the automatic aside. It had done its job.

Both of the huge dogs were lying in a bed of glass, lined with blood. One of them was whimpering with humanlike tones, trying unsuccessfully to rise. I placed the nose of the Cobra to its forehead, ending its misery.

The sound of footsteps racing up the veranda steps rushed through the shattered windows. I ran to a wide door. Peeking into a long hall, I satisfied myself that it was empty. Behind me, I swung the doors to the sitting room shut just as my pursuers began to spray the room with lead.

Quickly, I moved a table and a statue on a pedestal, overturned them, and propped them against the door which was being hailed with lead.

Down the long hall, I raced toward the center of the mansion, closer to the sound of a woman's screams.

A gunman stepped into the center of the hall. Before he could level his gun, I went flat, pulling off two shots. The first shot was high, but the second caught the man between his eyes.

Shortly after he crumpled into a heap, I was snatching the Uzi that lay by his side.

Behind me, my blockade against the sitting room door was surrendering its last gesture of defense. Following the same screams I had heard earlier, I raced past a majestic staircase with a water fountain at its base.

Following the desperate cries for help, I reached a door that had a key in its lock. Without hesitation, I unlocked the door. Keeping the key, I opened the door and rushed into the room just as my barricade lost all of its usefulness.

I closed the door behind me promptly and grabbed Karen, putting a hand over her mouth.

"If you want to stay alive," I hissed, "be quiet!"

Her eyes registered consent and disbelief at the same time.

I flipped a switch and darkened the room.

Placing an ear to the door, I could hear enough rushing footsteps to believe that an army was on the loose. Someone was barking commands over the sound of general confusion and doors being kicked in.

My mind strained as knots formed in my throat and stomach.

I grabbed Karen by a scrawny arm and pulled her to me.

"Start screaming again!"

She looked up at me like I had lost all touch with reality.

I tightened my grip on her arm.

"Start screaming. Like you were doing before. Scream!"

She started off tentatively but seemed encouraged when she saw me brace myself for the worst, aiming the automatic at the door—our only shield.

Presently, the sound of hard heels on a heavy pair of feet could be heard resounding on the hall's marble floor. The steps approached the door, then stopped.

Even with Karen's fake screams, there was an impending quiet. No gunfire.

My breathing seemed magnified, and against my will, my lungs and mouth continued to suck in and expel deep gushes of air.

I turned the automatic toward Karen, who had been screaming with less and less conviction. Instantly, she became more convincing, and the click of the hard heels soon retreated.

A moment after I congratulated myself in relief, the alarm went off again, sounding twice as loud as it previously had.

Hurried footsteps moved away from us toward a greater commotion. The gunfire that had been absent suddenly picked up intensity. In my mind's eye, I pictured Ross, Grant, and the rest of the task force storming the fortress.

I checked the time on my watch, trying to correlate it to the time that it would have taken for Delaney and his crew to arrive. Unfortunately, I'd forgotten to note the exact time that Kevin and I had chosen to act alone.

Meanwhile, sounds indicative of a small war reached my ears.

"I think you're safe now," I told Karen. "Wait here!"

I was moving cautiously along the wide hall toward the sound of uninterrupted gunfire when I turned to find Karen slinking along behind me. Instead of insisting that she turn back, I told her to follow me.

When we reached the center of the hall, some of the Dwarf's men were retreating up the stairs of the front entrance.

Fearfully, I grabbed Karen by her wrist and pulled her with me, running up the ornate winding staircase. The heels she wore slowed us down, but I wouldn't let go of her wrist.

We were halfway up the steps when I swung the automatic around and sprayed the chain of the massive crystal chandelier that hung above the center of the hall. It came crashing down with a tremendous roar, shattering broken crystals on the marble floor below.

In their haste, the Dwarf's men slipped and slid as if they were running on marbles.

Karen and I made it to the top of the stairs, ducking out of range.

A thunderous roar suddenly preempted the battle that continued. It took a few seconds for me to realize that the sound was that of a helicopter coming from the roof above.

Letting go of Karen, I raced up another pair of steps and found an open doorway leading to a narrow stairwell. Following the steps that led to the roof, I rushed out into the night air.

Immediately, I spied the chopper rising from the roof. The powerful rotors kicked up sharp, biting dust. Even with dust and the distance, I could make out a smug expression on the Dwarf's face as he looked down on the scene from the climbing helicopter. He appeared to be laughing as his eyes settled on me.

Nearby, I heard the report of a gun, and turned to find Kevin taking careful aim at the Dwarf's rapidly rising means of escape.

Quickly yet methodically, he fired off three more rounds.

The last one did the job.

Suddenly, with an immense explosion, the helicopter was transformed into a blazing ball of fire. For a fraction of a moment, the conflagration seemed suspended in the black air. Then came another explosion of even greater intensity. It sent me diving for cover, watching the fireball descend into a fiery heap, crashing near the back of the house.

Five of the Dwarf's surviving men surrendered before the fire department finally came to fight the blaze. The death count numbered twelve men, but only three of Delaney's men had suffered serious injury.

An extensive search of the mansion uncovered nearly fifty pounds of cocaine and a smaller amount of marijuana. Yet those discoveries were tame in comparison to the sickening discovery that came when the basement was searched. Living like animals in cages, ten abused, skeletallike children were released from their chains.

Feeling weak and sick to my stomach, I left Delaney and his crew to handle the members of the press who had dutifully showed up in full force.

Spotting me as I left the gates of the entrance, Collette Carter and her cameraman followed me as I headed toward K-21.

"Mr. Priester," she called, prancing up behind me. "Could you give me a minute."

"Not if my life depended on it!"

Chapter Nineteen

With Senior Agent Ted Delaney's recommendation, and FBI influence, the charges against me for assaulting Lieutenant Donner were dismissed.

Delaney also promised to speed up the paperwork that went into seeing that I got my $50,000 share of the reward for helping to bring an end to the Dwarf's wretched reign.

I figured that even after I gave half of the reward to Shorty's wife, there would be enough left over to open my own investigation agency.

I was disappointed that the Dwarf had died before he could be brought to trial, for there were still questions in my mind concerning exactly who had killed Jennifer.

Ultimately, I knew that the Dwarf had made the decision, even though someone else had most assuredly committed the act. Then I would think of the mansion's furnace and the young souls who had perished there, and the Dwarf's fiery demise somehow seemed justified, an ironic twist of fate.

Aster was happy that the case was over and I was now free to spend a month or so with her in Spain. The tickets were bought and our bags were packed.

There was only one commitment that I had to follow

up on. Then, within hours, I would be boarding a flight with Aster.

It was raining hard at noon when I pulled Silver Shadow into the parking lot of the Alcoholics Anonymous meeting house in Glendale. I found Pops at a table in the dining section, talking to a young bookworm type. The guy excused himself when I sat down.

"Thanks, Pops, I really appreciate your time," the guy said earnestly before leaving us.

"So how do you feel?" Pops asked me as he tapped the end of a cheroot on the face of his Rolex.

"Like I wish I wasn't here," I answered honestly.

"Look." He smiled through his wispy moustache. "So you fell off the wagon once in two years. Big deal. Think God loves you any less? Of course not," he answered his own question. "That's why I still think that you should stand up there today and talk about what all this means to you."

"I'll do it to satisfy you. I owe you that much."

"Not for me—for you!" he said. "And it might also be helpful to someone like that kid that just walked away. And besides, it's something that you have to do." He sighed heavily. "Not only for yourself but for the memory of Jocelyn, too. She can't always be your warden. You have to want to stay sober for you, not for anyone or anything else."

"Like I promised, I'm here," I said, trying to change the subject. "Aster was packed a week ago, but I knew that you'd be worrying your head off if I left before today."

"Right you are!" He lit his smoke.

Getting up from the table, I went and got some hot water and a tea bag, and sat back down at the table across from Pops.

Sipping at my tea, I watched Pops wringing his hands together nervously as though it was him instead of me that was to speak from the podium.

"Pops," I said cynically, "how the hell'd you wind up with the handle Pops?"

He smiled, blowing rings of smoke from his mouth. "Never told you about that, huh?"

"Nope," I said, "but I've got a funny feeling you're about to."

"I used to play ball, baseball, minor league—years ago." He smiled mischievously. "I was too small to make the majors. A pretty good little shortstop, though. Mostly known for what I did with a bat in my hand. I might ground out or pop up, but almost always I'd manage to get some wood on the ball—hardly ever went down swinging." He laughed to himself, then went on. "But as I got older, some of those home runs I used to blast out of the park started to fall a few feet short. That's when one of my coaches put the tag on me."

"Pops." I smiled. "Yeah, I can almost see you now."

"It's true, son," he said, "but every now and again, I'd get a bead on a sinker or slider and send that sucker flying high, up and out of the park. Then, as I was rounding the bases, it felt good to hear them shouting, 'Pops! Pops! All right, Pops!' "

I smiled at the thought. "You've got a ton of memories, huh?"

"Sure thing," he said, squirming slightly in his seat. "Not to change the subject." He bit his lower lip. "Look what Mom saved for you." He reached down to the floor and lifted up an old battered briefcase, laying it on the table. From inside, he pulled out a laminated copy of a story that had appeared in *Newsweek*. "She cut it out, saved it for you."

I took the plastic memento that showed Agent Delaney and Kevin outside the Dwarf's mansion on the night of the raid. In a smaller boxed caption was a picture of me.

"Tell her thanks a lot, I really appreciate it."

"Funny thing is . . ." Pops finally spoke again. "This!" He tapped a finger on Kevin's copper-skinned likeness. "Been trying to remember where I'd seen this guy before, and suddenly this morning, it all came rushing back."

"It's Kevin Carter, my friend," I offered lamely.

"I know that! But I used to see this same guy at the racetracks all the time, until about six months ago. Only . . . he looked different than he does here in the picture."

"Different how?"

"Like a high roller with a knack for losing."

Picking up the article, I studied Kevin's grim and superior expression as my mind raced in frantic, helter-skelter circles.

"Matter of fact," Pops said, "the last time that I took you to Hollywood Park with me, I saw him then. Looked like he was trying to avoid us—as I recall now."

"Are you sure?" I asked, doing my best to remain calm.

"Sure as I am about what day it is." Pops shrugged.

Without offering an explanation, I grabbed the magazine piece and stood up. "I got to go, Pops."

"What's up? Where're ya going?" I heard him call after me. "Sol?"

The grip of the storm had intensified, and the thick, low-hanging clouds darkened with every passing second as I drove toward Kevin's house in Echo Park.

As I neared it, I realized how irrational it would appear if I went to him voicing the hideous suspicions which were blanketing my every thought.

On his street, I pulled into a driveway and made a U-turn.

Twenty minutes later, I walked into the police department's downtown impounding depot. Soon I found the man I was looking for, a guy named Doug. Knowing that he had been questioned previously, I wasted no time getting to the point.

"You talked to the officer who came and requisitioned the cream-colored BMW, back in January—the one that ended up like a puff of smoke?"

"Yeah," he said, looking up from his lunch, wiping some coleslaw from his mouth. "That's right."

I gave him the laminated article. "Did he look like this?"

Doug studied the photo, still wiping at his lips, "Maybe, if he had sunglasses and longer, curlier, lighter hair."

I grabbed a Magic Marker from a cup on his desk and poised it above the photo, "About how long was the hair?"

Doug took the marker from my hand, and like a seasoned artist he drew light, curly hair and sunglasses on Kevin's face.

"Could be," Doug mused when he was done. "Yeah, it could be the same guy," he said, recapping the pen. "But it ain't my fault. Like I told everybody else that wanted to know, he had all the right papers, signed, sealed, and delivered."

As I walked away, he shouted at me, "What magazine was that picture in?"

"Time," I lied.

I pulled back onto Kevin's street. Through the heavy sheets of the downpouring rain, I thought for a moment that I'd seen the unmarked car that Lieutenant Donner and his partner used. It made a turn, disappearing before I could make certain that it was them.

I parked a half a block away from Kevin's house and walked up to his Le Mans, which was parked in his driveway.

Using a screwdriver on my keychain, I jimmied the

lock on the trunk. In a corner, next to the spare tire, I found a rainbow-colored beach towel. Opening it, I felt my heart sink. For there it was, a curly-haired wig.

I stuffed it into my waistband. Then I searched the trunk further, finding a nickel-plated .22 special. Hurriedly, I slipped it into one of my boots.

While I climbed the steps to his front door, all the pieces of what had been a puzzle seemed to fall into place, leaving no doubt that Kevin had been on the Dwarf's payroll.

I no longer wondered why he had risked his job rescuing me with the shotgun that night in front of Karen's house. The BMW had still been at the impound until that next morning. Obviously, he had been terrified that Donner would squeeze too much information out of me.

Instead of allowing that, he had broken his cover.

Now, no longer did I have to wonder who had fired two slugs into Bryan Mann's head. Nor did I have to guess at who the mysterious party was that Andre and Tarzan had expected the night that they had hustled me off to the soundstage.

It was obvious, also, that Kevin had set them up, eliminating them to hide all traces of their connection with Jennifer's kidnapping, and to erase the chance that it might all lead back to his boss, the Dwarf.

No doubt, he would have eliminated me that same night, or any other time, if he thought that I'd learned too much.

In our search for clues to the identity of Casey the Cowboy, the task force and I had not overlooked the possibility that the name might have come from the initials K.C., but the thought that Kevin Carter might be hiding behind the name never entered my mind.

Soaking wet, I knocked at his front door.

When no answer came, I tried the lock. It opened. I let myself in, leaving the door ajar.

I could hear a shower running and Kevin humming

some heavy-metal-like tune. I dropped the wig on the coffee table and sat down on the couch.

I called out, "Kev!"

Twice more I called his name. Then he answered with a note of concern in his voice, "Who's there?"

"Me. Sol."

Sounding surprised yet cheerful, he shouted back, "Make yourself at home. Be out in a minute."

Listening to the shower run and checking my watch, I realized that Aster would be wondering where I was. Our plane was to take off in less than an hour and a half.

Kevin's shower continued to pour as I stood facing the hall to the bathroom.

I dialed Aster's number. She answered on the first ring.

Skipping a greeting, she said, "This better be you, Solomon!"

"It's me."

"God, you had me worried! You're late! Where are you?"

"I can't talk now." I rushed my words together in hushed tones. "Catch a cab and I'll meet you at the airport."

There was a long pause on the line.

"Why? What's going on?"

"I can't answer now. Just do it. I'll meet you. I promise."

I took my ear away from the phone receiver to satisfy myself that the shower was still going. It was still pouring like the rain outside.

However, standing before me in the hall doorway, wearing nothing but a pair of old jeans, a wet Kevin stood training his .38 at a place somewhere between my eyes.

"Lay the phone down," he demanded in an evenly

controlled voice while pulling up the zipper on his pants with his free hand.

I could hear the faint sound of Aster's voice still questioning me as I laid the phone in its cradle.

Kevin pointed to the wig on the coffee table.

"How did you find out?" he asked through tightly clenched teeth.

"Just a bit of luck, K.C."

"I wouldn't call it luck," he said. Shaking his wet hair, he shouted, "Sit down and put your hands on top of your head."

"Why, Kevin? Why you?"

Raging across the room, he kicked the coffee table in front of me aside.

"It's a long story, buddy," he hissed as he trained his gun inches away from my heart. "Maybe I'll clue you in, after I take this."

He stripped me of my Cobra.

"You wouldn't be wearing a mike, would you?" he asked as he feverishly ripped through my shirt. After he had thoroughly patted me down, he stepped back, breathing hard.

"Figures!" He laughed, almost doubling over—like an evil caricature of himself. "You came here by yourself! Didn't you?"

Trying to find words that weren't there, I averted my eyes and shook my head. "Yes."

"Keep the hands up," he warned, backing away from me. "By now, you should know what a good shot I am!"

"That I do," I said, staring straight into his crazed eyes. "But how did this all come down to me sitting here with you about to blow my brains out?"

"Yes, indeed! You do understand," he said, walking toward the door I'd left ajar. A step before I thought he would reach and close it, he turned back to me. "There's a lot you don't know about me!"

Before I could say anything, he went on. "Nothing I like better than winning!" He shook his head several times, as though his own words made no sense to him. Then he continued, "You've got no idea of what it's like to win on the ponies. For a dollar or two at first. Then for more. Much more. But it's all right, 'cause I've been just waiting, storing my earnings away. Now, when I'm done with you, I'm out of here!"

He sat down, sliding into a squat position against the wall that faced me. His eyes closed for a second, then darted open, suspiciously alert.

"I was set back by twenty thousand dollars when some bookie introduced me to Andre and Tarzan—as you call them. Like it was no big thing, they said they'd handle my debt and give me fifty thousand dollars to play with. If . . . if," he repeated, "if I'd consider working with their boss."

"So you took the money?"

"How fuckin' smart you are!"

"And you paid them back by making sure they died that night at the soundstage."

"Again you're proving yourself to be a regular genius." he said, snorting as if the oxygen level in the room was running low, rising to his feet again. "They asked for it! When they caught the girl at the house, they got her to admit a lot. But when she spoke about Bryan wanting to blackmail her father, she talked to them in the third person—like she was talking about somebody else. So the fools, thinking they'd freelance some extra bucks, go straight to Collingsworth." He laughed fiendishly. "I think you know the rest."

"So right from the beginning," I ventured, "you've been undoing every single thread of evidence that I could come up with."

"I tried to warn you." His grin turned into a grimace. "But I knew that you were too stubborn and dumb to back down. There were times I wished that it had been any cabdriver in the world except you. But you . . . you were just too close to home."

"So you tried to get rid of me with the bomb that killed my driver, Shorty?" I asked with a shudder, reenvisioning the catastrophe, seeing Kevin as he appeared at my front door only hours before it happened.

"Yeah! That's right!" he shouted. "Lucky for you, unlucky for him. But all of your luck has run out, pal. 'Cause no way I can let you walk away now!"

"Why not?" I asked as casually as possible. "I could have called the police before I came here. As you can see"—I pointed to the light-haired wig—"I already guessed everything that you've told me. I just wanted to hear it from your lips." I stood up slowly. "You're the one that has to live with it. The shit you created. Think your conscience can handle that?" I asked with contempt. "Then go ahead, try."

"Stop," he screamed as I moved toward the door— glad I'd left it ajar. "Not another step, Sol!"

Taking two quick steps, I flung myself through the doorway. Hearing the report from his gun, I felt hot lead pierce my shoulder. The pain was masked by my racing heartbeat and fear.

I vaulted the railing of the porch and landed hard on my back some twenty feet below. Then I rolled beneath the steps as Kevin leaned over the rail's edge—too late for his aim.

Drawing the .22 from my boot, I fired two shots up through the wooden porch.

I heard a squeal of pain and fired two more rounds.

When the gun stopped firing, I could hear his naked feet scampering back into the house.

Then I heard nothing but the unceasing rain as it splashed and splattered on everything around me.

Checking my wound, I satisfied myself that though I was losing blood, the bullet had passed through the fleshy part of my shoulder.

Then a splat of Kevin's blood mixed with rainwater fell down on my face from a bullethole in the porch.

Straining my ears, I climbed unsteadily to my feet. The fall had twisted my right ankle. As I attempted to walk, the pain in my leg overshadowed that from the gunshot wound. Taking a few steps, I collapsed back under the staircase.

Opening the chamber of the .22, I checked to see how many rounds remained.

Then, like a flash, Kevin appeared from the side of the house. He was holding his .38 in both hands. Again, he aimed at my head, shouting through the pouring rain.

"Drop it! You son-of-a-bitch, better drop it!"

A steady stream of blood flowed from the heel of his left foot and mingled with the runoff of rain.

Letting the empty gun fall from my hand, I stared into Kevin's anguished eyes. "That's the .22 that killed Bryan, huh?"

"Get up!"

"For what?"

"Back, I want you back in the house!"

"Why should I make it easy for you? If you're going to kill me, you'll have to do it here."

"I'm only going to tell you once more," he said, his rainwashed face contorting into a demonic mask. "Up!"

From behind him, through the cascading sheets of rain, I spied a welcome sight. Lieutenant Peter Donner and his partner, Joe Nash.

Both of them had their guns drawn and were closing in on Kevin.

"Haven't you killed enough?" I challenged.

"Not yet, Sol! I've still got you to do!"

"Like the girl!? Like Jennifer!? Like you killed her!?"

"No, I strangled her. You, I think I'll—"

"You can't do jackshit!" I said, rising with great effort. "And if you look behind you, you'll know why!"

"Nice try, Sol," he hissed. "But it's not going to work!"

Donner and Nash were now only a few feet from Kevin, flanking him on both sides, sighting down their barrels.

"I'm telling you," I said, taking a few painful steps toward him. "It's over, K.C. It's all over! And you lose!"

"Drop it, Carter!" Lieutenant Donner growled.

Kevin's mouth flew open as he whirled to face Donner and Nash.

With no hesitation, both cops fired off four or five rounds apiece before Kevin finally sank to the ground, still clutching his gun.

Later, as I was being helped into an ambulance, a ruffled-looking, lanky Nash came over to me. He explained that a call from the guy at the impound, Doug, had sent them on a mission to question Kevin. He looked tired, casting his eyes down as he spoke.

"I'm sorry about all the misunderstandings," he said as he extended a wet hand my way. "But I guess now's as good a time as any to apologize."

I looked past his hand toward paunchy Donner, who was conferring with a couple of uniformed officers.

"Are you speaking for yourself or for both of you?" I asked, recalling the severe beating that Donner had laid on me in jail.

"For both of us." Nash sighed wearily, dropping his hand.

I shook my head with regret. "Why is it that you always have to do the dirty work?"

* * *

As the ambulance screamed away, my eyes were drawn to Kevin's lifeless body shrouded in a blood-stained sheet.

Knowing that it just as easily could have been my body instead of his, I raised an exultant fist and cried: "Thank you, Jah!"